PRAISE FOR COLLEEN COBLE

"*The Lightkeeper's Bride* is a wonderful story filled with mystery, intrigue, and romance. I loved every minute of it."

— Cindy Woodsmall, *New York Times* best-selling author of *The Hope of Refuge*

"Colleen Coble has long been a favorite storyteller of mine. I love the way she weaves intrigue and God's love into a story chock-full of carefully crafted characters. If you're looking for an awesome writer—I highly recommend her!"

— Tracie Peterson, best-selling author of *Dawn's Prelude*, Song of Alaska series

"Colleen delivers a heart-warming romance—and plot twists that will keep you guessing until the final pages! Perhaps best of all, her novels call us to a deeper, richer faith."

— Tamera Alexander, best-selling author of *The Inheritance*, regarding *The Lightkeeper's Daughter*

"*The Lightkeeper's Daughter* is a maze of twists and turns with an opening that grabs the reader instantly. With so many red herrings, the villain caught me by surprise."

— Lauraine Snelling, best-selling author of *A Measure of Mercy*

"A high stakes, fast-paced romance. I loved it!"

— Mary Connealy, best-selling author of *Montana Rose*, regarding *Lonestar Homecoming*

THE
LIGHTKEEPER'S
BALL

OTHER NOVELS BY COLLEEN COBLE INCLUDE

The Rock Harbor series
Without a Trace
Beyond a Doubt
Into the Deep
Cry in the Night

The Aloha Reef series
Distant Echoes
Black Sands
Dangerous Depths

Alaska Twilight
Fire Dancer
Midnight Sea
Abomination
Anathema

The Lonestar novels
Lonestar Sanctuary
Lonestar Secrets
Lonestar Homecoming

The Mercy Falls series
The Lightkeeper's Daughter
The Lightkeeper's Bride

THE LIGHTKEEPER'S BALL

A Mercy Falls Novel

Colleen Coble

THOMAS NELSON
Since 1798

NASHVILLE DALLAS MEXICO CITY RIO DE JANEIRO

Published in Nashville, Tennessee, by Thomas Nelson. Thomas Nelson is a registered trademark of Thomas Nelson, Inc.

Thomas Nelson, Inc., titles may be purchased in bulk for educational, business, fund-raising, or sales promotional use. For information, please e-mail SpecialMarkets@ThomasNelson.com.

Scripture quotations are taken from the KING JAMES VERSION.

Publisher's note: This novel is a work of fiction. Names, characters, places, and incidents are either products of the author's imagination or used fictitiously. All characters are fictional, and any similarity to people, living or dead, is purely coincidental.

ISBN 978-1-4016-8781-6 (CRS)

Library of Congress Cataloging-in-Publication Data

Coble, Colleen.
　　The lightkeeper's ball / Colleen Coble.
　　　　p. cm. — (A Mercy Falls novel ; 3)
　　ISBN 978-1-59554-268-7 (tradepaper)
　　1. California—History—1850–1950—Fiction. I. Title.
PS3553.O2285L5 2011
813'.54—dc22   2010054395

Printed in the United States of America

12 13 14 15 16 QG 5 4 3 2 1

For Ami

ONE

THE NEW YORK brownstone was just half a block down from the Astor mansion on Fifth Avenue, the most prestigious address in the country. The carriage, monogrammed with the Stewart emblem, rattled through the iron gates and came to a halt in front of the ornate doors. Assisted by the doorman, Olivia Stewart descended and rushed for the steps of her home. She was late for tea, and her mother would be furious. Mrs. Astor herself had agreed to join them today.

Olivia handed her hat to the maid, who opened the door. "They're in the drawing room, Miss Olivia," Goldia whispered. "Your mama is ready to pace the floor."

Olivia patted at her hair, straightened her shoulders, and pinned a smile in place as she forced her stride to a ladylike stroll to join the other women. Two women turned to face her as she entered: her mother and Mrs. Astor. They wore identical expressions of disapproval.

"Olivia, there you are," her mother said. "Sit down before your tea gets cold."

Olivia pulled off her gloves as she settled into the Queen Anne chair beside Mrs. Astor. "I apologize for my tardiness," she said. "A lorry filled with tomatoes overturned in the street, and my driver couldn't get around it."

Mrs. Astor's face cleared. "Of course, my dear." She sipped her tea from the delicate blue-and-white china. "Your dear mother and I were just discussing your prospects. It's time you married."

Oh dear. She'd hoped to engage in light conversation that had nothing to do with the fact that she was twenty-five and still unmarried. Her unmarried state distressed her if she let it, but every man her father brought to her wanted only her status. She doubted any of them had ever looked into her soul. "I'm honored you would care about my marital status, Mrs. Astor," Olivia said.

"Mrs. Astor wants to hold a ball in your honor, Olivia," her mother gushed. "She has a distant cousin coming to town whom she wants you to meet."

Mrs. Astor nodded. "I believe you and Matthew would suit. He owns property just down the street."

Olivia didn't mistake the reference to the man's money. Wealth would be sure to impact her mother. She opened her mouth to ask if the man was her age, then closed it at the warning glint in her mother's eyes.

"He's been widowed for fifteen years and is long overdue for a suitable wife," Mrs. Astor said.

Olivia barely suppressed a sigh. So he was another of the decrepit gentlemen who showed up from time to time. "You're very kind," she said.

"He's most suitable," her mother said. "*Most* suitable."

Olivia caught the implication. They spent the next half hour discussing the date and the location. She tried to enter into the conversation with interest, but all she could do was imagine some gray-whiskered blue blood dancing her around the ballroom. She stifled a sigh of relief when Mrs. Astor took her leave and called for her carriage.

"I'll be happy when you're settled, Olivia," her mother said when they returned to the drawing room. "Mrs. Astor is most kind."

"She is indeed." Olivia pleated her skirt with her fingers. "Do you ever wish you could go somewhere incognito, Mother? Where no one has expectations of you because you are a Stewart?"

Her mother put down her saucer with a clatter. "Whatever are you babbling about, my dear?"

"Haven't you noticed that people look at us differently because we're Stewarts? How is a man ever to love me for myself when all he sees is what my name can gain him? Men never see inside to the real me. They notice only that I'm a Stewart."

"Have you been reading those novels again?" Her mother sniffed and narrowed her gaze on Olivia. "Marriage is about making suitable connections. You owe it to your future children to consider the life you give them. Love comes from respect. I would find it quite difficult to respect someone who didn't have the gumption to make his way in the world. Besides, we *need* you to marry well. You're twenty-five years old and I've indulged your romantic notions long enough. Heaven knows your sister's marriage isn't what I had in mind, essential though it may be. Someone has to keep the family name in good standing."

Olivia knew what her duty demanded, but she didn't have to like it. "Do all the suitable men have to be in their dotage?"

Her mother's eyes sparked fire, but before she spoke, Goldia appeared in the doorway. "Mr. Bennett is here, Mrs. Stewart."

Olivia straightened in her chair. "Show him in. He'll have news of Eleanor."

Bennett appeared in the doorway moments later. He shouldn't have been imposing. He stood only five foot three in his shoes, which were always freshly polished. He was slim, nearly gaunt, with a patrician nose and obsidian eyes. He'd always reminded Olivia of a snake about to strike. His expression never betrayed any emotion, and today was no exception. She'd never understood why her father entertained an acquaintance with the man, let alone desired their families to be joined.

"Mr. Bennett." She rose and extended her hand and tried not to flinch as he brushed his lips across it.

"Miss Olivia," he said, releasing her hand. He moved to her mother's chair and bowed over her extended hand.

Olivia sank back into her chair. "What do you hear of my sister? I have received no answer to any of my letters."

He took a seat, steepled his fingers, and leaned forward. "That's the reason for our meeting today. I fear I have bad news to impart."

Her pulse thumped erratically against her rib cage. She wet her lips and drew in a deep breath. "What news of Eleanor?" How bad could it be? Eleanor had gone to marry Harrison, a man she hardly knew. But she was in love with the idea of the Wild West, and therefore more than happy to marry the son of her father's business partner.

He never blinked. "I shall just have to blurt it out then. I'm sorry to inform you that Eleanor is dead."

Her mother moaned. Olivia stared at him. "I don't believe it," she said.

"I know, it's a shock."

There must have been some mistake. She searched his face for some clue that this was a jest. "What happened?"

He didn't hold her gaze. "She drowned."

"How?"

"No one knows. I'm sorry."

Her mother stood and swayed. "What are you saying?" Her voice rose in a shriek. "Eleanor can't be dead! Are you quite mad?"

He stood and took her arm. "I suggest you lie down, Mrs. Stewart. You're quite pale."

Her mother put her hands to her cheeks. "Tell me it isn't true," she begged. Then she keeled over in a dead faint.

❦

Harrison Bennett tugged on his tie, glanced at his shoes to make sure no speck of dirt marred their perfection, then disembarked from his motorcar in front of the mansion. The vehicle had rolled up Nob Hill much too quickly for him to gather his courage to face the party. Electric lights pushed back the darkness from the curving brick driveway to the porch with its impressive white pillars. Doormen flanked the double doors at the entry. Through the large windows, he saw the ballroom. Ladies in luxurious gowns and gentlemen in tuxedos danced under glittering chandeliers, and their laughter tinkled on the wind.

His valet, Eugene, exited behind him. "I'll wait in the kitchen, sir."

Harrison adjusted his hat and strode with all the confidence he could muster to the front door. "Mr. Harrison Bennett," he said to the doorman.

The man scanned the paper in his hand. "Welcome, Mr. Bennett. Mr. Rothschild is in the ballroom."

Harrison thanked him and stepped into the opulent hall papered in gold foil. He went in the direction of the voices with a sense of purpose. This night could change his future. He glanced around the enormous ballroom, and he recognized no one among the glittering gowns and expensive suits. In subtle ways, these nobs would try to keep him in his place. It would take all his gumption not to let them. It was a miracle he'd received an invitation. Only the very wealthy or titled were invited to the Rothschilds' annual ball in San Francisco. Harrison was determined to do whatever was necessary to secure the contract inside his coat pocket.

A young woman in an evening gown fluttered her lashes at him over the top of her fan. When she lowered it, she approached with a coaxing smile on her lips. "Mr. Bennett, I'd hoped to see you here tonight."

He struggled to remember her name. Miss Kessler. She'd made her interest in him known at Eleanor's funeral. Hardly a suitable time. He took her gloved hand and bowed over it. "Miss Kessler. I wasn't expecting to see you here."

"I came when I heard you were on the guest list."

He ignored her brazen remark. "It's good to see you again. I have some business to attend to. Perhaps later?"

Her eyes darkened and she withdrew her hand. "I shall watch for you," she said.

And he'd do the same, with the intent to avoid her. "If you'll excuse me." He didn't wait for an answer but strolled through the crowd. He finally spied his host standing in front of a marble fireplace. A flame danced in the eight-foot hearth. Harrison stepped through the crowd to join the four men clustered around the wealthy Rothschild.

The man closest to Harrison was in his fifties and had a curling mustache. "They'll never get that amendment ratified," he said. "An income tax! It's quite ridiculous to expect us to pay something so outrageous."

A younger man in a gray suit shook his head. "If it means better roads, I'll gladly write them a check. The potholes outside of town ruined my front axles."

"We can take care of our own roads," Rothschild said. "I have no need of the government in my affairs. At least until we're all using flying machines." He snickered, then glanced at Harrison. "You look familiar, young man. Have we met?"

Flying machines. Maybe this meeting was something God had arranged. Harrison thrust out his hand. "Harrison Bennett."

"Claude's son?"

Was that distaste in the twist of Rothschild's mouth? Harrison put confidence into his grip. "Yes, sir."

"How is your father?"

"Quite well. He's back in New York by now."

"I heard about your fiancée's death. I'm sorry for your loss."

Harrison managed not to wince. "Thank you." He pushed away his memories of that terrible day, the day he'd seen Eleanor Stewart for what she really was.

"Your father was most insistent I meet you. He seems to think you have a business proposition I might be interested in."

Harrison smiled and began to tell the men of the new diamond mines that Bennett and Bennett had found in Africa. A mere week after Mr. Stewart's passing, Mr. Bennett had renamed the venture to include Harrison. An hour later, he had appointments set up with three of the men as possible investors. His father would be pleased.

Harrison smiled and retraced his steps to the front door but was waylaid by four women in brightly colored silk. They swooped around him, and Miss Kessler took him by the hand and led him to a quiet corner.

"Let's not talk about anything boring like work," she said, her blue eyes sparkling. "Tell me what you love to do most."

He glanced at the other women clustered around. "I'm building an aeroplane. I'd like to have it in the air by the time earth passes through the tail of Halley's Comet."

She gasped. "Do you have a death wish, Mr. Bennett? You would be breathing the poisonous fumes directly. No one even knows if the earth will survive this."

He'd heard this before. "The scientists I've discussed this with believe we shall be just fine," Harrison said.

"I assume you've purchased comet pills?" the blonde closest to him said.

"I have no fear."

The brunette in red silk smiled. "If man were meant to fly, God would have given him wings. Or so I've heard the minister say."

He finally placed the brunette. Her uncle was Rothschild. No wonder she had such contempt for Harrison's tone. All the nobs cared for were trains and ships. "It's just a matter of perfecting the machine," Harrison said. "Someday aeroplanes will be the main mode of trans-continental transportation."

The brunette laughed. "Transcontinental? My uncle would call it balderdash."

He glanced at his pocket watch without replying. "I fear I must leave you lovely ladies. Thank you for the conversation."

He found Eugene in the kitchen and beckoned to his valet.

Eugene put down his coffee cup and followed. "You didn't stay long, sir," he said. "Is everything all right?"

Harrison stalked out the door and toward the car. "Are there no visionaries left in the country?"

Eugene followed a step behind. "You spoke of your flying machine?"

"The world is changing, Eugene, right under their noses—and they don't see it."

Eugene opened the door for Harrison. "You will show them the future, sir."

He set his jaw. "I shall indeed."

"I have a small savings set aside, Mr. Bennett. I'd like to invest in your company. With your permission, of course."

Eugene's trust bolstered Harrison's determination. "I'd be honored to partner with you, Eugene. We are going to change the world."

Two

BIRDS SANG IN the shrubs that surrounded the tiny courtyard. Olivia hadn't thought her mother would be up to eating dinner, but once the matron was revived, she had taken charge again. Mr. Bennett joined them for the meal on the terrace, but there was little conversation after the servants dished up the soup.

Olivia fingered the locket with her sister's picture in it and wished she would awaken and find this all a bad dream. *I don't believe it.* She must have spoken, because Mr. Bennett's dark eyes were on her face when she put down her soupspoon.

"Eleanor was buried in Mercy Falls, California, yesterday. Those are the facts, Miss Olivia."

Did he not even care? His dark eyes held no emotion. "With none of her family there to mourn her?" she choked out. "Why were we not informed of her death before now?" She clutched her skirt in her fists.

"I asked Harrison to leave the conveyance of the news to me. In any event, you could not have arrived before her interment. I didn't wish you to receive this news via a telephone call or a telegram."

"What were the circumstances of her drowning? Did a boat capsize?"

He shrugged. "It appears she went swimming alone."

"That's impossible! Eleanor hated the water. She has never gone swimming in her life."

"Olivia, stop your interrogation at once," her mother said. "Nothing will bring your sister back to us." Her mother took a dainty spoonful of soup. "It is through no fault of ours that the marriage will not take place, Mr. Bennett. I expect you to uphold your part of the arrangement and sign the papers transferring fifty percent of the new mine to us."

Her mother's audacity dried Olivia's welling tears. She waited to see how Mr. Bennett would respond.

Mr. Bennett stirred sugar into his tea, then put his spoon back on the saucer. "I'm afraid that's impossible, Mrs. Stewart. It's too bad your husband's dearest wish is unable to be fulfilled." He pursed his thin lips. "There will be no property transferred without a wedding."

Her mother's smile was ingratiating. She glanced from Mr. Bennett to Olivia. "Well then, I still have a marriageable daughter. Without a blue-blooded wife, Harrison will always be merely nouveau riche and outside the best society."

The man nodded. "The agreement between your husband and I was that the two families be joined. I do not care how that is achieved. One daughter is as good as the next."

"Your son can't possibly change his affections so hastily," Olivia said.

The man shrugged his slim shoulders. His mustache twitched. "He'd barely met Eleanor before her death. He is amenable to doing what is best for his family. He will still be agreeable."

Olivia hardly knew what to say, how to stop this insane proposal. She knew her mother was stressed. Six months ago her father had died when the tunnels of a newly acquired African diamond mine collapsed on him. His body was never recovered, nor were his financial investments, which had been exhausted along with the old mines. Time since then had seemed an eternity of watching pennies and struggling to pay the servants while keeping whispers of their change in fortune secret from the society in which they moved. A well-made marriage would give Olivia the power to change their circumstances. But the cost was so high.

Mr. Bennett's gaze flickered back to her mother. A cold smile lifted his lips. "You are willing to send Olivia to marry Harrison?"

"It is what my husband wished. I assume you will draw up the papers to give me a share of the mine?" She dabbed her lips again. "I still don't quite understand what happened to the first mine. My husband had such high hopes for it."

Mr. Bennett shrugged. "Mines play out, as this one did. The new black-diamond mine has many years of production ahead of it. An inheritance from my late grandfather is what enabled me to purchase it. As I've mentioned, Mr. Stewart's agreement to join the families was his contribution to the investment. You'll never want for anything."

She was being sold off like a piece of jewelry at an auction. Olivia leaped to her feet. "No one has asked me if I am willing." She rushed across the flagstone and jerked open the door that led into the house. Her mother called after her, but Olivia ignored the summons and raced up the steps to her room, where she collapsed onto her bed.

Tears scalded her cheeks, and she punched her pillow. "I *won't* marry him! I won't!" she said fiercely to the china doll in the middle of the bed. She sat up and rubbed her wet face with the back of her hand. How would she get out of this?

She noticed the mail on her bed table, and the slanted writing on the top envelope made her breath catch in her throat. It almost looked like Eleanor's bold cursive. She picked it up, her pulse hammering. It *was* Eleanor's handwriting. Olivia ripped open the envelope and glanced at the date. A week ago. She must have written it just before she died.

The letter was short and to the point.

My dearest sister, Olivia,

   I am in dire straits and I need you to come to me at once. I don't know where else to turn. Please don't think it my usual exaggeration when I say I fear for my future, and it will be Harrison's fault. Come at once. Tell no one.

Your loving sister,
Eleanor

Harrison's fault? What could she mean? Olivia remembered the last time she'd seen her sister. Eleanor had been dancing around her bedroom in a new blue gown. She'd been so delighted in the adventure of moving clear across the country. Eleanor had been a shooting star in Olivia's life. How could she ignore this plea, even from the grave?

Could Eleanor have been murdered?

"I shall find out," she said to the doll staring at her. "If Harrison is responsible for her death, I shall have him brought to justice."

She rose and went downstairs to make a proposal to her mother. Bennett had left, and her mother was still on the terrace.

"Mr. Bennett is gone?" Olivia asked.

"He left after your most childish outburst." Her mother rubbed her forehead.

"A migraine?" When her mother nodded, Olivia took a deep breath. "I'll go to Mercy Falls." She held up her hand when her mother opened her mouth. "But only on one condition. Don't tell Mr. Bennett just yet. I want to see if Harrison and I will suit first."

Her mother's smile faded. "And if you don't?"

"Then I'll come home. I want until summer to decide. Surely you can get by for that long. Go stay with Mrs. Astor. She would be glad to welcome you for the season."

Her mother shifted in her chair. "I imagine she would. I could close the house and save that expense." She studied Olivia's face. "But I suspect there is something you are not telling me, my dear."

It was better for her mother not to know of Eleanor's plea. If Mother knew of the danger, she would forbid Olivia to go. "I'll be fine."

Her mother sighed. "If only I'd borne your father a son, I would not be in this situation. We would have a man to lean on, but I have only you now. I fear I have no choice but to agree to this harebrained scheme. Otherwise you will reject the marriage outright, correct?"

Olivia folded her hands in her lap and nodded. Her mother leaned back in her chair. "Very well. I hope you know what you're doing," her mother said. "If you refuse Harrison, we'll be unable to keep our change of fortune secret any longer. You'll be forced to accept the first swell who offers for you."

Olivia could only pray for divine providence.

Olivia leaned on the ship's railing and watched the dark landscape slide past. She had traveled across the country in Mrs. Astor's private train car. When Olivia and Goldia reached San Francisco, they caught the packet to Mercy Falls, though what she really wanted was to reboard the train and go home. Everything in this faraway land was alien to her, from the wild Pacific Ocean foaming on the rocks to the rough stevedores working at the wharf.

They were nearly to Mercy Falls, and she wanted nothing more than to see the buildings of New York instead of the towering trees of this thickly forested coastline. The fog curling from the base of the trees and over the whitecaps made her shudder.

She sighed and toyed with the strings of her hat. She already missed home, though there would be much to see and do here. For the first time she would see the manor house her father had built in this town four years ago. It was a way of being closer to him.

"Are you frightened, Miss Olivia?" Goldia asked, joining her at the rail.

She shook her head. "I've an idea though, Goldia. I'm going to be known here as Lady Devonworth."

"I thought you hated using your title."

"I do. But I'd rather not be known as Olivia Stewart. Harrison will be on his guard if he knows I'm in town. With a different name, I can observe him unhindered. I boarded this ship as Lady Devonworth, so please remember not to call me Miss Olivia."

Goldia's lips pursed. "I don't like it, miss. If someone really harmed Miss Eleanor, you could be in danger."

To Olivia, the plan seemed straightforward. Her maid's vapors were quite silly. "Not if I'm able to keep my identity a secret. I'll find out what happened and bring the culprit to justice."

"Well, I'm scared," the girl said. Olivia turned away from the waters to face her.

Was that a man in the shadows? Olivia squinted into the darkness. "Who's there?" she called. No answer came, but a cat strolled into the wash of light, and she relaxed. "It's so damp here. Could you fetch my shawl?" she asked her maid.

Goldia nodded and hurried away. The fog quickly muffled the sound of her footsteps. Olivia stared at the lighthouse twinkling in the distance. Everything would change soon, and she would have to assume a role.

A sound came behind her, and she assumed it was Goldia until she smelled a man's cologne. She half turned at the furtive, sliding noise, but before she could see who was joining her, hard hands seized her from behind. The man's breath smelled of mint. She flailed at the assailant, but her fists struck only air. Her slippers slid along the polished deck, and the next moment she found herself bent over the railing, facing the turbulent water. The hard rail dug into her stomach and stole her breath. She tried to scream, but panic closed her throat as her balance tipped toward the water and away from the boat. With a last push from her assailant, she was plunging into the waves with her arms pinwheeling.

Cold water closed over her head. She fought the pull of the sea on her soaked skirt. A current took her deeper. Panicked, she kicked toward where she thought the surface was, though there was no light to guide her. Her head broke through, and she drew in the sweetest breath she'd ever known before the waves grabbed her. Before she went under again, she saw a light winking to her right. With her lungs full of air, she groped at her laces. Before she managed to get her boots off, her chest began to burn with the need to breathe. With that weight removed, she was able to rocket back to the surface. Gasping, she dog-paddled in the waves. She gulped in air, gathered her strength, then struck out toward the blinking light.

Her arms and legs ached as she fought the current. A cramp struck her calf and she cried out. Her head went under the waves and she gulped salty water. She was going to drown, just like her sister. She struggled for the surface.

A hand grabbed her arm and yanked her up, pulling her out of the depths. Hands flipped her onto her back, then a rough palm cupped her chin. The next thing she knew she was being towed toward shore.

Her bottom hit sand. She smelled kelp and felt seaweed around her waist. Then arms dragged her forward until she lay across hard thighs. She gagged up seawater.

"Are you all right?" a deep voice asked. The man sat her up.

She blinked water out of her eyes and realized she was still sitting on his lap. His hands gripped her forearms.

Water dripped from his dark hair down his face, and his breathing was as ragged as hers. "Were you trying to kill yourself?" he demanded.

"Someone pushed me," she said. "A man. You were on the ship?"

"I didn't see anyone push you." His tone indicated he doubted her words. "I heard you scream and I ran to the railing."

"You jumped in to save me?"

He shrugged. "I could hardly do anything else. It was clear you were not going to make it to shore by yourself."

Something about him was familiar, but it was too dark to make out much more than the tilt of his head and his dark hair and eyes. She struggled to stand. "Thank you," she said. "You can let me up now."

He moved her off his lap onto the shore, then stood and offered her a hand. She allowed him to help her up. "Is that the lighthouse?" she asked, pointing toward the beacon on the hill.

"Yes, I'll get help. Stay here." He jogged off into the darkness.

She wasn't about to sit and wait when someone had just tried to kill her, but he didn't answer when she called out after him. He was quick, and her voice was too raw and thin from the salt water to be heard over the waves. She walked on wobbly legs toward the lighthouse.

❦

Harrison pounded on the door to the lighthouse and Will Jesperson answered the summons. Harrison had been friends with the light-keeper ever since Will moved to town, and the keeper was quick to grab a lantern and a blanket.

"The woman says she was deliberately thrown overboard?" Will asked as they picked their way back down the rocky slope.

"That's what she said."

"You believe her?"

Harrison paused to catch his breath as Will swept the light around the area. "I saw her in the water and thought she might have jumped, but she seemed panicked. She's lucky I was there."

"Her skirts might have dragged her down," Will agreed.

Harrison frowned and stared at the landscape. "I know this is where I left her. I told her to wait here."

"Maybe she went to the dock to try to rendezvous with her family. Let's look there."

Harrison went in the direction of the stevedores' shouts as they carried crates from the ship that had just docked. "Why would she run off?"

"She didn't know you. Not likely to obey the orders of a stranger." Will held the lantern aloft, but the yellow glow revealed nothing but a few crabs scuttling out of the way.

What might have made her leave? He didn't like the direction his thoughts led. What if she really had been attacked? "You suppose whoever attacked her came back?" Harrison asked.

"The thought crossed my mind too. It's worrisome," Will said.

They reached the quay. Harrison stopped several men alighting from the ferry and explained what had happened. Two men pushed a dinghy into the waves and shoved off. Harrison prayed they didn't find the pretty lady's body.

It took Olivia much longer than she anticipated to make it to the brick residence attached to the light tower. She was shaking and winded by the time she reached the top, probably because she had been unable to find a path and climbed awkwardly over rocks instead. She heard a shout in the distance and realized the man had gone back another way to find her. He and someone else were shouting for her, but she didn't have the strength to answer them.

Her arm shook as she raised her fist and pounded on the door. Inside, a child squealed, and the happy sound put her at ease.

The door opened, and a pretty brunette stood wiping floury hands on an apron. A little girl of about three stood by her feet. The woman's smile faded as she registered Olivia's condition. "You're soaking wet! Come in." She stepped aside.

Olivia stepped into the welcoming warmth of the hall. Some kind of beef dish was on the stove for dinner, and her stomach gave a rumble at the aroma of onions and tomatoes. She shivered as the young woman led her to the fire in the parlor. The little girl scampered after them.

The woman draped a throw around Olivia's shoulders. "Was there a shipwreck? Will was called out to help a victim."

"No, no, there was a man." Olivia clutched the warmth of the wool to her. "H-He threw me overboard." It had really happened, hadn't it? Some man had tried to kill her and nearly succeeded.

The other woman gasped. "Oh my dear! We need to get you out of those wet clothes. We're of a similar build. Let me get you a towel. You stay by the fire." She rushed from the room and her feet pounded up the stairs.

Olivia's eyes burned, and she fought the sting of tears, aware it was a reaction to her near drowning. She managed to smile down at the little girl who regarded her with big, dark eyes. "Might I ask your name, little one? You're very cute."

"I'm Jennie," the little one said, reaching a chubby hand to Olivia's wet skirt.

The other woman's footsteps came back down the stairs, and she entered the parlor with a cotton dress and a towel slung across her arm. "I took the liberty of bringing you a change of clothing. Here you are. I'll take Jennie into the kitchen with me. No one will disturb you while you change."

The strength ran out of Olivia's legs and she nearly fell. "I-I think I shall need your assistance," she said.

"Of course." The young woman stepped behind Olivia and released the laces on the back. "What's your name?"

"I'm Olivia Stewart." Too late she realized she'd revealed her true identity.

"I'm Katie Jesperson. My husband is the lightkeeper here." She helped Olivia step out of her ruined clothes, then dropped a clean dress over her head.

The warmth of the fabric enveloped her, and Olivia let out a sigh. "I'm so cold," she said.

"Sit by the fire." Katie pushed her gently into the folds of an overstuffed chair. "Let me dry your hair." She took out what pins hadn't been removed by the sea until the heavy dark locks hung on Olivia's shoulders. Katie toweled it briskly. "Your hair is so lovely."

"Thank you." Shuddering, Olivia sank back into the warmth of the chair. Katie put down the towel, then tucked a quilt around Olivia. "I shall call the constable as soon as we get you settled. What was the name of your ship? Do you have companions who will be worried about you?"

"It's the *Atlantis*. My maid will be quite upset when she can't find me."

"I'll make sure she is informed of your whereabouts when Will gets back."

Who would have thrown her overboard? She hadn't spoken to anyone but Goldia. When the cat at her feet meowed, she remembered the cat on the ship and the shadowy figure of a man she thought she'd seen. What if someone had overheard her talking to Goldia and realized she was really Olivia Stewart? Could the man have had something to do with Eleanor's death? Maybe it was even Harrison. And the man who had rescued her. He'd come from the ship. Had he seen something in spite of his statement to the contrary?

Olivia reached toward Katie as she started for the door. "I'm registered as Lady Devonworth. May I ask you not to mention the name Olivia Stewart to anyone?"

Katie stopped and stared. "I don't understand."

Olivia hardly knew where to begin. "I'd rather people know me by my formal title," she said. "My father was a duke who came to New York in his twenties."

Katie frowned. "Stewart. Are you related to Eleanor Stewart?"

Olivia couldn't lie. Not when the woman had been so kind. "She was my sister. But no one must know that. Not yet."

Katie bit her lip. "I don't like deception."

"Please, only for a little while," Olivia begged. "I need to find out who wants me dead. I want to find out what happened to Eleanor. What did you hear of her death?"

"I know only that she drowned while swimming."

Olivia shook her head. "Eleanor was terrified of the water. She would never have put one toe in the ocean."

Katie's eyes widened. "You fear she was murdered?"

Murder. Such an ugly word. Olivia nodded. "I know of no other explanation."

"She was not herself the week before she died. Somber and unhappy. Could she have done away with herself?"

"Not Eleanor! And even if I could be persuaded of such a fate for her, she would not have drowned herself. Not with her overwhelming fear of water."

"Someone tried to harm you. I must admit that bolsters your suspicions. You must tell the constable."

"Not yet," Olivia said. "I don't want to run the risk of anyone finding out I'm investigating. We can tell him of the attack, but he only needs to know my formal title. I intend to keep it that way for now."

"Very well. But may I tell my husband?"

Olivia wanted to ask her to keep it to herself, but she could hardly come between a man and his wife. "He will keep it to himself?"

"Of course. Will is a man of honor."

"Very well." At least she'd found a friend and ally her first day in Mercy Falls.

THREE

HARRISON STRODE ALONG the quay under the glow from the street lamps. The *Atlantis* bobbed offshore. Several dinghies plied the waters with lanterns, but he heard no shouts of discovery. The wind freshened and brought the scent of rain to his nose. The first drops fell moments later.

Will glanced at him. "It's been more than an hour."

Rain began to patter harder, and Harrison adjusted his hat to keep the moisture off his face. "Now that she's missing, I'm beginning to rethink her account. Maybe someone really did toss her into the sea."

"You told the constable her story?"

"Yes. He seemed to give it as little credence as I first did."

Will shrugged. "She'll turn up sooner or later. Nothing we can do with the storm coming in. Come to the house for coffee. Katie made cookies this afternoon. And fresh bread."

Going back to the empty manor house didn't appeal. Since Eleanor's death, Harrison found himself seeking out friends. Being with Will and Katie held more allure than he could resist. "My thanks. If you're sure I wouldn't be intruding."

"You're one of Katie's favorite people. And Jennie's. My daughter will be in your lap before you can take your first bite of cookie."

Harrison's spirits lifted at the thought of the little girl. She'd taken a liking to him last summer. Will and Katie had thrown a party on their anniversary and the whole town had come out for it. Jennie had attached herself to his leg all evening.

He'd thought he might have a little one of his own in the next year. Until he saw Eleanor's true nature.

He noticed a captain approaching along the shore with another sailor and hailed them. "Are you in charge of this ship?" he asked, gesturing to the floating hulk in the waves.

"Yes," the man said.

"I pulled the woman out of the sea. What have you heard?"

The captain tipped his hat back on his forehead. "I didn't see her go overboard, but First Officer Nettles here did. Nettles, tell this man what you saw."

The other man was about forty. Slim, with a weathered face and a hooked nose. "Wasn't much. I heard a shout and rushed to the railing. I saw Lady Devonworth in the water. A few minutes later a man dived overboard."

"That was me. She screamed?"

Nettles shrugged. "A scream or a shout. Not sure what it was."

The same shout he'd heard. "Was the sea rough enough to cause her fall?" He hadn't thought it that rough, but perhaps a woman leaning on the railing could have been pitched overboard.

The captain shook his head. "This was before the storm moved in. Mild seas and just a little wind. Not even any rain."

"Then how did she get into the water?" When the men glanced at one another uneasily, Harrison stared at Nettles. "Did you see anyone else at the railing?"

"No, sir."

"No footsteps, nothing?"

The man hesitated. "There's often folks on deck, sir. There's always footsteps."

Lady Devonworth. She was titled, so maybe she had money. A kidnapping might have netted a blackguard some money, but she was worthless dead. Unless it was a kidnapping gone wrong?

"Thank you for your time," he told the men. When they walked away, he turned back to Will. "That coffee is sounding better and better."

❧

Flames danced in the fireplace. Dry now, Olivia's hair lay on her shoulders and she'd finally stopped shivering. Katie's simple blue dress fit Olivia's slim figure perfectly. What was she going to do? It was clear someone wanted her dead. If the man discovered he'd failed, he would try again. She was tempted to get on a boat and head back up the coast, then take the first train home. But no. She was here to find out what had happened to Eleanor.

Katie bustled back into the room with more tea on a tray. "Now that Jennie is down for the night, we can chat. You have color in your cheeks now," she said, putting the tray on a table. "My, you're quite beautiful. Your hair is lovely. And such dark eyes. Like a Spanish dancer."

Heat rose in Olivia's cheeks, and she began to wind her hair back up on her head. "I can't thank you enough for your hospitality. I'm so sorry to impose in this way."

Katie poured tea into a cup and handed it to her. "It's not an imposition at all! I shall quite enjoy feminine company."

Olivia glanced at the clock on the mantel. "It's only eight? It feels like much later."

"You nearly drowned. That would wear anyone out. There are fresh linens on the bed in the guest room. Whenever you are ready for sleep, I'll show you to your room."

"You're too kind." Olivia was ready to lay her head on the pillow and forget a murderer stalked her. She added sugar to her tea, then heard steps and male voices outside on the porch.

Katie rose. "That's probably Will. Let me tell him what's happened."

"Who is with him?"

"Let me check." She went to the window and pulled back the lace curtain. "Will has Harrison Bennett with him."

Olivia held back a gasp. "You can't tell him I'm here!"

"Will he recognize you?"

The front door opened and footsteps came down the hall. "I don't think so. I was only ten the last time I saw him, and he barely noticed me."

Katie stepped toward the door. "Stay calm. You have to meet him sooner or later."

Olivia rose and nodded as two men stepped into the room. She studied the face of the man who had caused her so much heartache. Harrison's shoulders were broad under the cotton shirt he wore. She'd expected him to be in a suit and exuding wealth and power. His dark hair curled above his ears and along the nape of his neck. He reminded her of a sleek panther that hid its power and true danger until one least expected it.

He stopped when he saw her. "There you are," he said.

She recognized the voice at once. Harrison Bennett was the man who had rescued her from certain death. Her words left her and all she could do was stare.

"We've been scouring the sand and the dock for you, Lady Devonworth," he said, glowering. "I told you to stay put. Do you have any idea how much worry you've caused?"

She found her tongue. "I could hardly stay alone on a dark beach when someone had just tried to kill me. And I must say I resent your tone, sir. You hardly have the right to order me to do anything."

His scowl deepened. Then his dark gaze lightened and he laughed. "You've got a temper, Lady Devonworth."

Katie stepped between her and the men. "It's good to see you, Harrison. I'm sorry to say Jennie is in bed. She'll be so disappointed to have missed you."

Olivia didn't care for the amusement on Harrison's face. And she did *not* have a temper.

The other man chuckled feebly at the obvious tension in the air. "You must be the mermaid Harrison pulled from the sea. I'm Will Jesperson."

Olivia smiled and held out her hand. "Your wife has befriended me when I needed it most, Mr. Jesperson. Thank you for your hospitality."

"We're honored to have you in our home," he said. "How did you end up here?"

Katie helped him out of his anorak. "You can interrogate her by the fire. I'll get some cookies and coffee."

Olivia watched Harrison. Surely women flocked to him. Confidence oozed from his broad shoulders. His square jaw was clean shaven, and his black hair curled a bit on his collar. He returned her perusal, and she averted her gaze.

His brown eyes held no recognition, just curiosity. She extended her hand and glanced at Katie. "You know my name, but you have not introduced yourself."

He took her hand. "Harrison Bennett."

Olivia managed not to snatch her fingers away as he bent. When his lips brushed her skin, she nearly yelped. As soon as it was seemly, she put her hand behind her back. "Are you a businessman, Mr. Bennett?"

"My father and I own some diamond mines in Africa," he said. "We also have a silver mine or two and a few lumber tracts. Our newest acquisition is a black-diamond mine."

With his deep voice and smooth manners, she had no doubt he managed to sell investors on anything he wanted. "I've never seen a black diamond. How interesting. I should like to see one."

"The local jewelry designer recently purchased some. I should be delighted to show them to you."

Jewelry wasn't something she was able to buy right now, but the ruse would allow her to spend time around him. "I need to let the servants at the Stewart manor know I've arrived and am unharmed. If you wouldn't mind escorting me to the residence tomorrow, perhaps we could stop by the jewelry store on the way."

His brows rose. "There is no one in residence there."

"No indeed," she said. "Mrs. Stewart is still mourning the death of her daughter, but she urged me to stay as long as I like. I'm quite tired of the season's parties. The idea of spending time in the country is most alluring."

His smile faded. "If you are close friends of the Stewarts, why did you not immediately indicate you recognized my name?"

"You're right. I should have done so at once. I'm sorry for your loss." The words of condolence nearly choked her, but she managed to keep her smile fixed in place. She settled into the chair by the fire.

"Thank you."

His curt reply made her curl her fingers into her palms. Didn't he care at all about Eleanor's death? "What were you doing on the ship?" she asked.

His brows rose. "The same as you. Coming here. I was returning from business in San Francisco."

Her cheeks heated. "Of course." Could he have been the man who threw her overboard? How convenient he was on the same boat. What better way to gain her trust than to rescue her?

FOUR

THE MOTORCAR HIT a muddy pothole, and if not for Harrison's quick grasp of her arm, Olivia would have gone flying. They sat in the backseat as the driver, Thurman, navigated the rough road, and she was conscious of his elbow brushing hers.

The glowering clouds had temporarily stopped spitting rain, and she could only hope they reached shelter before the storm hit. The rain would ruin her new gown. The canvas top would block little of the elements. At least Will had retrieved her belongings from the ship.

She grabbed the side and hung on for dear life as the open-body Cadillac bounced along the rough streets. She craned her neck to take in the town of Mercy Falls. It was quite attractive to her dazzled eyes. She'd expected nothing more than wooden storefronts in what she considered a backwater, but it was a bustling town with well-dressed men and women strolling the brick sidewalks.

Being with Harrison Bennett set her on edge, but the only way to find out what happened to Eleanor was to spend time in his presence. He would make a slipup that would lead her to the truth.

Thurman parked the automobile in front of a stately stone storefront that boasted a large display of jewelry in its picture window. Harrison leaped over the side of the car and came around to assist her. "The pieces in the window are of paste," he said. "The real items are in the safe."

She lifted her silk skirt free of the mud puddle outside the motorcar and stepped onto the sidewalk with his assistance. "What a pretty town," she said, staring at a charming white church with a tower.

"I like it." The bell tinkled as he opened the door for her.

She stepped onto marble floors. Gold foil papered the walls. The tin ceiling was painted gold as well.

A woman behind the counter discreetly poured tea into delicate china. "Would you care for sugar, Lady Devonworth?"

He must have alerted the staff to her visit. "Two sugars, please." She accepted the tea and sipped it as she moved toward the glass counters. Sparkling jewels captured the light from the chandeliers overhead. She caught her breath at one necklace. "That almost looks like lace," she said, pausing over the display.

The woman beamed. "The platinum adds to that illusion. The weight of diamonds in this piece is five carats total, though they are small to grab the light in a lacelike display."

What was she doing here? She couldn't afford any of this jewelry, not until Bennett made good on his promise. All she had was the small sum she'd brought with her, and that had to last for the summer.

The woman lifted the necklace onto the glass. Harrison lifted it from its black velvet home and draped it around Olivia's neck. It was cold at first but quickly warmed on her skin. She touched the delicate filigree and fingered the glittering diamonds. They were of top quality and picked up facets of light from every direction.

"I quite adore it," she said.

He clipped dangling diamond earrings to her ears. The brush of his warm fingers against her neck made her shiver. She forced herself to stand her ground. He turned her toward the light from the windows and motioned to a full-length mirror. She was not a covetous woman, but seeing her reflection made her long to keep the necklace. "I've never seen anything so lovely."

His gaze never left hers in the mirror. "Nor have I."

Her cheeks burned at the intent in his gaze. What a rogue he was. "And the price?"

"Five thousand dollars."

"I'll think about it," she said, turning away from the mirror. "If you don't mind, we could stop at the manor and let the servants know where to pick up my things."

"Of course."

"If you would be so kind as to undo the clasp." His warm fingers grazed the back of her neck again. She didn't like the way her pulse leaped. The cad knew how to make a woman respond to his touch. No wonder Eleanor had been so enamored. Olivia vowed not to be as weak as her sister. She could see through this man's mask.

He handed the necklace to the sales clerk, and Olivia stepped away before he could remove the earrings. "I can get these." She quickly took them off and handed them to the other woman.

When his fingers touched her elbow, she didn't move toward the door. Not when she had so many questions. She hovered over the display case. "Where are those black diamonds you praised?"

"Right here." He pointed to a bracelet studded with black and white stones.

The black diamonds glittered against the white ones. "Did you buy any of these lovely pieces for your fiancée?" She glanced at him from under her lashes and saw him flinch.

"Unfortunately, I saw Eleanor very little," he said, his tone frosty. "When she arrived, I was on a trip to Africa. She died four days after I returned."

"It was an arranged marriage?"

His brows lowered and his lips thinned. "I'm sure you know it was, Lady Devonworth. If you're such a close friend of the family, you would be quite aware of these things."

"I beg your pardon. I didn't mean to offend you," she said. When his glower didn't diminish, she turned up the wattage on her smile until his lips twitched. She moved toward the door with him.

So, Eleanor had seen little of him, yet she died four days after his arrival from Africa. What did it all mean? And how could Olivia get the truth out of him?

Harrison guided the young woman past the manicured lawns to the sweeping portico of Stewart Hall. The high surf from the approaching storm pounded on the rocks below. The woman's pointed questions about Eleanor left him on edge. He quite detested high-society women who were only interested in gossip.

"The front door is open," Lady Devonworth said.

A man carrying rugs emerged from the open door. Harrison recognized him as footman Jerry Bagley. The young man didn't see them and carried the rugs to the line at the side of the house. A rug beater lay on the ground. He draped the rugs over the line and picked up the beater.

"Jerry, if you have a moment," Harrison called.

Jerry whirled with the beater held up like a weapon. His pug-nosed face relaxed in a smile when he saw them. He struck a pose and dropped the tool. "A woman drove me to drink and I never had the courtesy to thank her for it," he said in a snide drawl.

"W. C. Fields," Harrison said. "Good job."

The young man grinned and picked up the beater again. "He's easy to do. I've got a part in a vaudeville that debuts in two weeks. I hope you can come."

"I wouldn't miss it."

Jerry glanced at Lady Devonworth and his eyes widened. Harrison knew he was taking in the luxury of her silk gown. "This is Lady Devonworth. I assume the house has been prepared for her visit."

"Yes, sir. Mrs. Stewart called several days ago. Mama has been cracking the whip over all of us." He glanced at Lady Devonworth. "She told us to expect—"

"I'm so glad she called to let you know to expect me," Lady Devonworth said. "I'm at the lighthouse right now, but I wanted to make sure you were ready for my arrival."

Harrison stepped past Jerry. "I'll introduce Lady Devonworth to your mother." He guided Lady Devonworth toward the door. "This is your first visit, correct?"

"Yes. Mr. Stewart had the place built four years ago. Or so I was told," she said. "Mrs. Stewart has not seen the manor." Ever since she'd stepped from the car, she'd been aloof. She also hadn't looked at him.

"It's quite large," he said, mounting the steps. He noticed her eyes widen as they stepped into the grand hall. Silk papered the walls. The redwood floors gleamed. A sweeping staircase six feet wide rose to their left. The ceiling in the foyer was fifteen feet high. "The parlor is this way," he said, touching his fingers to her elbow again. She flinched at his touch, and he frowned. He guided her to the large parlor on the right, where they found the housekeeper furiously dusting the items in the china cupboard.

"Mrs. Bagley," he said. She whirled to face him. Her face hardened when she saw him. He pretended not to notice. "This is Lady Devonworth. She had a bit of an adventure yesterday, but she's quite all right."

The older woman wiped her hands on her apron and studied the young lady. Thora's faded blue eyes brightened, and she gave a slight nod as if she approved. "As soon as that lazy son of mine brings in the rugs, the house is ready. Your room has been prepared, Lady Devonworth." She didn't look at Harrison again and did not address him.

Her dislike was nothing new to Harrison. "I'll be pleased to fetch your belongings, Lady Devonworth. You can rest in the parlor and I'll be back with them."

She flushed and shook her head. "That won't be necessary. I can hardly vacate the lighthouse without thanking Will and Katie for their hospitality. If you'll run me back to their home, I'll spend a final evening with them and come tomorrow. If that's all right," she said, directing her question to Thora.

"Of course, your ladyship," Thora said. "If you'd like, I can show you around before you go."

"I should like that." The young woman fell into step beside the housekeeper. Neither looked back at him.

Harrison started to go after them, then decided against it. He didn't care to force his presence on them. "I'll wait here," he said.

He stepped to the window and watched Jerry beat the dirt from the rugs with vigor. The last time he'd been here was the day Eleanor disappeared. He'd come to take her to lunch, and she was pale and quiet. She said hardly anything to him over the meal and had been quick to ask to return home. Now he knew she had to have been planning her suicide.

He was lost in thought for so long he barely registered the women's return. When Lady Devonworth stepped back into the parlor, he was struck with her beauty. Her hair was so dark it was almost black. Her eyes were large and brown, shining with curiosity and a zest for life he found quite appealing. The warm tones of her skin paired with her eyes gave her a stunning beauty that was accentuated by her high cheekbones.

She must have noticed him staring, because faint color tinged her cheeks. "Is everything all right?" she asked.

He liked her voice too, husky and vibrant. It was too bad she made little pretense of hiding her distaste of him. He was unsure what he'd done to displease her. "Is everything to your liking?"

"It's an exquisite home. The ballroom on the third floor is the largest I've ever seen. It would hold nearly the whole town. I don't believe Mrs. Stewart realizes how lovely this place is."

He had no interest in the ballroom. "I'll take you back to the lighthouse if you're ready."

"Of course. I'll return tomorrow," she told Thora. Lady Devonworth put her hand on his arm and allowed him to escort her to the motorcar.

The driver started the Cadillac. Harrison climbed into the backseat with her. "Are you angry about something, Lady Devonworth? Your eyes have been spitting fire at me."

She turned those magnificent eyes on him. "I've been wondering why your fiancée would choose to drown herself," she said.

He stiffened at the rudeness of her comment. "You're very outspoken," he said. "And you don't know me, certainly not well enough to ask such pointed questions about something that is none of your concern. Your set may enjoy gossiping about such a horrific tragedy, but I do not. I'll take you home now and I'll thank you to keep your questions about my personal life to yourself."

FIVE

OLIVIA'S CHEEKS WERE still burning when Harrison stopped the motorcar on the road at the bottom of the hill to the lighthouse. He couldn't let her out fast enough. The surf roared off to their left. Her questions must seem to be extremely rude to him, but she refused to let his opinion matter to her. Not until she was sure of his innocence or guilt. An apology was necessary to smooth things over, but it would pain her to make it.

"Thank you for the day," she said when he opened the door for her. "I beg your pardon for my rudeness. It was quite unconscionable. I can only plead fatigue has addled my brain."

A muscle in his jaw twitched, and pain twisted his mouth. "I accept your apology, Lady Devonworth." He escorted her up the steep steps to the lighthouse. "I'll leave you here, if I may?"

"Of course," she said. She watched him retreat to his auto. He got in front with Thurman. Something like remorse stirred in her, but she ignored it. He deserved every bit of discomfort she might bring him. She would *not* regret anything she said. She pushed open the door.

She met Will in the yard. He wore a distracted expression. "Is there something wrong?" she asked.

"I fear we have a major gale heading our way."

She glanced at the sky, clearing now. "How can you tell? It looks fine."

"The calm before the storm. The barometric pressure is very

low. I must prepare. You'll find Katie inside." He hurried toward the foghorn.

Olivia stepped into the foyer. "Hello?" she called.

"In here, Olivia." Katie's voice floated down the hall. She stepped into view through the doorway and met Olivia before she reached it. "My best friend, Addie, is here."

"You told her about me?"

Katie shook her head. "I've told her nothing, though it pained me to be secretive with her. I assure you anything you wish to discuss is safe with her though. She is most trustworthy."

"Thank you for keeping my secret." Olivia followed Katie into the parlor, where she saw another young woman seated on the sofa. The woman's dark auburn hair was on top of her head, and she wore the latest style of hobble skirt. Olivia hated the style. It was difficult to walk with the hem so tight around the ankles.

"Lady Devonworth, this is Addie North, my best friend," Katie said. "Addie, L-Lady Devonworth from New York." Her bright smile faded as she stumbled over Olivia's title.

Olivia exchanged a glance with Katie. She didn't want her to feel constrained by the lack of candor. "I appreciate the way Katie has helped me, Addie. If I may call you Addie?"

"Of course," the young woman said, glancing at Katie with a question in her eyes. Katie looked away.

Olivia liked the looks of this young woman, and she needed friends right now. She felt so alone. And frightened. She glanced at Katie and gave a slight nod before seating herself in the armchair by the fireplace. "Katie has quickly become a friend when I was in dire need of one," she said. "She assures me you are trustworthy."

"Any friend of Katie's is someone I would defend with my last breath," Addie said. "I hope you will rest in the care we can give you. Katie told me of your near drowning. I hope you're feeling quite recovered."

"I am, thank you." Olivia studied the woman's earnest expression. "My name is Olivia Stewart," she said. "Lady Devonworth is a title I seldom use, but I would plead for your discretion. Let me tell you what has happened." She plunged into the fearful circumstances that had ended with her arrival at the lighthouse. "Someone did his best to ensure I never reached these shores, so I must keep my survival quiet for now."

The color had leached from Addie's cheeks. She smoothed her silk skirt. "My lips are sealed," she said. "This is horrible."

"I gave Katie permission to tell Will. I would not want to come between you and your husband, so you may tell him. I need some allies."

"You can trust my Will and Addie's John," Katie said. She handed Jennie her dolly.

"Do you have any idea who might have done this?" Addie asked. "Did your sister have any enemies?"

Olivia exhaled. "I suspect Mr. Bennett."

Katie's worn boots hit the ground and she stood. "I must disagree most vehemently, Olivia. We have often had Harrison in our home. I don't believe he has one evil bone in his body. Will thinks most highly of him, and Jennie quite adores him."

"Don't you find it most peculiar that someone threw me overboard, and Harrison was on the ship with ample motive and opportunity?"

"But he saved you!"

"It might have been a ruse. Some men are good at hiding their true character. Something happened to my sister, and I mean to find out the truth."

Addie's hand went to her throat. "You fear foul play?"

"She was terrified of water."

Addie's eyes widened. "Ah. So she wouldn't have been out swimming. The attack on your own person bolsters your belief as well," Addie said. "But I agree with Katie. Harrison is an honorable man. He would never have hurt Eleanor. Nor you."

"Harrison was in Africa when she arrived," Katie said. "She came to tea with us a few times at Addie's house. I liked her very much."

"What about . . . suicide?" Addie asked.

Olivia swallowed hard. "She was full of laughter. Marrying Mr. Bennett was all she talked about before she left. I've never seen Eleanor despondent. Never once in her twenty-three years."

Katie took a bite of her cookie. "Perhaps she heard lies about him. I believe you're quite wrong about Harrison. We'll help you get to the bottom of it though. Harrison is one of the most eligible bachelors in town. The unmarried girls were downcast when Eleanor showed up."

Olivia could well believe it. His dark good looks drew attention. "Did Eleanor say anything to either of you about him?" she asked.

Addie paused. "We last saw her two days before she died. She was more quiet than usual. She said something about a letter she'd received from her father."

Olivia's jaw dropped. "From our *father*? He died six months ago."

"That's what she said, from her father."

The blood rushed from Olivia's head and she felt faint. "I don't understand. That was all my sister said?"

Katie bit her lip and glanced at Addie. "Didn't she say something about asking Harrison to explain?" She rubbed her head. "I can't quite remember."

"That's right!" Addie said. "I'd forgotten too. She said Harrison would be able to explain it all, and that she couldn't wait for him to get home."

"I must find that letter," Olivia said slowly.

❧

The lighthouse accommodations were more rustic than Olivia was used to. A handmade quilt covered the mattress on the iron bedstead in her room. Matching curtains hung in the windows. There was no closet, only a chifforobe against one wall. A bowl and pitcher of water rested atop the dresser.

But the room held a warmth she'd never experienced in the elegant mansion on Fifth Avenue. These people were different too. Accepting of who she was. They didn't know she knew the Astors or that she hailed from one of New York's most prominent families. Olivia suspected they wouldn't care if they did know.

She jotted down in her journal her impressions of Mercy Falls, then put down her pen when a knock came at the door. "Come in," she called, knowing it had to be Katie.

But it was little Jennie who popped through the door. "I came for a good-night kiss," she said. She ran to Olivia and tried to climb into her lap.

Olivia lifted the little girl onto her knees. Jennie wrapped her arms around Olivia's neck and turned her cheek up for a kiss. The feel of the warm little body in her arms was quite delightful. She hadn't been around children much, and hugging Jennie, she wished it had been different. The child's trusting expression and round cheeks touched her heart in a way she'd never experienced.

Olivia brushed her lips over the soft cheek smelling of talcum. "Good night, darling." She glanced up to see Katie in the door.

"I hope she didn't disturb you." Katie stepped into the room and held out her arms to her daughter.

Olivia handed Jennie up to Katie. "I loved it."

The wind picked up outside and rattled the windowpanes. Katie frowned when the first spatters of rain struck the glass. "Will says we're in for a bad gale, not just a rainstorm."

"How does he know?"

"He's a weatherman. Always playing with his weather balloons and instruments. He calls in his findings to the weather bureau." She smiled. "Good night."

"Good night." Olivia turned out the light when the other woman shut the door. She tried to settle in for sleep, but her thoughts churned. Could she be wrong about Harrison, or was he just very good at charming his way into women's graces?

She realized the wind had increased in velocity. The gale howled, and she sat up and watched the rain sheeting down the glass. The window rattled, then the glass broke. Rain came in a straight line through the opening. She leaped from the bed and called for the Jespersons. She wrenched open the door and in the hall met Katie, who had Jennie in her arms.

Katie thrust her daughter to Olivia. "Get downstairs! I'll try to cover this hole."

Thunder rumbled and the wind howled again. Jennie clutched Olivia and whimpered. "It's okay," Olivia said, patting the little girl's back awkwardly. The child's sobs ratcheted up with the storm.

She rushed down the steps with the child. When she reached the parlor, sparks were flying onto the floor from the wind churning down the chimney. Olivia set the little girl on a chair and grabbed a rug. She beat out the embers, then took the poker and separated the logs so the fire could die down. Sparks flew out and burned her dress, but she quickly extinguished them. The windows all over the house rattled, and the howling of the wind made her want to cover her ears.

She scooped up the sobbing child. "It's okay, Jennie. The fire is out." Olivia ran to the steps. "Katie, are you all right?"

Katie rushed down the steps. "I couldn't get it covered. I've never seen a storm like this. I wish Will were inside." She plucked her daughter from Olivia's arms.

"Where is he?" Olivia asked.

"In the light tower. I'd insist he come down, but it would do no good. He'll stay up there until the ship that crosses this time of night has passed safely." She paced the floor, humming to Jennie as the wind intensified.

Olivia grabbed an afghan from the back of the sofa as the chill seeped into the room. The storm continued to beat against the building. In spite of the storm's fury, the little girl put her head on her mother's shoulder and slept.

A horrendous crash came from somewhere above them. Katie turned wide eyes on Olivia, then thrust her wailing daughter at her. "I have to check on Will!"

Before she ran up the stairs, more crashes came, then a door banged. Footsteps ran toward them and Will took the final three steps in a leap.

"Get out! The whole thing is coming down." He grabbed Jennie from Olivia, then herded them all to the door.

Olivia paused, not wanting to go out into the storm. How bad could it be?

Katie plucked at her sleeve. "We must get out, Olivia. Come now."

Olivia allowed her friend to lead her out of the lighthouse.

Glass shattered and timbers creaked. They exited into driving rain. The wind nearly knocked Olivia over as she struggled to see through the downpour that instantly drenched her. A huge crash sounded behind them, and she whirled to see the lighthouse collapsing. Every window in the house had been blown out. The tower toppled to the ground.

SIX

WIND AND RAIN lashed Harrison's motorcar as his driver navigated the flooded road from Ferndale to Mercy Falls. It was a wonder the driver could see, though this Cadillac model had a windshield. Still, sheets of rain came in all around the canvas top. Harrison couldn't even see the beacon from the lighthouse in the storm. They were on the outskirts of town. He had responded to a call to help transport a family driven from their home by a flash flood to a relative in Ferndale.

Thurman braked abruptly, and Harrison leaned forward. "What's wrong?"

"Look, sir." The driver indicated a bedraggled column of people out in the storm.

"Good heavens, it's the Jespersons," Harrison said when he saw the man's face. He got out into the drenching rain. "Get in!" he shouted above the din of the storm.

He ushered them into the backseat, then realized there were three adults plus Jennie. Lady Devonworth was with them. He climbed into the front beside his driver. He put his arm on the seat back and turned around to stare at his passengers. Lady Devonworth wore only a nightgown. She shivered in the soaked garment.

"This isn't any drier, but it might warm you," he said as he shrugged off his wet jacket. He handed it back to her, and she murmured her thanks as she slid her arms into it.

Even with dripping hair, she was the most beautiful woman he'd ever seen. Those gypsy black eyes were exotic and compelling, even with her lashes dripping wet and water running down her cheeks.

"What's happened?" he asked.

"The storm blew down the lighthouse," Will said. "I knew it had some weak areas, but I hadn't been able to get money from the Bureau of Lighthouses for repairs."

"Totally gone?" Harrison asked. Will nodded. "No wonder I couldn't see the beacon. I thought it was because the storm was so bad."

"I just pray no ships were grounded out there without it. I think the *Lucy* had already gone past."

"Thank God you were all uninjured. You were in the building when it came down?"

Will nodded. "I was in the tower and barely escaped. I got the women out, and the next gust caved in the roof. It's totally destroyed."

"You're all unhurt. That's the important thing." Harrison glanced at Thurman. "Let's get everyone to my house."

His driver nodded. "We'll be home in five minutes."

"Turn up the heat," Harrison told Will. "The gas burner is by your feet."

Will complied, and the burner sputtered. The rain blew in on everyone in the backseat. He tucked his coat around his daughter, then slipped his arm around his wife. "I've never seen a storm like this. The wind speeds topped a hundred miles an hour."

"You're welcome to spend the night at my house," Harrison said. "You too, Lady Devonworth. Unless you'd rather I have my driver take you to the Stewart manor?"

She hesitated. A wary expression crossed her face, then she shook her head. "I don't want to rouse the household at this hour. Thank you for your kind offer. I shall take you up on it."

The car reached his home, and Thurman braked at the sidewalk. "I have an umbrella, sir," he said.

"I think we're all too wet for it to matter," Harrison said. "Don't trouble yourself. The rain is slowing. Ready to make a run for it?" he asked his guests.

When they nodded, he got out, then helped Lady Devonworth out while Will lifted Katie and Jennie from the motorcar. They all ran for the front door. Harrison held on to Lady Devonworth's elbow and hurried her toward the haven inside. They burst into the warmth of the foyer and shook water all over the floor.

He saw Lady Devonworth take in the opulent hall and the curving staircase to the second floor. "It's more grand than I need," he said. "But my father insists on the best of everything."

Mrs. Lindrum rushed toward them with towels. "Oh goodness, Mr. Harrison, you're all going to catch your death of cold. Come in by the fire." His housekeeper motioned to the ladies to follow her.

His collie, Nealy, bounded to meet him. He rubbed his dog's head, and Nealy whined, then went to greet the women. Lady Devonworth jumped back when she saw the dog. Her eyes went wide.

She darted behind Will. "Get him away!"

"Nealy won't hurt you," Harrison assured her.

Her face went even more pale. "I was bitten when I was a child," she said softly. "Dogs terrify me."

He clucked his tongue. "Nealy, come." The dog came to his side and lay down by his feet.

Katie and Lady Devonworth left the wet towels on the floor and disappeared through the parlor door. Harrison toweled off his hair, then followed with Will, who still had Jennie in his arms. She lay quietly with her head on his shoulder and her eyes wide as the thunder roared outside.

"Want some cookies and milk, honey?" Harrison asked her. She nodded and reached for him. He took her and held her close. "You're cold. I'll get you a blanket." He carried her into the parlor with the women and asked Mrs. Lindrum to fetch refreshments. An afghan was on the sofa, and he wrapped it around the little girl.

When she snuggled her head against him, he saw Lady Devonworth's attention fixed on them. "She likes me," he said.

"Obviously," she said.

There was a note in her voice he didn't quite understand. Surprise or disquiet? She seemed wary around him too, and he'd given her no reason to distrust him. He couldn't figure her out.

~∗~

The hot chocolate warmed Olivia's insides and her teeth finally quit chattering. Mrs. Lindrum had found clothing for the ladies to change into. The dressing gowns could have covered her and Katie twice over. They were darned and worn, obviously the housekeeper's, but at least they were dry and clean.

Olivia pushed aside one of the blankets Mrs. Lindrum had wrapped around her, then glanced around the guest room. It had been newly redecorated. Had Eleanor ever stayed here? Olivia could have gone to Stewart Hall, but she couldn't resist this opportunity to learn more about Harrison, to explore his house for clues.

She put down her mug and went to the door. Putting her ear to the wood, she listened. Nothing. Hopefully everyone was in bed. It was after ten. She eased open the door and stepped into the hall. Darkness cloaked the space. She didn't know the house so it was going to be hard to find her way to the staircase. Inching along with her hand on the wall, she felt her way to the end of the hallway. The wall under her fingers ended, and the staircase opened in front of her. Pale light shone from below. Her feet made no sound as she tiptoed down the runner covering the polished wood steps.

Once she reached the foyer, she paused and looked both directions. She'd already been to the left, so this time she turned right and found a doorway opening into a library. Not even knowing what she was looking for, she stepped in and shut the door behind her.

The room was dark, but she'd seen electric lights in the parlor, so she ran her hand beside the door and twisted the knob she found. The room flooded with light. She glanced at the shelves. It was not the typical library for a man. The glass shelves held a mishmash of popular titles. Dog-eared and worn, they weren't the leather-bound copies that were only for show. The desk wasn't the ornate object so often chosen for its imposing size. It was austere, but more of the Arts and Crafts movement. Papers littered the battered top. Harrison actually used this desk. He didn't bring people in here to impress them with his furnishings.

She moved deeper into the room and glanced at the titles. A complete collection of Mark Twain filled a shelf, and Jack London novels crowded another. The next shelf held Doyle novels. She raised her brows at the collection of Austen novels, and a smile lifted her lips. The man had a romantic side? He seemed all business.

The door creaked behind her, and she whirled to see Harrison standing in the doorway. He was in his dressing gown, and his hair stood on end like a boy's.

He stopped and stared. "Lady Devonworth? Is something wrong?"

She stepped away from the shelves. "Not at all. I . . . I couldn't sleep."

"Ah, I am in the same predicament. I see your solution is the same as mine." He gestured to the shelves. "Find a good book to read."

"I'm sorry if I am intruding."

"Feel free to choose what you like."

"You have read all these books?"

"Most of them." He moved to the shelves and pulled down *The Call of the Wild*.

She couldn't help the smile that curved her lips. "Even Jane Austen?" She touched the spine of *Pride and Prejudice*. "This looks well read." He chuckled, and she found her smile widening. The man was much too charming. She pulled the book down. "Afraid to answer me?"

He nodded. "I can see it now—you'll announce it at a party some time. My reputation will be ruined."

She laughed. "Seriously, you've read Austen?"

"Of course. I undertook a study of your fair sex some years ago. Women are most bewildering."

"Did the books help?"

He shook his head. "I still find women indecipherable."

Her smile stilled, but the question on her lips sprang out. "Do you agree that a man with a fortune is in need of a wife?"

His smile vanished. "So might say women who are only interested in a man's wallet." He stepped to the door. "I'll bid you good night and leave you to choose your own reading material."

She warned herself not to be taken in by him, as her sister had been. He was not the man he presented to the world. She just had to prove it.

SEVEN

THE BREEZE LIFTED the hair on the back of Harrison's neck as he bent over the aeroplane's engine. He tightened a bolt, then closed the hatch. Perfect afternoon for flying. And it would wash away the last of the bad taste left in his mouth from that woman's nosiness. What was she doing in his library last night? He doubted it had been to look for a book.

"Let's get in the air!" Jerry Bagley yelled from the open-air cockpit of the biplane. "Sundown will be here too soon. And Mama will be after your hide if I'm late."

Harrison nodded and cranked the propeller over. Mrs. Bagley thought he was going to get her son killed, and she worried whenever Jerry was away from the house. Harrison cranked the propeller again until it caught and began to whirl.

He ducked under the wing and climbed in front of the young footman. He waved at his mother, who sat in her wheelchair at the edge of the field. She waved back, and he prayed he'd make her proud today. Her attendant, Mary Grace, maneuvered the chair into a better position and adjusted the black blanket around his mother's knees. The ribbons on his mother's straw hat fluttered in the breeze, and she wore a bright smile.

Jerry slapped him on the back and gave him a thumbs-up. Harrison opened the throttle as far as he dared, and the aeroplane began to roll over the uneven ground of the meadow. It picked up momentum as it went. The wind nearly snatched his leather hat from his head, and he hunkered down and watched the trees coming much too fast. He'd have to brake if he didn't get lift soon.

He leaned forward. "Come on, come on," he whispered. The wheels on the flying machine bounced, then didn't touch ground. He guided the nose up. Just like that, they were in the air. Five feet above the ground, then ten, then twenty. Moments later the machine was soaring over the tops of the trees. His grin nearly split his face, and he shrieked his elation into the howling wind as he pumped his fist in the air. He grinned back at Jerry, whose eyes were huge in his freckled face.

He waggled the biplane's wings at the speck far below that was his mother. His chest was near to bursting. It was the highest he'd ever successfully lifted a flying machine into the air. He guided the plane over the ocean's whitecaps, then down to land on the field. The wheels bumped and the plane went aloft again before settling down. Once the machine slowed and stopped, he leaped from the seat and clambered down.

His mother's face shone with pride and she waved to him. Mary Grace rolled her chair toward the plane.

Harrison rushed to meet them. "We made it over the trees, Mother!"

Esther Bennett had been in the wheelchair for ten years—ever since she was struck by a carriage—but Harrison had never heard her complain once. Though she didn't understand his passion for flight, to her credit, she'd given up trying to talk him out of working with the plane.

"You're a real birdman, Harrison," she said when he reached her. "I'm so proud of you. I'll telephone your father tonight."

His grin faded. "I'd rather you didn't. When he comes to visit, I'll have to endure one of his lectures about not wasting my time."

She gripped his hands. "He only wants what's best for you, Harrison. He's very proud."

"He has a strange way of showing it," he said. "All I ever hear is how much time and money I waste on my 'little hobby,' as he calls it."

"Everything your father has, he fought for. He wants you to have all the advantages he never had. I'm sure he will be quite proud of you when he hears this news."

Harrison nodded but said nothing more. This was a topic they would never come to agreement on. "Did you hear the lighthouse blew down last night?" he asked. "The Jespersons and their guest spent the night with me."

His mother gasped. "Are they all right?"

"Yes. They escaped the structure before it fell, and I found them standing in the downpour. They were all having breakfast when I left this morning."

His mother adjusted her hat. "A guest was with them, you say? Who is it?"

"A Lady Devonworth from New York."

She pursed her lips. "I thought I knew all the peerage who resided in the city. I've never heard of her."

"She was staying with the Jespersons temporarily but is going to reside at Stewart Hall. I believe she plans to take up residence today. She appears to be a close friend of theirs."

"It's quite odd she would be staying there with none of the Stewarts in town. Especially considering the circumstances. Was she a friend of Eleanor's?"

"I don't believe so." Now that he thought about it, he wasn't sure of that at all. She'd offered her condolences but said nothing about her relationship to the young woman. Lady Devonworth said very little about herself, in fact.

"What is she like?"

He shrugged. "Typical for that set. Interested in balls and parties." He stared back at the aeroplane. The comet was coming soon, and he planned to make history. He'd be soaring above the treetops when that star grew bright, and if the colors of the tail flashed in the sky as he hoped, flying into it would be the ultimate test for him, proof that he was more than his father's mouthpiece. He'd be proud of himself even if his father rolled his eyes at his accomplishments.

⌘

Debris littered the sand and rocks. Olivia grabbed a tattered dress that the wind had draped across a tree limb. Tears rolled down Katie's cheeks as she stared at the wreckage. Jennie didn't seem to notice her mother's distress. She scampered through the mess, retrieving toys.

Will shouted and waved his arms. "Farther out!" he shrieked at the ship offshore. The boat veered closer to the dangerous rocks. He ran to the edge of the cliff, but the vessel seemed to pay no attention.

A grinding noise split the air. Will groaned. "They're grounded. I'd better get help." He jogged down the slope and off toward the pier.

Katie stooped to pick up a battered pot. "What are we going to do?" she asked. "Will called the Bureau of Lighthouses. There is no money to rebuild right now. We have to wait until they can ask Congress for money."

"B-But where will you live? Do they know it's completely uninhabitable?"

She nodded. "They know. We could stay with Addie and John, but they have guests right now. I suppose we'll have to find a place to rent."

"You can stay with me," Olivia said. "There's plenty of room at Stewart Hall, and I'd like the company." When she saw she had Katie's attention, she smiled. "I need protection too, remember? You'd be doing me a favor. With Will in the house, an attacker would be less likely to strike again."

"You're sure?" Katie asked. "It might be several months."

"You can stay until the lighthouse is rebuilt, even if it's a year or two." Her gaze swept the destruction. "The whole thing is gone."

Katie's gaze was on the grounded ship. "Men will die while we wait."

Olivia had come close to dying in that water. Shuddering, she stared at the waves rolling to shore. "What about raising the money yourself?"

Katie scooped up her daughter. "An ice-cream social isn't going to raise the kind of funds we need."

Olivia stared at the Fresnel lens shattered on the ground. "I have an idea," she said slowly. "I'll host a ball at the manor house! A masquerade. We'll call it the Lightkeeper's Ball. I'll invite all my friends from New York. It will be a huge event and a way for them to see the Wild West. My friends will *love* it!"

"Why would your friends travel three thousand miles to attend a ball?" Katie asked, her brow furrowed.

"You don't know how bored my set gets. The summer season is coming, and they are always looking for something new to do or try. Anything that is remotely different or adventurous will have them rushing to join in."

The more she thought about the idea, the more she knew it would work. The bored New York set was always up for the unexpected. Instead of going to Newport for the summer, she would talk them into coming here for a May ball, then a summer on the Pacific shore.

"How much money would it take to rebuild?" Olivia asked.

"At least fifteen thousand, according to Will. The lens will have to be replaced."

She waved her hand. "That's nothing to my friends. Just one of them could pay that."

Katie's tears had dried and a smile made its way to her face. "Seriously, Olivia? You'd really be able to do this?"

"I've planned dozens of parties. This will be no problem."

Katie hugged her. "Thank God he brought you here when he did!"

Olivia wasn't used to physical displays, but there was something about her friend's fierce embrace that warmed her. People in her set tried not to show emotion. It felt good to know she could do something for these friends who had helped her when she needed it most.

They spent the morning picking through their things to see what was salvageable. Addie and John North arrived to help as well. Olivia wished she'd had her trunk delivered to Stewart Hall instead of to the lighthouse. Nearly everything was ruined. Most of Katie's things were torn and ripped as well, and she sniffled occasionally as the extreme damage became apparent.

Olivia heard a man's voice hail them and turned to see Harrison loping up the slope in their direction. He stopped when he reached her, his mouth gaping as he took in the destruction.

He stooped to pick up a broken doll.

"There isn't much left," Olivia said.

He turned the doll over in his hands. "I bought this for Jennie. I must buy her another."

He had bought the doll for Jennie? She studied his crestfallen expression. How much of his concern was real? Could she be wrong about him?

EIGHT

STEWART HALL SEEMED cold and lonely. The Jespersons were purchasing necessary items in town. Olivia arranged the skirt of her dress, one of Eleanor's she'd found upstairs, on the velvet sofa in the parlor and sipped her tea. Scones lay untouched on the silver tray.

Servants hurried past in the hallway, and the scent of dinner being prepared wafted into the room. The aroma of roast beef was no more appetizing than the scones to her. She closed her eyes and imagined herself back home. At this time of the afternoon, her mother would be attending to correspondence and going over household bills with her secretary. The birds would be chirping on the cherry trees out back, and her cat would be lying in wait on the patio in hopes one of them would lose all caution. Before her departure, Eleanor would have been chattering about the latest party or the new dress she'd ordered.

Olivia almost thought she could feel her sister's presence here. She'd sensed it yesterday too. Closing her eyes, she imagined Eleanor running through these halls. She would have livened the stuffy rooms and brought excitement into every corner. Putting down the cup of tea, she rose and moved to the window. The housekeeper would know where Eleanor had been buried. Olivia intended to visit the grave this afternoon. It was something she'd been dreading. She'd much rather remember her sister with her blue eyes alight with life and laughter.

She went to find Mrs. Bagley. The woman was supervising the

polishing of silver in the butler's pantry. Footmen rubbed at the forks and barely glanced up when Olivia stepped into the doorway.

Mrs. Bagley turned with an armload of linens in her hands. "Lady Devonworth. I didn't see you there. Is there something I can do for you?" The doorbell rang. "Jerry, would you get that? You'll have to sign my name for the delivery." She put down the linens. "How can I help you?"

"I'd like a moment of your time, please." Olivia walked back into the dining room with the housekeeper following her. The rest of the servants didn't need to overhear their conversation.

"Is something wrong, miss? Your room is not to your satisfaction?" the woman asked. "I put you in the room we'd prepared for Miss Olivia. Is she coming at all now?"

"I'll be the only one in residence for now," Olivia said, skirting an outright lie. "The room is lovely, thank you. You've been here a long time, Mrs. Bagley?"

Thora bobbed her head. "Ever since Mr. Stewart built the manor four years ago."

"Then you were present when Eleanor Stewart resided here?"

"Of course. Much too good for the likes of Mr. Bennett."

"You don't like Mr. Bennett?"

"It's not my place to say anything."

Olivia didn't point out that the woman had just said that very thing in so many words. "Did he not treat Miss Eleanor well?"

Mrs. Bagley sniffed. "He's an adventurer, that one. He'll never settle down. I fear he's going to get my son killed one of these days."

"Killed? How?"

"Him and his flying machine. He's turned Jerry's head with it."

"Harrison has a flying machine? He seems all businessman and not at all an adventurer."

"He's not what you think."

"What is he like, then?" At some point Olivia knew the woman would clam up, but at least she was talking for now.

"Full of notions and big plans. All the ladies cluster when he's around."

Olivia could well believe that. "Did he get along with Eleanor?"

"Miss Eleanor didn't see much of him. He was gone when she first arrived. Quite unforgivable for him to be off gallivanting when his bride was coming."

"Did you see her the day she died?"

The woman glanced up, then back to the rug on the floor. "Yes, miss." Her tone was sullen. Though she didn't have the nerve to question Olivia's interest, her tense shoulders and reticent manner told the story.

Olivia said, "I told her mother I would see what I could find out about the circumstances leading up to Eleanor's death."

"As you wish, miss."

"So how did she seem?" Olivia asked, letting her impatience show in her voice.

"Perfectly normal. She ate her breakfast, then called for the open motorcar to be brought around. She had a luncheon engagement."

"With whom?"

"She didn't say."

"She was home for dinner?"

Mrs. Bagley shook her head. "When I heard the front door, it was after midnight. I had the maid take her breakfast up, but the bed was empty. It didn't appear to have been slept in."

"I want to visit Miss Eleanor's grave. Where might I find it?"

"There's a graveyard beside the Mercy Falls Community Church. She's along the iron fence at the back. Near the biggest tree."

"One more question. I heard Eleanor received a letter from her father. Can you confirm that?"

"I don't snoop in the mail, Lady Devonworth," Mrs. Bagley said, her tone offended.

"Of course not. I didn't mean to imply you did. Thank you, Mrs. Bagley." Olivia rushed away, not wanting the housekeeper to see her impending tears.

She reached the entry and started for the parlor. The sound of carriage wheels rattled through the window. She glanced toward the circular drive and saw Goldia alight from a cab. It would be just like her to blurt out Olivia's real name in the excitement of being reunited. It would be best for their first meeting here to be in private so the servants wouldn't be made aware.

"I'm going to my room for a few minutes," she told the footman. When confusion clouded his eyes, she brushed past him and rushed up the steps. He would wonder why she was explaining her movements to him.

In the sanctuary of her chamber, she sat in the upholstered chair by the window and listened for her maid's footsteps. Olivia had chosen this room the moment she saw it. The colors of palest blue with touches of yellow were her favorite.

Goldia's quarters would be on the third floor at the back of the house. Perhaps Olivia could creep up the back stairway and find her. She waited for ten minutes, then opened her door and slipped into the hall. No one was about. The rooms and halls were confusing, and she got turned around twice before she found the door to the third floor. The steps creaked under her feet, and she winced, then reminded herself it would be perfectly natural for her to be exploring the manor.

The third floor was well lit. She went from door to door and realized the entire floor was a ballroom with the exception of a bathroom and enormous butler's pantry. She'd seen the ballroom when Harrison first brought her here, but she'd thought the servants' rooms would be up here too. She found another set of stairs and ascended them to the attic. As soon as she stepped onto the wide, unpainted boards, she heard voices. The servants' quarters had to be here. She ducked down a hall as the door ahead opened and the chambermaid stepped out. Once the woman went down the steps, Olivia tiptoed to the room the woman had vacated.

Goldia stood by the window. A white cap covered her blond hair, and her normally pink cheeks were pale. Olivia gave a curious glance around the room. She'd never been in a servant's room before. Her mother had always taken care of the staff. The starkness surprised her. No rug on the floor, minimal furnishings, and an iron bed with peeling paint were the only furnishings.

She shut the door behind her. "Goldia," she whispered, holding a finger to her lips as her maid whirled to face her with wide eyes.

"M-Miss Olivia?" the girl stammered. "Oh my dear Miss Olivia! I thought you were dead until that nice lightkeeper told me different!" She flew across the room to throw her arms around Olivia in an extravagant gesture. "I was so relieved when I got the message."

Olivia hugged her back, relishing the relief in the tight embrace. "Shh, Goldia, remember that you can't tell anyone who I am."

Goldia rubbed her forehead. "I don't see how you can fool anyone for long, Miss Olivia. Someone is bound to figure it out."

Olivia bit her lip. "I fear the news getting out after that man tried to drown me."

"Hire a bodyguard," the maid suggested.

Olivia shook her head. "It's more than the danger. I am quite determined to find out who killed Eleanor."

"Mr. Harrison would help you," Goldia said. "He cared about her."

"I suspect he had something to do with her death," Olivia said, her voice hardening. "He is the last person I would ask for help."

"What can I do, miss?"

Olivia stared at her maid. Goldia had been a stalwart champion and constant companion for three years. "Some friends of Eleanor's told me she received a letter from our father that distressed her. I need to find that correspondence. It must be here in this house."

Goldia put her hand to her mouth. "That's impossible, Miss Olivia. Mr. Stewart is dead."

"I know it seems unlikely, but I believe the woman who told me about it. Perhaps it was sent before Father's death and was delayed somehow. You must help me find it."

❧

Harrison knocked on the door of the mansion with a doll for Jennie in his hand. His eyes burned from the late-night work the past two days. The doorman showed him to the parlor, where he found Lady Devonworth on the sofa. The deep garnet in her dress made her dark eyes look even more magnificent. She was a most annoying woman, but he couldn't deny she was one of the most beautiful ones he'd ever seen.

"Good afternoon, Mr. Bennett," she said.

"Lady Devonworth." He brushed his lips across the back of the hand she extended to him.

"You look a bit tired, sir. Are you well?"

"Quite well. I've been working late."

She motioned to the space beside her. "Please join me for tea and dessert. The cook here is very talented. The cranberry trifles are delightful."

He sat gingerly on the edge of the sofa. The delicate perfume she wore wafted to his nose. He would never fit in with her kind of high society. Why did his father even wish it? Harrison would much rather be soaring on the wind.

"Where are Katie and Will? I brought a new doll for Jennie." He showed it to Olivia.

She took the bisque doll and traced the cheeks and nose. "Is this a Kestner doll?"

"It is. Don't you think she looks like Jennie?" The eyes and tiny teeth had caught his attention the moment he walked past its department-store shelf.

"She does, yes. Jennie will be thrilled." She handed it back to him. "Katie took her to buy some shoes. Will is meeting with someone from the Bureau of Lighthouses. I don't expect either of them home for several hours."

He took a treat when she offered the plate. The cranberry trifle flooded his tongue with flavor as he searched for some kind of light conversation. He was used to talking with men where the topics ranged from politics to the approaching comet.

"Are you settling into the house?" he asked, desperate to break the silence.

"Oh yes. It's quite lovely. Not exactly my taste," she said, glancing around the parlor. "I'd love to get rid of the velvet and replace it with damask or silk. It's a little heavy and stiff. But redecorating is hardly worth the cost when so many people are out of work and struggling to put food on the table."

He raised his brows but said nothing.

"You look surprised, Mr. Bennett. I do have thoughts in my head beyond fashion and parties. For example, I've been watching the comet's approach. Do you think we shall all die if the earth passes through the tail? There was a peddler here yesterday trying to sell us comet pills. The silly housekeeper actually bought some."

"So you doubt our danger?" Harrison asked.

"Don't you?" Her full lips tilted in a smile. "I see nothing in the Bible to indicate the earth's demise will be from poisonous gas."

She was more intelligent than he'd given her credit for. "I've talked to several scientists. Some believe our destruction is imminent and others laugh it off."

"What about you?"

He shrugged. "I intend to be in the air if we are lucky enough to pass through the tail."

Her hand holding the cup of tea paused on its way to her mouth. "The air? In your flying machine?"

"That's right. I'm a birdman," he said. "I got it to four thousand feet this week."

She glanced down and said nothing for a long moment. "I've longed to experience a flying machine ever since I saw one three years ago."

"You're not afraid?"

She leaned forward. "No. I should like to go up sometime."

He eyed her. "I'm looking for investors. Would you be interested in being part of the venture?"

She sipped her tea. "I'm interested, Mr. Bennett. I had a small stake in a flying machine in San Francisco, but it crashed and the pilot decided he had no more interest in it."

To Harrison's shock, he discovered he was enjoying talking to the woman. She was interesting and articulate. "I'd be honored to show you my plane. I envision someday there will be air travel between here and New York." When she didn't laugh, he went on. "Even between New York and Paris."

She nodded, her dark eyes grave. "I have no doubt you're right. We're on the cusp of great discoveries. Our nation is full of inventive, intelligent people. The changes we shall see in the next twenty years will be amazing." She took up her tea again. "Did Eleanor go up in your plane?"

"She did not." Until she'd brought up Eleanor's name, he'd actually begun to like her.

NINE

OLIVIA SIPPED HER tea and watched him with Jennie on his lap. The little girl was exclaiming over her new doll. Who was he under that businessman's attire? Had his dangerous streak frightened off Eleanor?

"You're looking quite pensive," Katie said, taking off her gloves. A whiff of fresh air clung to her clothing. She handed over her purchases to a maid before joining Olivia on the sofa.

Olivia forced a smile. "It's been a tiring few days. Have you heard how Will's meeting went?"

Katie selected a trifle, then shook her head. "I didn't see him in town." She smiled at Harrison. "You are a hero in Jennie's eyes. All she's talked about today is how sad she was about her broken dolly."

"Mommy, she has eyes that move!" Jennie rocked the doll back and forth.

Katie got up to examine the doll. "She looks a little like you, sweetheart."

Olivia worried about Katie's pale cheeks and the circles under her eyes. "Are you all right? Perhaps you need to rest."

She nodded. "I shall do that in a little while. I'm quite hungry." She nibbled on the cranberry trifle.

Olivia looked back at Harrison. Could a man who was so tender with a child actually be a murderer? It seemed so out of character. She hadn't expected to find anything that challenged her views of the man. Especially within days of setting foot in Mercy Falls.

"How is your mother?" Katie asked him.

"Quite well. She came out to watch me fly the other day."

"What does your aeroplane look like?" Olivia asked.

"Why are you so interested in flight, Lady Devonworth?" he asked. "I must say, it's a bit peculiar."

There was more than curiosity in his face. It sounded like admiration in his tone too. "There's something so—free—about not being tethered to the earth," she said. "It appears to me that you would have an entirely different perspective on the earth from up there too. I peruse any pictures taken from an aeroplane. I'd love to see the ground from high up like that myself."

"It's a rather dangerous pastime."

She sipped her tea. "There have been accidents but few fatalities. Have any women learned to fly yet?"

"Not to my knowledge."

Though she wanted to proclaim her intention to be the first, she knew it was impossible. Her friends would be scandalized if she learned to fly. Something so outrageous wasn't done. "Jennie is asleep," she observed.

"I don't mind."

"Perhaps you should put her in her bed," Katie said.

He glanced down at the child with the doll still clutched in her arms. "If you would be so kind as to show me to her room?"

"I'll do it," she told Katie when she stared to rise. "Rest."

Olivia led the way up the staircase to the small room that held Jennie's things. It was outfitted in pink and white. The white bedstead was small and low to the ground, perfect for a three-year-old. She pulled back the covers. He laid the little girl on the sheet, then unlaced her shoes and gently tugged them from her feet.

A lump formed in her throat as she watched him exercise such love and tenderness toward the child. She reminded herself that even murderers were sometimes fathers. Loving a child had nothing to do with his true character.

He tucked the doll into her arms, then pulled the covers up around Jennie. When he turned to exit the room, his dark eyes were gentle. The gentleness vanished when he looked at Olivia. "What do you have against me, Lady Devonworth? We've only just met, yet you bait me at every turn. Do you enjoy seeing me squirm when Eleanor's name is mentioned? I know what people say—that she would rather die than marry me. It's all gossip. I would have thought an intelligent woman like yourself would look deeper."

"People think she killed herself?" Though Katie and Addie had mentioned the possibility, Olivia hadn't realized it was the speculation of the public.

"The topic has been mentioned."

"Why do you care what I think?"

He pressed his lips together. "I have no idea why I care," he said. "For some reason it grates that you would be so quick to believe the worst."

Her pulse jumped in her throat. She examined his expression. Was that genuine hurt in his eyes? Surely he wouldn't really care what she thought. Was he attempting to use his charm on her?

"I don't really know you, Mr. Bennett. I apologize if you thought I was being judgmental. I told Eleanor's mother I would try to discover more about what happened to her."

His lips pressed together. He brushed past her. "Good night, Lady Devonworth."

She followed as he stalked down the stairs. The front door slammed. That had been awkward. She feared the coldness between them would thwart her investigation. She had to take more care to hide her disdain.

Katie met her at the doorway when she entered the parlor. "It sounded as though Harrison slammed the door on his way out."

"I fear I angered him with too many questions about Eleanor."

"Oh dear. He's really a wonderful man, Olivia. Why are you so sure he murdered Eleanor?"

"Don't you find it odd that she died within days of his return to town? It was an arranged marriage. Perhaps he objected."

"That doesn't mean he murdered her."

"Harrison said others in town have speculated she killed herself rather than marry him. Is this true?"

Katie nodded. "No one really knows what happened, so they talk."

"I don't believe it. Something happened to her. I intend to find out what." She realized her friend was even more pale. "Are you all right?"

"I . . . I need the bathroom." Katie rushed down the hall to the room on the left.

Olivia heard her retching and followed. "You're ill."

Katie was white as she turned from rinsing her mouth in the sink. "I'm increasing."

"How lovely!" Olivia hugged her and led her back to the parlor. "Does Will know?"

Katie shook her head. "I didn't want to tell him until I was sure. I saw Dr. Lambertson today, and he confirmed it."

Olivia guided her to the sofa and lifted her feet onto the cushions. "All the more reason for the ball to be a success, so we can get to planning the nursery."

❧

Stewart Hall was quiet. The Jespersons weren't up yet, though Olivia supposed the servants were busy below on the first floor. She crept down the hall to her sister's room. It still held the essence of Eleanor's perfume. Olivia stood by the bed and closed her eyes. She could nearly hear her sister's laughter.

Goldia touched her hand and broke the spell. "Are you all right, Miss Olivia?"

Olivia opened her eyes. "I miss her, Goldia."

The maid's eyes were moist. "She's in a better place."

"I hope so." The prospect of heaven always confused Olivia. How could a person know when she was good enough to get there? She'd gone to church all her life but never had a sense of knowing who God was, or that he really knew her soul. Eleanor's death made Olivia think more about her own life.

She went to the closet and opened the door. The space was nearly as big as a room. Pink and blue silk dresses festooned with lace hung inside. Hatboxes were stacked nearly to the ceiling. Slippers lined the floors. Eleanor's perfume wafted into the air, even stronger now. She'd culled the dresses suitable for her own figure the day she arrived, but it was time to search for clues.

Olivia caught the sleeve of the closest dress, a royal-blue satin with a white lace overlay. "I remember when she wore this to the Astors' ball last season," she said.

"I'm surprised she brought it with her," Goldia said.

"I think she wanted to recapture that night. I expect she found an occasion to wear it here. No one would have seen her in it before."

Goldia nodded. "What are we looking for? Just an envelope?"

Olivia began to rummage through the clothing. "I assume she left it in the envelope, but she might not have. If it was truly important, she would have hidden it somewhere."

"Maybe with her jewels," Goldia suggested.

Olivia shook her head. "It's the first place someone would look." She stepped deeper into the closet, allowed the aromas to envelop her. The dresses rustled as she brushed past them. She ran her fingers along the luxurious fabrics. Eleanor was so much more equipped for this life than she was. Most of the time she felt she was living someone else's life. Wasn't there more to her existence than the next party and the latest fashion? Though she was ashamed to admit it to herself, she felt a real purpose in tracking down who had harmed Eleanor. She found her mind and spirit quite engaged with the puzzle. Though of course it was so much more than a puzzle. She wanted whoever had killed her sister brought to justice.

Pushing aside several dresses, she studied the back of the closet. Plain plaster walls painted pink were all she saw. She studied the floor and baseboard. Nothing.

"I'd like you to go through all the hatboxes," she told Goldia. "Perhaps she hid something there."

Goldia cast a dubious glance at the shelves. "That will take a fair amount of time, Miss Olivia."

"Lady Devonworth," Olivia reminded her. "You must get into the habit. Oh, and let's be quick about it. I intend to visit Eleanor's grave later this morning. You will accompany me?"

"Yes, miss."

"You start on the boxes. I shall examine the bureau drawers." Olivia was only too glad to leave the closet behind with its lingering essence of Eleanor. She glanced around the lavish bedroom. Had Eleanor redone this herself? The decor appeared newer, more feminine, than any other room except Olivia's own chamber. The paper on the walls was a delicate basket pattern in pale pink and ivory. The bedspread was pink silk with a lace skirt. The Persian rug under the bed appeared new, as did the furniture, the newest Arts and Crafts style.

She eyed the bed, then lifted the skirt and thrust her hand under the mattress as far as she could get it. Her fingers touched nothing but the springs. She knelt and peered under the bed. Not even dust. She rose and went to the dresser. The mirror bounced her reflection back at her. She quite loathed her olive coloring. Her mother had called her a little gypsy when she was a child. She'd wanted hair like sunshine, just like her mother's and Eleanor's. Instead, she'd taken after her father's mother, who was of French descent.

Olivia picked up the picture on the dresser. It was of the two sisters on Olivia's last birthday. They'd been told not to smile, and the somber expressions on their faces contrasted with the merriment in their eyes. Had it been only three months ago? She felt so much older now than twenty-five. Grief would do that. In quick succession she'd lost her father and her sister.

"Lady Devonworth," Goldia said. "I found this in the crown of a hat." She held out a vellum dance card.

Olivia stepped to the closet and took the card. "She appears to have danced more than once with Mr. Frederick Fosberg," she said. "I don't recognize the name. Mr. Bennett's name is not on here."

"Maybe the dance took place before he returned from Africa. Miss Eleanor was here for nearly three months. She came right after your birthday."

Olivia studied the scrawled names on the card. "She danced with the gentleman four times. That's hardly proper when she was engaged to be married."

Could she have been wrong? Maybe Eleanor had fallen in love with another man in Harrison's absence. And why hide this dance card? A memento of a forbidden romance, perhaps?

"I'm surprised Katie or Addie didn't mention it to me. Surely the whole town noticed. I need to find this man and see what he meant to Eleanor." She rubbed her head. "Maybe I'm wrong and Eleanor did throw herself in the sea rather than be married to a man she did not love."

"I don't believe it," Goldia said.

Olivia heard noises in the hall. "Let's go." She pulled the door shut behind them.

Jennie ran toward her, and Olivia scooped her up. The child still had her new doll clutched under her arm. She planted a kiss on Olivia's cheek. "Are you hungry? I think breakfast should be ready." When the little girl nodded, Olivia set her down. Jennie took off for the staircase.

Katie joined Olivia at the top of the stairs. She smiled a good-morning. "You look like you're feeling better."

"I'm actually hungry."

"How did Will take the good news?"

"He's over the moon!"

Before she went downstairs, Olivia laid her hand on her friend's arm. "I found this." She showed Katie the dance card. "Do you know this man?"

"Mr. Fosberg. I met him at this same party. I saw Eleanor with him, but I thought they were discussing business."

"So she did not seem overly friendly with him?"

Katie bit her lip. "Well, there was some talk at Addie's party," she admitted. "I did my best to squelch it, but you know how gossip can spread."

"Did Eleanor say anything to you about seeing him again?"

Katie shook her head. "She was soon caught up in a whirlwind of social engagements. I didn't see her nearly so often after the party."

Olivia thanked her and the two women went down to the dining room for breakfast. She saw the morning post and snatched the new edition of *Woman's Home Companion*.

"I love that magazine," Katie said. "I like the Kewpie pages."

"That's what I wanted to read," Olivia said. She motioned to the servants to begin serving as she seated herself at the long table. Toying with her water glass, she glanced at her friend. "Sometimes I think I'm just like one of the Kewpies. Expected to be cute and accomplished on the outside and perfect in every action. Posed for the most advantage without a thought in my head."

Katie leaned over and patted her hand. "You're more than a Kewpie. You have wit and insight. You challenge the status quo. You're quite remarkable."

"I should have been born a man," Olivia said. "My insight does me no good when I'm stuck in a box."

"God expects you to use those gifts. You just have to be brave enough to do it. Ask God how he wants you to use your gifts."

She'd never considered asking God something so personal. He was, well, God. He couldn't be bothered with mundane problems. Did Katie really talk to him on such an intimate level? It was much too personal a question to ask.

TEN

BIRDS SANG IN the oleander bushes lining the graveyard. Some sweet flower left its presence on the wind. Olivia had dreaded yet longed to come today. The grave would be fresh, still uncovered by grass.

Goldia walked beside her with a basket of flowers. Neither of them spoke in the somber moment. The minister had said Eleanor rested under a live oak tree overlooking the ocean. She scanned the cemetery and walked in the direction of the waves' murmur. There was the iron fence Mrs. Bagley had mentioned.

Goldia pointed to a huge tree. "There it is, Lady Devonworth."

Olivia spotted it at the same time. The mound of dirt appeared so stark and lonely. Tears came to Olivia's eyes, and she quickened her steps though she longed to run away. She reached the grave and sank onto her knees. The scent of raw dirt stung her nose. "Oh, Eleanor," she whispered. "I can't bear it."

"Miss Olivia," Goldia whispered.

Olivia lifted her head and started to correct the maid when she saw the reason for Goldia's alarm. Harrison Bennett was striding toward them with his collie in tow.

She hastily rose and brushed the dirt from her skirt. How dare he intrude on this moment? And with a *dog*?

"Mr. Bennett," she said when he reached them. "I didn't expect to see you here."

She didn't care for the way he studied her expression. She was much too vulnerable right now to hide her agitation. And tears hung dangerously close.

He grabbed the dog as it started toward her. "I could say the same, Lady Devonworth," he said. "Though I suppose propriety demanded you bring flowers. Did you know Eleanor personally or are you just interested because you are using their home?"

"I knew her very well," she said, not caring if she revealed too much. "I've known her since she was a child. She was a lovely girl."

"So she was," he said. "You've never said how you know the Stewarts. Are you neighbors?"

She bit her lip, wishing she were more prepared for the questions. She should have thought of how to explain her connection.

"I'm surprised Eleanor never mentioned you," he said.

"You hardly spent much time with her," she said. "You yourself told me you'd only come back to Mercy Falls four days before she died."

"True enough."

"So what are you doing here?" she countered.

He glanced away as if he didn't know how to answer her. "I saw the Stewart crest on your carriage," he mumbled. "My mother asked me to issue an invitation."

If he only knew how they would have to sell everything, even the manor and the carriage, if she didn't make an advantageous marriage. "Invitation?"

He proffered a card. "She'd like to have you to tea."

"I didn't realize your mother was still alive," she said, then when his brows rose she wished she could call back the words. "I mean, your father is often in New York but he makes no mention of a wife. I'd heard of the accident and assumed . . ."

Lines of pain creased the skin around his mouth. "I believe he's rather ashamed of her since she's been in the wheelchair."

"I'm sorry," she said. "I meant no harm."

"I'm sure there are even more rumors than I know about," he said, his voice harsh.

"I should be honored to have tea with your mother," she said, wanting to ease the darkness in his eyes. "This afternoon?"

"If you please."

"Where does she live?"

"In the house across the street from mine. I've tried to convince her there is plenty of room in my home for her, but she abhors the idea of being a burden. Besides, Father comes every few months, and he and I . . ." He shrugged.

"You don't get along with your father?"

"You could say that." He grinned. "I see what you're doing, Lady Devonworth. We had been talking about you and you so adroitly changed the subject."

Her cheeks warmed. "Not at all. I'm an open book, Mr. Bennett."

"More like murky water," he said, grinning. He glanced at Goldia. "I don't believe we've met."

It was uncommon for someone to want to be introduced to a servant. Was his concern all a show? "This is Goldia. She was employed by Miss Olivia Stewart, a-and was looking for a new position. I was happy to give her one as I was in need of a good lady's maid. Olivia spoke very highly of her."

"So you know Olivia as well. You never said."

Why had she mentioned the name Olivia? It was a disastrous mistake. He was focusing too much attention on her relationship with the Stewarts. Surely he couldn't suspect her real identity, could he? "I know the Stewart family quite well, all of them. Why else would they give me free access to their home?"

"Why indeed," he said. The glint in his eyes vanished. "I'd be pleased to escort you to tea at Mother's. Shall I call for you at twelve thirty?"

"Yes," she said. His mother might reveal something. And surely she'd met Eleanor.

He bowed. "I'll leave you now until this afternoon." His long legs quickly carried him away.

"He knows something, miss," Goldia said. "That one is too smart for his own good."

Olivia waved away the concern. "I'm more interested in finding out what his mother knows about Eleanor's death."

❧❧❧

"I'm sure we shall find Mother in the parlor," Harrison said as he led Lady Devonworth down the hall. Had he ever been so aware of a woman's presence before? The slightest movement of her hand on his arm made him uncomfortable. "I am most grateful you agreed to my mother's request. She doesn't have many friends."

"Because of being crippled?" she asked. She paused to take in the portraits of his ancestors in the foyer.

He nodded. "It's difficult for her to meet for lunch or tea, and the sidewalks are not always easy for her attendant to navigate with the wheelchair."

She turned back toward him. "You are her only child?"

"I had a younger brother who fell from a tree when he was ten. He died of a broken neck."

"I'm so sorry."

The odd thing was she seemed to mean it. Her husky voice was soft, and the dark eyes she turned on him were liquid with warmth. There was so much about her that he didn't understand. Her presence in the graveyard raised so many questions. Her reddened eyes and obvious distress were out of place. She herself had said the Stewarts were friends, not relatives, so why such obvious grief? And every time he tried to dig into her background, she turned the conversation away from herself.

Piano music tinkled out from the parlor. "Your mother?" Lady Devonworth asked.

He nodded. "She's very accomplished."

He led her to the parlor, where he found his mother seated at the grand piano. Her fingers danced over the keys in Liszt's "Dante Symphony," and her eyes were dreamy. She wore her hair up and even had a hint of rouge on her face.

His mother stopped playing when she saw them in the door. A smile brightened her eyes. "Hello! I lost track of time, my dear."

The dog rose when he saw them. Lady Devonworth flinched, and he ordered the dog to lie down. "He won't hurt you," he said. "Collies are great dogs."

"It was a collie that bit me."

"That's quite unusual. Were you teasing it?"

She frowned. "I don't remember. I was a child. But it should have been trained not to attack."

"True enough," he said.

"Give me a moment to get settled on the sofa," his mother said.

"Of course." Harrison raised a brow in Lady Devonworth's direction, then led her back to the hall. "She doesn't like others to see her struggle," he said. "Shall I show you around the house until her attendant helps her to the sofa?"

"I should like to see it."

With her fingers on his forearm, he felt tongue-tied and awkward, but he escorted her toward the morning room. The house was so large and grand, he often felt lost in it, but Lady Devonworth would be quite at home with its silk-covered walls and plush carpets.

"Did your mother get along with Eleanor?" Lady Devonworth asked.

Her preoccupation with Eleanor truly annoyed him. "This is where Mother does her morning correspondence," he said, indicating the white desk by the window. Her questions were entirely inappropriate. A lady of her caliber should have realized by now that her persistent questions were the definition of rudeness.

"It's quite lovely," she said, glancing around the blue room.

Mary Grace appeared behind them. "Mrs. Bennett is ready to receive you," the nurse said.

At least he didn't have to hear any more of Lady Devonworth's questions. He escorted her back to the parlor. His mother was pouring out the tea. Blueberry scones were arranged on a silver tray. "Mother, this is Lady Devonworth. Lady Devonworth, I'd like you to meet my mother, Mrs. Esther Bennett."

"I've been longing to meet you, Lady Devonworth," his mother said. "Come sit beside me and tell me all about yourself."

He suppressed a smile. This had been a grand idea. His mother could pry the slightest secret from the most reticent person. Once Lady Devonworth was seated beside his mother, he dropped into the leather chair by the fireplace and settled back to watch his mother do her magic.

Wariness flickered in Lady Devonworth's eyes as she sipped her tea and studied the older woman. "You have a lovely home, Mrs. Bennett."

"I'm sure you're used to much grander surroundings," his mother said. "My son tells me you are a longtime friend of the Stewarts. What does your father do, my dear?"

Lady Devonworth took a sip of tea. Harrison was sure it was a delay to gather her thoughts. And he was certain her cheeks paled. His tense muscles relaxed. Watching this unfold would provide much entertainment. He'd been no match for the lady's questioning, but his mother was a master.

"Might I have a scone?" Lady Devonworth asked.

"Of course." His mother lifted the silver tray to the young woman, then put it back on the table after Lady Devonworth had selected a pastry. "About your father?"

Harrison's lips twitched. His mother was not about to let the young woman slip out of the net.

"Business is so boring, don't you think? My father has often spoken of his various interests, but it goes right over my head." She laughed daintily. "I'd much rather talk about this charming town. I quite adore Mercy Falls already. I'm sure Eleanor Stewart loved it the moment she saw it. I'm surprised she didn't stay here with you, though. To help you in any way she could."

Spots of color appeared on his mother's cheeks at the implied condemnation. "Of course I invited her! But the girl loved parties and wanted to plan several luncheons and evening soirees. It was too much for a lady in my condition. We both agreed it was best for her to have her own space."

Harrison gaped, then shut his mouth. Lady Devonworth had slipped through the snare with no effort.

"Oh, Eleanor loved parties. I can see how such merriment day and night would be quite wearing for you," Lady Devonworth said. "She was quite the chatterbox."

"The girl talked incessantly," his mother said. "In quite an entertaining way, of course," she added hastily.

"Of course. Eleanor was a most charming girl," the younger woman said.

Harrison had no idea that his mother hadn't liked Eleanor. He stared at Lady Devonworth and saw the frown crouching between her eyes. The silence was beginning to be awkward.

Lady Devonworth sipped her tea. "Do you know Frederick Fosberg?" she asked him.

"The attorney from the city who owns a house up the mountain?"

"Yes, the attorney," she said.

He shook his head. "Not personally. How did you hear of him?"

She nibbled on her scone. A delaying tactic, of course. She was quick to ask questions but less apt to answer them. "I may need his services, and I wondered if you would recommend him."

"I've met Fred a few times," his mother said. "He has done some business with your father on occasion, Harrison. A fine young man.

In fact, he's due to come to town in a few days. If you'd like to meet him, Lady Devonworth, he'll be our dinner guest on Friday night. Do come."

"I'd be delighted," she said quickly.

"My husband thinks the world of him. He's a hit with the ladies in town. A most eligible bachelor."

Lady Devonworth smiled. "I'm only interested in his business acumen."

Harrison resolved to find out what he could about this Fosberg. The lady had a purpose in her questions.

ELEVEN

OLIVIA HAD LIKED Harrison's mother, but the stress of navigating dangerous questions had drained her. She rubbed her aching head. She'd been prowling the second floor since the servants retired for the night. She should seek some rest herself, but she needed to find the letter. Eleanor was a pack rat, and Olivia knew she wouldn't have destroyed it. It had to be in this house somewhere.

She glanced around the last bedroom on this floor. Goldia had made subtle inquiries of the other servants, and this room had never been occupied. It was at the end of the hall. The hissing gaslight cast a yellow glow over the burgundy wallpaper. She'd poked through the empty closet and pulled out every drawer in the dresser but found nothing.

"Olivia."

She flinched and her head came up. The whispered voice came from nowhere. She strained to see through the shadows in the room. "Who's there?" The man had called her by name, a name she'd taken great care to conceal.

"It's me, Olivia."

Her heart leaped against her ribs. Her throat went tight. The voice sounded vaguely familiar, almost like her father. Was it a ghost? She backed toward the door. She needed to get to safety. She grasped the doorknob and yanked on it. The door refused to open. She tugged on it again, the muscles in her throat still blocking any sound.

"Olivia," the voice whispered again. Something clanged.

It was no ghost. That's when she realized whoever it was had to be using the mansion's speaking tube. She yanked on the door again, but it refused to budge. Had he locked her in? She knelt on the redwood floor and peered through the keyhole. No light. Something blocked it from the other side. Her breath came fast. Could someone be hanging on to the doorknob, laughing at her puny efforts to escape?

The mental image washed away her fear and released the tightness of her throat. She pounded on the door. "Let me out!" She twisted the knob again but the door held fast. The window. She rushed to the window and threw up the sash. Salt air tugged loose strands of her hair.

Leaning out the window, she searched the dark yard below her. There was nothing to enable her to climb down from this height. She would find no purchase on the smooth stone of the facade. When she pulled her head back inside and went back to the door, she thought she heard a slight click. She twisted the knob again, and this time it turned easily. Her initial impulse was to yank the door open, but what if the man waited on the other side?

She snatched her hand back and stared at the closed door. She couldn't stay here all night. Forcing herself to turn the knob again and pull, she peeked into the shadowed hall. Empty. She twisted the knob to extinguish the lamp, then rushed down the deserted hall toward her bedroom. The hallway was better lit here, and the tightness in her chest eased as the shadows fled. Outside her door, she paused. What if he was waiting inside? She needed assistance.

The servants were already abed, but there was a speaking tube in all the bedrooms. She could summon Jerry or one of the other footmen. Will was nearby also. She could call for him, but the thought of rousing the entire family deterred her. She went past her door to Eleanor's bedroom. She felt along the dark wall. *The knob for the lights should be here somewhere.* Her fingers encountered the round switch and she twisted it. Light illuminated the room. It was empty. She went to the speaking tube by the bed.

"Thora, we have an intruder in the house. Please send Jerry or one of the men to my room immediately." She didn't like the way her voice shook.

There was silence, then her housekeeper's sleepy voice answered her. "Right away, Lady Devonworth."

Olivia went back to the hall and waited under the wash of light. She was safer out of the shadows. Moments later footsteps pounded down the steps from the third floor.

Still buttoning his shirt, Jerry burst out of the enclosed stairway. He was barefoot. "Lady Devonworth, you said there is an intruder?"

Her limbs had begun to tremble. Olivia nodded and fought the burning in her eyes. It was just a reaction, but she couldn't give in to it. "He spoke into the speaking tube."

"What did he say?"

She bit her lip. "He just whispered my name."

He herded her to her room and opened the door. "Wait here until I check the house."

"What if he's in my room? I . . . I was elsewhere."

He glanced at her with a question in his eyes but didn't ask where she'd been. Flipping on the light, he left her standing in the doorway while he examined her bedroom, including the closet. When he found nothing, she entered and sank onto the chair by the dresser.

"Thank you," she said. "I shall lock the door after you."

"I'll report back after examining the rest of the house. The other footmen are scouring the grounds."

When he left, she rose and threw the lock on the knob. It couldn't have been her father's voice. He had been dead for six months.

The tree would provide the perfect frame for his new aeroplane. Harrison pointed out the specimen he wanted, and the lumberjacks set to work. He would never admit it to his father, but he enjoyed getting out of the office and seeing how men worked with their hands. When he was a teenager working here to learn the ropes of his father's latest acquisition, he'd liked exercising his muscles hauling timber and running his end of a saw. It gave him a chance to clear his head and be one with God. Even now, he liked doing more than pushing papers.

His valet, Eugene, worked alongside him as he loaded some boards for the wings onto a trailer. "You've been quiet today, sir," Eugene said.

"Just thinking about the new flying machine. I've come up with a new idea. What would you think about something on the bottom? Like skis. Something that allowed it to land on water?"

"On water? You mean the ocean?"

He shook his head, "Probably not the ocean. The waves would upend it. I was thinking about a lake. The weather would have to be calm."

Eugene paused and wiped his brow with a red kerchief. "It might work. Are you going to attempt to build it on this machine?"

"I believe so." Eugene's calm gaze lingered on Harrison's face. "What is it?" Harrison asked.

"You're a true visionary, sir. I never realized until now."

Harrison stopped and tugged on his collar. "Hardly a visionary, Eugene. It's interesting though, no?"

"The world is changing, as you've said," his valet said. "Men like you will help shape it, if you have the courage to lead."

Harrison thought of his father's hard face. "Some expectations are hard to break."

"They are. Even your father's expectation for you to marry a Stewart lady. What will you do now, sir?"

"I know one thing. I'm not going to marry some highbrow just to satisfy my father's desire to be part of the nobs."

"What will become of Mrs. Stewart?"

"I wouldn't want Mrs. Stewart to be deprived of her fortune."

"Perhaps your father will give her a fair part of the mine anyway."

"I don't see him ever being willing to do that."

"Did Mr. Stewart ever discuss this matter with you personally? The marriage, I mean."

"No." That fact had always bothered Harrison. Arrangements had been made while his father and Mr. Stewart were in Africa. His father had come home from that trip with the agreement in his pocket. And Mr. Stewart was dead.

"I'm going to tell Father to pay her anyway," he said.

Eugene nodded.

Harrison pressed his lips together. In the past five years he'd seen the desire for more and more money consume his father. They were comfortable. There was no need for more. But his father wanted to be accepted as one of the premier families in America. He lusted after that power to an unhealthy degree.

TWELVE

THERE WAS A brook around here somewhere. Olivia could hear it gurgling and churning over the rocks. Redwoods towered overhead, their leaves so high she nearly couldn't see them. Addie held little Edward's hand, guiding her son as the women picked their way along the path through the forest. His German shepherd, Gideon, nosed after a ground squirrel, and Olivia kept an eye on the dog.

"Are we almost there?" Olivia asked. Something about the mist curling around her boots and the lack of city noise had her glancing over her shoulder.

"Nearly there," Katie called. She was the vanguard of the little group.

Olivia heard it then—the roar she'd mistaken for the wind in the trees became more prominent. The falls came into view. Clear water tumbled from the black rocks to the pool of water at the base. The dog barked and raced to leap into the clear lake.

"The perfect spot to plan the ball," Addie said. She set down the basket she carried and withdrew a red-and-white checkered tablecloth from it. Once she spread it on the ground, she began to lift sandwiches wrapped in waxed paper from the basket.

Olivia settled beside her and watched the little boy and his dog frolic in the water. She glanced into the shadows of the trees. Their location was exposed and dangerous. She needed to tell her friends about last night's intruder. At least Jerry had come with them. She felt safer with a man in attendance. He hovered a discreet distance from their little picnic.

"Have you had any success in finding the letter?" Katie asked.

Olivia shook her head. "I've poked through every corner of Eleanor's room, and most of the other bedrooms. I can't imagine where she hid it. I'm beginning to consider the possibility that it might not be in the house," she admitted. "If I don't find it, I'm not sure how I shall find out what so disturbed her. But there's more."

She told Addie about finding the dance card. "I thought you might offer insight, Addie, since you attend more parties. Katie doesn't really know Mr. Fosberg. Do you know the man?"

"Oh yes. Every matchmaking mama in town has her claws out. I'm surprised he hasn't gained twenty pounds from all the dinners he's been invited to."

"He has accepted all the invitations?"

Addie handed her a sandwich. "Indeed he has, though I haven't heard he's paid any particular attention to one young woman over another. He's opening a branch of his law office in town, and he's happy to make the acquaintance of anyone who might need his services."

"You've met him personally?"

Addie nodded. "I spoke with Eleanor in the garden the night he came to that dance you mentioned. I asked her about him when we spoke. She said they were discussing business."

"That was Katie's impression too," Olivia said. Katie nodded. "What kind of business could she possibly have? Our attorney handles everything. Even Mother has no head for business."

"She didn't elaborate," Addie said.

Olivia bit her lip. "There was an intruder in the house last night," she said. She told her friends about the whispers from the speaking tube.

Katie shuddered. "I'm most fearful for you, Olivia. You should have roused Will."

"I should have done just that." She tipped her head to the side. "Do you hear something?"

"What did it sound like?" Katie asked. "I hear only the wind."

"Almost like a child crying." The noise came again, a plaintive wail that lifted the hair on the back of her neck. "It sounds like it's coming from that tree." She rose and went to the base of a giant redwood. The trunk's diameter was so wide that if she stood with her arms outstretched, her fingers would not reach the outer edges.

She peered up the rough red bark. The pungent odor of the crushed needles under her feet filled the air. Something moved in the high branches. Squinting, she tried to make out what it was.

Katie stared up into the treetops too. "I do believe it's a kitten," she said.

"How could a kitten get so high?" Olivia asked. Another wail floated down from the treetops.

"It probably climbed."

"How can we get it down?"

"We would need a lumberjack," Addie said, joining them. "He could shimmy up with no problem."

"There is some activity going on at the lumber camp," Katie said. "I'll run over there and fetch help."

"Not by yourself," Olivia said.

"I'm quite used to hiking in the forest."

"I shall go with you," Olivia said. "Addie can stay with Edward so his enjoyment of the lake isn't cut short."

"As you wish." Katie pointed toward a trail through the redwoods. "It's that way."

The women set off. At first the trail followed the river, cutting a swath through the valley far below them. Then it began to climb out of the gully until they walked a track barely wide enough for their boots. One misstep and Olivia knew she could plunge to her death. She soon felt a blister on her right foot. Insects buzzed in her ears, and a light mist hung in the air that made it seem she breathed liquid.

"Are you managing all right?" Katie asked. She didn't even appear to be out of breath.

"I'm perfectly fine," Olivia said, biting back a request to stop a moment. She forced one foot in front of the other. This was no stroll on well-tended sidewalks.

They reached a break in the trees overhead, and Olivia looked down at the mass of the lumber site. It hurt her heart to see the majestic trees lying broken on the forest floor.

Her attention was caught by a familiar set of broad shoulders. Instead of a blue morning coat, Harrison wore a red-and-black checkered shirt and trousers held up with suspenders.

She pointed. "What's he doing here?"

"His father owns this camp. I suspect he's here overseeing." Katie started down the trail.

Olivia followed. She told herself the only reason her pulse had leaped when she saw Harrison was from fear.

⌘

A movement caught Harrison's eye on the trail and he realized two women were picking their way along the narrow track to the camp. Alone. Squinting against the sun in his eyes, he frowned when he realized it was Lady Devonworth and Katie.

He moved to intercept them with Nealy on his heels. Lady Devonworth stepped into a shaft of sunlight. Her hair gleamed like a raven's wing. Her skin held a blush of color from her hike through the forest. He couldn't take his eyes from her. Since when did a lady hike through a redwood forest? Since when did she visit a lumber camp full of loud men?

He joined them. "Good afternoon, ladies. What drives you to such a rough place?"

Lady Devonworth eyed his dog and stayed back. "We found a kitten up a very tall tree. Only a lumberjack could get it down."

He could only stare at her. She'd come all this way for . . . for a cat? The moment stretched out. She held his attention until he recovered himself.

"I can get it down," he said before he could help himself. He wouldn't miss seeing what this was all about. "Let me get climbing hooks and a rope."

"You can climb a tree that high?"

"I worked every summer of my youth here at the camp. My father thought it important I learned to work. I was a tree topper." He liked the shock on her face. There was more to him than met the eye as well.

After he fetched the equipment and rejoined them, he pointed to the path. "Lead on, ladies."

Olivia's color was still high when she turned and walked back the way she'd come. Katie shot him a quick glance and smiled. There was sympathy in her eyes and he wasn't quite sure where it had come from. Or why.

Lifting her skirts, Olivia kept her head down and her gaze on the ground. She stumbled over a tree root. Her foot slipped toward the ravine. She screamed and threw out her hands but missed the branch that hung low.

Harrison leaped toward her, but Nealy dived past him. The dog latched onto her skirt. Harrison heard the cloth rip, but it held until he could seize her hand and pull her back to the path.

Her chest heaved as she fought for breath. She glanced past him to Nealy. "The dog saved me."

"He's trained to save," he said, putting his arm around her. He led her to a tree trunk. "Rest here a minute."

Katie rushed back to where he stood over Lady Devonworth. "Is she all right?"

"I nearly went over the edge." The lady swatted at a fly with a shaking hand. "Nealy grabbed me."

"Good boy," Katie crooned, rubbing the dog's ears. "See, a dog isn't so bad. Not all dogs are like the one that bit you, my dear. Pat him. He won't hurt you."

Nealy turned his dark eyes on the lady, and Harrison saw her shudder. He didn't think she would touch the dog, but she reached out her hand. Nealy took a step closer and pushed his long nose against her hand. She snatched her hand back, then moved it to his ears. She gave him a perfunctory pat. He wagged his tail.

She smiled. "I think that means he likes me."

"He likes everybody," Harrison said. "Are you strong enough to proceed?"

She nodded, and he helped her up. "Let me go first," he said when they reached a narrow path that led down. "I can assist you both." When she stood aside, he brushed past her and clambered down the incline, then turned and extended his hand. Her gloves were looking a bit worse for the wear. "I hope this creature is worth the loss of your gloves," he said. "I doubt your maid can remove the stains."

"I have others," she said, clutching his hand as she half slid, half stepped down the path.

They stood toe to toe, and he saw gold flecks in her dark eyes. Her breath was as sweet as the scent of the camellia blooming along the path. He should step away, but he stood frozen with her hand in his.

She pulled her hand free. "You need to help Katie."

"Of course." His face burned as she moved past him. He assisted Katie down the slope. "We are heading to the falls?" he asked her.

"We are. Addie stayed behind so Edward and Gideon could swim."

"We're not far now."

He let the women go ahead of him while he tried to figure out why he was acting such a fool. Was he so discomfited because she had a title? He'd never been one to take note of such inconsequential things. There was something different about Lady Devonworth.

He quickened his step to catch up with the ladies. The roar of the falls sifted through the trees, and he heard the dog bark and a child giggle. Nearly there. He reached the ladies and together they entered the clearing where Addie sat beside the lake. Edward splashed and swam with Gideon while she looked on. Nealy barked and ran past them to join the fun.

"We're back," Katie called.

Addie scrambled to her feet and hurried toward them with a smile. "That kitten is nearly hoarse from crying."

Harrison heard it then—the wail was faint and scratchy but frantic. "Which tree?"

"Here." Lady Devonworth stepped to the other side of the path and laid her hand on a giant redwood. "Up there." She pointed and he looked up. A tiny face was visible through the leaves. Three hundred feet up.

He whistled. "How'd that cat get up that high?"

Lady Devonworth raised a brow. "Climbed, I presume."

"Brilliant deduction, Sherlock," he said, grinning. She blushed and glanced away.

He dropped the rope from his shoulder, then strapped on the leather belt. After connecting all the hooks, he handed her the strap. "Circle the tree and bring it back to me on the other side."

He expected her to hold the grimy thing like she might a snake, but she gripped it firmly in her hands and hurried to do his bidding. Moments later she was on his other side.

"Is it big enough?"

He nodded and snapped the ring into his belt. Placing his feet against the rough bark, he began to shimmy up the tree. Though he wasn't about to admit it to her, it had been a good five years since he'd climbed a tree. And it was a long way up. Inch by inch, he traversed the big tree. The kitten cried all the more as he got closer.

His chest burned and his breath came hard by the time he reached the feline. "You're fine, cat," he said when the kitten backed away.

Grabbing it by the scruff of its neck to avoid being bitten or scratched, he tucked it inside his shirt. Its claws dug through his undershirt into his skin and he nearly howled himself. "Stupid cat, I'm trying to help you," he muttered.

The kitten loosened its claws, then snuggled under his armpit. Nothing like making it even more difficult to get down. He tried to reposition it, but it complained and grabbed him again, so he gave up and began to climb down. The muscles in his thighs cramped, and his hands were developing blisters, but he pressed on. The more he hurried, the sooner he could get rid of this cat. He was perspiring by the time he reached the ground. With a last shove, he dropped his booted feet to the soil and stood gasping at the foot of the tree.

"Great fun," he said, masking his rough breathing.

"Is the cat all right?"

He reached inside his shirt and grabbed the feline. "Youch! You little tiger, let go of me," he said. He succeeded in unhooking the kitten's sharp claws from his skin and pulled it out to view.

"Oh you poor darling," Lady Devonworth said, her voice soft.

The gentle sound of her voice went straight to his gut. He'd like to hear her use that tone with him.

THIRTEEN

JUST WATCHING HARRISON'S gentleness with the kitten did something to Olivia's midsection. In his common garb, she noticed the way his biceps bulged under his shirt and the mass of muscle in his thighs as he'd climbed the tree. Averting her eyes as he approached, she reminded herself that it was quite unseemly to notice such things.

"How about some sympathy for me?" he asked. "The wretched beast clawed me all the way down. I risked my life for it with no gratitude."

"I'm most grateful," she said. "Do your scratches need attention?" She made sure her tone dripped with impudence.

He grinned. "You're offering to tend to my wounds? I might take you up on that."

Her cheeks flamed at the flirtation in his voice. He was smooth, very smooth. "I'm sure you shall live," she said. "And thanks to you, so will Tiger here."

"I wouldn't name the monster if I were you. It's hard to let go once you name them."

"I have every intention of keeping Tiger," she said. "Such an adventurous animal deserves a home."

"He might not be happy cooped up after he's been allowed to roam free."

"You say that as though you have experienced it," she said. "Do you not enjoy your work?"

91

He lifted a brow. "A man can be good at something and still long for more."

"Are your planes what you long for?"

His expression sharpened. "I see the flash of interest every time the subject is brought up, yet you seem perfectly happy in your gilded cage."

She glanced away, unable to hold the intensity in his eyes. "I'm quite content with my place."

"What is your place? To be the fashion expert? To arrange flowers so beautifully your friends are astonished? Somehow you seem more ambitious than that. And much more intelligent."

She tried to hide her shock. "Ambition is more fitting for a man than a woman."

His grin widened. "A rather old-fashioned view. Your father's or your own? The times are changing."

"My father was a disciplinarian who felt women were pretty baubles for a man's arm. Somehow I think you share that view."

His lips tightened. "If you knew me at all, you would know how absurd that statement is."

She smiled, trying to defuse his anger. "My spies tell me every woman in town has her cap set for you."

His dark eyes flashed. "It's my money they are interested in."

She found that hard to believe. He had a magnetism that would draw any woman. Except her, of course. "Then you could have your pick of women to marry."

"I may never marry. I want a woman who will see me and not my bankroll." He raised a brow. "I think you are trying to deflect the conversation away from my question. What would you like to do if you could be more than that pretty bauble?"

What if she could be more than a debutante pursued for her title? What would she do with her life? For a long moment she allowed herself to dream of actually flying a plane herself, not just riding in one. But it was quite impossible. Her mother would be scandalized. Not that this man would understand.

"I can see you're thinking of something you'd like to do. What is it?"

"We have extra sandwiches if you'd like to share our lunch," she said.

"Coward," he said softly as she turned away.

She kept her gaze straight ahead and marched away with the kitten in her arms. The man was entirely too attractive. If she were the kind to notice something like that. Which she was most decidedly *not*.

Tiger began to knead her forearm where he lay nestled. She rubbed the kitten's head and he settled down on her chest.

Harrison fell into step beside her. "What are you ladies doing here in the first place?"

"Taking some fresh air while we plan the Lightkeeper's Ball."

"I'm sure you're most adept at planning such things. I suspect you could plan a ball or organize a suffragette march with equal accomplishment."

"I'm sure you have little experience with suffragette marches."

"More than you, I would wager. I'm on the board of the Mercy Falls group. I've marched in more events than you can count."

She stopped and stared. His expression was grave as if daring her to question his statement. "You support the woman's right to vote?"

"My mother is the smartest person I know. She knows more about the issues than my father does. Why shouldn't she have the vote? It's ludicrous it's not allowed yet."

He was serious. She closed her open mouth. What did she say to that? She could hardly express how much she admired him for that simple thing.

She stepped toward the pool of water. The clear stream gurgled over the rocks most charmingly. Her leather-bound journal lay on a rock where she'd dropped it. It was open to the list of things she planned for the ball. She stepped forward to grab it, and her foot slipped into an unseen hole and she toppled forward. Sharp pain seized her left wrist as she went down hard. The cat's claws dug into her arm. Her wrist throbbed in unison with the kitten's wails.

He knelt beside her with his hand slipping around her waist. "Are you injured?"

"My wrist," she managed to gasp out as she gripped it with her good hand.

He touched her forearm. "May I?"

Gritting her teeth, she nodded. His fingers probed the flesh of her wrist, already swelling. "I don't think it's broken, but it's a bad sprain. We should have it looked at."

"There's a doctor at Eaton Manor," Addie said. "It's not far."

Olivia had forgotten the consumption hospital was so close. "Perhaps we should go there. It's quite painful," she said.

The pain encasing her wrist spread up her arm. Eaton Manor would have something to help with the pain. Harrison pulled out a handkerchief and tied the ends together, then slipped it over her neck and under her elbow to support her arm. The pain began to ease. She was close enough to see the way his thick dark hair curled over his collar. Close enough to smell his bay rum pomade. She averted her eyes and prayed for this journey to soon be over.

⎯✢⎯

Olivia's wrist throbbed in time with every step she took. Harrison led them over the uneven ground toward the large stone house looming in the distance. Nealy bounded ahead, then turned back occasionally as if to ask if they were coming.

"It's quite lovely," she said when the three-story manor home came into view. The kitten purred against her chest.

Addie and Katie walked on either side of Harrison. "It used to belong to Addie," Katie said. "She sold it to a group who turned it into a home for consumptives."

"How admirable," Olivia murmured. Perhaps John hadn't wanted to maintain such a palatial home. It was the most elaborate structure she'd seen in Mercy Falls since she arrived, rivaling the finest New York residences. Harrison helped her mount the wide steps to the double doors.

"Stay," he told the dogs.

"Let me warn them that we need assistance," Addie said, brushing past them. "Nann," she called out as she stepped into the hall.

A smiling woman hurried to greet them. In her forties, her merry blue eyes radiated welcome and interest. Her hair was still mostly light brown and coiled into a bun at the nape of her neck. She wore a high-collared gray gown with a cameo at the neck.

"Mrs. North, how lovely to see you."

"My friend is injured, Mrs. Whittaker," Katie said, gesturing to Olivia. "This is Lady Devonworth from Stewart Hall. We could use some assistance."

Nann's smile turned to an expression of concern. "Bring her into the waiting room," she said. "Dr. Lambertson is here right now. He's with one of our residents, but I'll fetch him at once. This way." She turned a bright smile Olivia's direction. "My daughter Brigitte is in service at the Stewart home. She's one of the chambermaids."

Olivia managed to smile past the pain. "I shall have to seek her out and say hello."

Harrison steered her forward to the doorway where Nann stood waiting.

"The waiting room is here," Nann said. "I'll have an empty exam room ready shortly. I need to disinfect it first."

Olivia could see the table in the examination room. "What is this place?" she whispered to her friends.

"It's a healing place for consumptives. They've done wonderful work here," Addie said. "Nann was a consumptive herself. She's in such good health now that she wanted to help others in her situation and was quick to accept this position when it was offered."

"She seems very nice, but you can smell the sickness here."

Katie nodded and put her handkerchief to her nose. Her face was pale. "I shall have to wait on the porch. I'm feeling a bit poorly."

"Oh my dear, do you want me to come with you?" Addie asked.

"I just need some fresh air."

"Edward can play. I'll come with you." Addie patted Olivia's hand. "You'll be fine. Harrison will take good care of you."

Her lungs squeezed. "I want to go home," she begged. "Please. I'm fine."

Addie glanced from her to the doorway where Katie had gone. "Let me check on Katie. I'll arrange for a car to get us. You can go home very soon."

Nann Whittaker stepped out of the exam room. "We're ready for you, Lady Devonworth."

"Really, I don't want to trouble the doctor," she protested as the woman led her to the examining room and helped her sit. "It's merely a sprain. Rest and ice are all I need." She started to slide from the table, but Harrison seized her arm.

"You'll be home soon enough. The doctor will be here in a moment," he said. His hand touched her back, and he cradled her head to his chest.

She could hear the *thump-thump* of his heart against her ear. Something about his touch drained the pain from her wrist.

"It won't hurt to have the doctor take a look," he said.

Her teeth began to chatter. Was it from the pain? "I'm cold," she said.

Harrison released her a moment. He shucked his flannel shirt, revealing a white undershirt beneath it. He placed the warm flannel around Olivia's shoulders. "Better?"

The flannel encased Olivia and the warmth that lingered from his body seeped into her skin. She nodded as the shaking began to subside. "Thank you," she whispered, clutching the edges of the shirt to her throat. His manly scent lingered in the cloth and calmed her.

"Here's the doctor now," he said, stepping back after a final embrace.

Olivia glanced up to see a gray-haired gentleman with erect shoulders step into the room. He had a stethoscope around his neck, and his necktie was askew. But his kindly expression did much to calm the last of her jitters. A woman in her fifties with a kind face and graying hair in a bun was on his heels.

"A slight accident, I see?" He stepped to the examination table and took Olivia's arm in his warm hands.

She winced when his fingers probed the swollen flesh of her wrist. "I fell."

He nodded and continued to press on her wrist and arm. "No real harm done. It's a severe sprain though, and you need to rest it for at least three days. I'm going to send some powder home with you for the pain. Keep ice on it and keep it elevated on a pillow. I'll stop and check on you tomorrow. Where might I find you?"

"This is Lady Devonworth," Harrison put in. "She's staying at Stewart Hall."

The doctor turned to his nurse. "Mrs. Fosberg, would you fetch some pain powder? I'll write out instructions on its use."

As the woman hurried from the room, Olivia stared after her. Fosberg? Could she be related to the Frederick Fosberg who had danced so often with Eleanor? Surely Fosberg was a very common name, especially in this area so settled with those of Scandinavian descent.

It seemed an eternity before the older woman came back with a bag of white powder in her hand. Olivia accepted it with a smile. "Mrs. Fosberg, I've heard your last name before in connection with a young man by the name of Frederick. Is he any relation?"

The woman's smile broadened and she stood taller. "That would be my boy. I'm so proud of him. He worked his way through college to become a well-respected barrister in the city. How did you hear of him?"

"I mentioned that I was in need of an attorney, and he was recommended."

"You couldn't go wrong with hiring my boy. He has his own office in San Francisco. After the Great Earthquake, he kept right on working when the other barristers abandoned the city. He's brave, that one. Handsome too. He's due to town in two days. Shall I have him call on you?"

"Please do. I have much to discuss with him." It would be a better way to find out about him than at Mrs. Bennett's dinner party. And she'd start by finding out what the young man's relationship had been with her sister.

FOURTEEN

HARRISON TOOK THE bumps as lightly as possible, but the woman beside him still winced when they hit the unavoidable potholes. He breathed a sigh of relief when Stewart Hall came into sight. He let the dog out on his side and told him to stay.

He parked the automobile by the front door. "Don't forget your blasted cat." He deposited the kitten in her good arm.

"I very much appreciate your kindness in making sure I got home," Lady Devonworth said. The cat meowed and she gasped, holding it out from her. "It's got sharp claws. It's going to ruin my dress."

"Give it to me." He grabbed the kitten and stuck it inside his undershirt. "Stupid cat," he muttered.

A young woman with a white apron over her black dress opened the door. "Poor Lady Devonworth," she said. "I have your bed turned down and ready."

"I really don't want to take to my bed. It's barely three," she protested. "Goldia, show us to parlor."

Harrison shook his head. "The doctor said to keep your arm elevated on a pillow. Besides, you've had a shock and need to rest. Show me her room, Goldia."

The maid glanced at her mistress, then scurried up the stairs. He ignored Lady Devonworth's objections and propelled her up the sweeping staircase. The maid gestured to him from a door halfway down the wide hall decorated with gold foil. "This is Miss Olivia's bedroom," he said.

Lady Devonworth stopped and stared up at him. "How would you know such a thing?" she whispered.

Her face paled, and he realized how his remark had sounded. "Please don't misunderstand. At Eleanor's last party, she showed her guests around the mansion and remarked that no one was allowed to stay in this room except her sister. Eleanor said she'd had it decorated to Olivia's tastes and was eager to see how her sister liked it."

"I see." The woman's voice seemed choked.

Were those tears in Lady Devonworth's eyes? He led her to the bed and stepped back. She was most decidedly pale and shaken. "Are you in pain?"

She glanced away and straightened her skirt. "A bit, yes. I shall have Goldia prepare me a pain draught."

She started to remove his flannel shirt, but he put his hand on her arm and shook his head. "Keep it until your maid helps you change into something warmer. I'll get it later."

She stopped and hugged the shirt close again. "Thank you for your kindness, Mr. Bennett."

He bowed. "I'm happy to be of assistance, Lady Devonworth. If you are in need of me at any time, ring me and I will be here in minutes."

"You're too kind," she said, not looking at him.

He studied her a moment before backing out of the room and taking his leave. Her manner had changed most abruptly when he mentioned she was in Olivia's room. Perhaps it was the pain in her wrist. What else could it be? He strode down the hall to the stairs. At the top of the steps, he hesitated when he heard Goldia call his name.

She was huffing by the time she reached him. "Mr. Bennett, sir."

"Is she all right, Goldia?"

Her hazel eyes narrowed. "She wants that kitten."

He'd forgotten he still had the blasted cat tucked into his shirt. He yanked the cat out into the light of day. It yowled its misery to the world and tried to claw its way back inside his shirt. He hastily handed it to the maid.

Goldia curtsied. "Thank you, sir. Miss, uh, Lady Devonworth was most upset at the thought that she wouldn't have the kitten in her possession."

He watched her scurry back down the hall with the cat nestled against her. He found to his dismay that he really didn't want to leave.

❧

Cradling the kitten, Olivia fell back against the pillow. Her eyes burned, and she gulped back the sob building in her throat. Eleanor had decorated this room for her and she hadn't known it. She glanced around the lavishly appointed bedroom. The silk, blue and white with touches of palest yellow, had spoken to her the moment she'd taken stock of her surroundings. No wonder. Eleanor had known exactly what Olivia would like.

Goldia touched her hand. "Miss Olivia?"

Olivia didn't have the heart to remind her to call her Lady Devonworth. "I'm all right, Goldia. Just shaken up. Could you fetch me some tea?"

"Yes, ma'am, but I wanted to tell you I found this while you were out." Her hand went to her pocket and she held up a letter addressed to Eleanor. "I recognized your daddy's handwriting. I think this is what we've been searching for."

Olivia stared at the thin envelope in her maid's hand. Even from here, the familiar loop of the letter *J* made her pulse leap. Her hand shook as she reached for it. The paper felt fragile in her fingers. She slipped the letter from the envelope. It wasn't her father's usual thick vellum but a cheap, coarse paper. No monogram, just plain paper. She unfolded it and began to read.

Dear Eleanor,

I know this letter will come as a distinct shock to your sensibilities, as you have believed me dead for six months. Through no fault of Bennett's, I'm very much alive. Take every precaution against him. Avoid him at all costs. His son as well. You must break off the engagement immediately and return home. But take care, daughter! Surround yourself with those you can trust. Make sure you are on guard every moment. I fear for your life. I am nearby and I shall be in touch. In the meantime, depart from Mercy Falls immediately!

Your Loving Father

Olivia stared at the date at the top of the letter. A mere month before Eleanor died. Eleanor hadn't run from town soon enough. She must have been reeling from the shock of realizing her father was alive. *Or had been, a month ago.* Where was he? According to the letter, he was nearby. But where?

"Miss Olivia?" Goldia said. "You're scaring me. What's the letter say?"

"You didn't read it?"

"Of course not, miss. Weren't my place to read it. Besides, it's hard for me."

Olivia studied her maid's face. Did she dare tell Goldia the contents of the letter? Goldia had been with her since Olivia was twelve. If she wasn't trustworthy, who was? "It's from my father," she said.

"I was right!" Goldia smiled and clapped her hands.

"He's alive. He warned Eleanor to leave town. He said that Mr. Bennett had something to do with the circumstances and is dangerous."

Goldia's smile faded. "What about Mr. Harrison?"

Olivia hadn't wanted to think about Harrison. "Father says he's dangerous as well."

Goldia shuddered. "Handsome men sometime are."

"Father told Eleanor to avoid him and to break off her engagement. He must have had a good reason for such a drastic order."

An inner warning sounded at her father's lack of clear explanation, and she realized she didn't *want* to believe Harrison could be guilty of any devious behavior. Something in her rebelled at her father's autocratic orders as well. She'd spent her whole life trying to make up for the fact that she wasn't the son he wanted, and she realized she was tired of being treated as a lesser human being.

Goldia clasped her hands together. "Maybe he was mistaken. Did the letter say why he hasn't let your mama and you know that he was alive?"

Olivia inhaled as if that would stop the pain that swept over her. "He didn't mention me or my mother." What possible reason could he have for cutting them off so completely? Hadn't he realized how devastated they were by the news of his death? Her memories of her father were conflicted. She adored him, but he seldom noticed her.

She had to notify her mother at once. "I need to place a telephone call," she said.

"The only telephone on this floor is in the big bedroom at the end of the hall. Where your sister stayed."

Olivia swung her legs to the side of the bed, dislodging the kitten, who gave a protesting yowl. Her wrist throbbed at the movement, and she held it in the air with her other hand as she followed Goldia to their destination. She collapsed into a chair by the bed next to the stand that held the telephone.

"I could use that tea now, Goldia," she said. In truth, she wanted to be alone for this conversation. Once her maid nodded and scurried down the hall, Olivia lifted the receiver and rang for central. She gave the number to the friendly-sounding woman on the other end and waited. A transcontinental call took longer than local connections.

"Ringing now, Lady Devonworth," the operator said.

Olivia's fingers tightened on the earpiece, and she pressed it tightly against her head. Her mother was bound to be overcome by the news. And what if the operator listened in? "Hello?" she asked cautiously. When the operator didn't answer, she relaxed.

"Stewart residence," the housekeeper said.

"Iola, it's Olivia. I'd like to speak to my mother, please."

"Oh, Miss Olivia! I'm so relieved to hear your voice. I will fetch your mother straightaway."

Olivia waited through a clunk and much fumbling on the other end of the line. Even after several years of answering the phone, Iola was still uncomfortable with the instrument.

Her mother came on the line. "Olivia, is that you?"

"Yes, it's me."

"I expected you to call before now. Have you met with Harrison?"

Olivia suppressed a sigh. All her mother cared about was marrying Olivia off to money. "Yes, but he doesn't know I'm Olivia Stewart."

"What?"

"I'm using my proper title of Lady Devonworth. I wanted time to get to know him with no expectations."

Her mother tut-tutted. "You're behaving in a ridiculous manner. How will he know if you suit if he's not thinking of a future alliance?"

"I'm trying to find out what happened to Eleanor."

"She drowned, Olivia. That's it. You can't bring her back. I miss her too, but we must look to the future. I suspected you would need my assistance. I'm making arrangements for a train now. I should be there by week's end."

"I thought you were going to spend the season with Mrs. Astor."

"So did I, but in spite of my hints, I never received an invitation. I suspect she's heard whispers of our financial situation. Which is why it is all the more imperative that you make a suitable marriage. I suspect she is no longer willing to introduce you to her friend either. This may be your last chance, Olivia."

"Have you seen Mr. Bennett? Is he still in town?"

"I have neither seen nor heard from him. I assume he's not in New York at the present time."

"If you see him, remember not to tell him that I'm in Mercy Falls."

Her mother let out a sigh of exasperation. "It's a good thing I'm coming out. You need a firm hand and guidance."

"I shall be happy to see you." As long as she could convince her mother not to divulge her identity. "I could use your help in planning a charity ball as well."

"Ah, I should love that. What's it for?"

Olivia told her about the destroyed lighthouse. "But there is much happening here you don't know, Mother. I'm not quite sure how to tell you this."

"What is it?"

Olivia drew in a breath. "I have most astounding news, Mother. Father is still alive."

FIFTEEN

THE NEXT DAY Harrison made a courtesy call to Lady Devonworth to inquire about her wrist. Her maid told him she was resting and couldn't be disturbed, but he couldn't help but wonder if the lady was avoiding him. He set to work on his aeroplane.

On Friday he finished reviewing a signed contract for a new acquisition for Bennett and Bennett. He knew the contract was fair, but his father would say he should have been harder on the buyout. Harrison knew God had given him the talent to work with numbers and money. Why then did he yearn for something more than creating this? Why did his spirit long to be in his machine soaring above the clouds? His mother said he was throwing away God's gift by not tending to his talent in the boardroom. Did God always expect a man to use a gift? What about his own desires?

Frowning, he pushed away the ledger. A movement caught his eye and he looked up to see his father standing in the doorway.

Harrison pasted on a welcoming smile and rose with his hand outstretched. "Father, when did you arrive?"

"An hour ago." The elder Bennett shook Harrison's hand. "What are you working on, son?"

"Just filing the purchase papers of Riley Hardware."

"Excellent! May I see them?" He settled in the chair on the other side of the desk and pulled the papers toward him. His smile faded as he looked them over. "You paid them more than I specified."

"I wanted to be fair."

His father sighed. "They agreed to the price."

"Only because they were in financial straits with a sick child. We can afford it."

"That's not the point! The sale affects our bottom line. I want you to redo this."

"No. I've already spoken with Mr. Riley, and he's most apprecia-tive. The papers are signed. This deal will allow him to take his daughter to New York for treatment. And I've already authorized the money to be transferred to his account."

His father's face reddened and his lips tightened. "We've spoken about this before, Harrison. You have got to quit this kind of behavior or you will pauper us."

"Not much chance of that. Do you even *know* how much we have in the bank? It's astronomical. Almost obscene."

His father smiled thinly. "There is no such thing as too much money. Even with all our wealth, we still are not accepted in the high-est echelon of society. *That* is my goal. With Eleanor dead, we have to find another woman in that set. Mrs. Stewart is trying to convince Olivia to take Eleanor's place."

Harrison folded his arms across his chest. "I'm not agreeing to anything like that again, Father. I'm tired of being auctioned off like a cow. I'll find my own wife, thank you. And I can assure you it will *not* be a Stewart. I'd rather be single than marry Olivia."

His father studied his face. "What has gotten into you, boy? This is important for your future."

"Eleanor betrayed me. I wouldn't trust a Stewart woman again."

"I'm sure your mother will be distressed to hear this."

Harrison wasn't about to let his father leverage the usual excuse of upsetting his mother, not when the older man cared not a whit about her feelings. He had all but abandoned her. "Mother wants me to be happy."

"She tells me you've been keeping company with a woman from New York. A Lady Devonworth."

"I'd hardly call it 'keeping company.' She's merely an acquaintance."

"Your mother says she believes her family is one of the Four Hundred."

The Four Hundred were the most elite families in America. They were the ones invited to the upper echelon of society balls, the ones who were invited to the best homes and the most elite clubs.

"Why do you do this, Father?" he asked. "Why do you care what a bunch of nobs think? To them we'll always be swells who are getting too big for our britches. We're doing all right. Making money, gaining a reputation. We don't need to be part of that set."

His father's jaw hardened. "Let me explain something to you, boy. General Marshall invited me to attend a luncheon at the Vanderbilt's. I arrived to find the invitation had been rescinded. I will not tolerate a humiliation such as that again. I *will* be accepted!"

There was no more to be said. It would do no good to point out how prideful it was to insist on being accepted by the nobs.

"What of this Lady Devonworth? She is unmarried, is she not?" his father asked.

"She is unmarried and I like her."

His father scowled. "I've never heard of the Devonworths. I doubt the woman carries the social clout of a Stewart, and I'm determined for you to marry a woman of quality who will allow you to walk in the highest levels of society. Most couples live separate lives anyway. Look at your mother and me."

"I'd like more from my marriage than what you two have." He knew it was the wrong thing to say the second the words left his lips.

His father drew himself up and huffed. "I don't know where you've gotten these romantic notions, boy. From that riffraff you hang out with, I presume. A lightkeeper and his wife. What kind of example is that for you to follow?"

"The best kind," Harrison said. "And what of that agreement with the Stewarts about the mine?"

His father's eyes glittered. "I shall continue to own controlling interest in the diamond mine. That was the agreement."

"But that would leave Mrs. Stewart and her daughter in desperate straits."

His father shrugged. "That's hardly my problem."

"You sound as though you hate her."

"She could champion me, introduce me to her set."

"She has tried that. She's had you to their dinners. It's hardly her fault the others don't include you on their guest lists."

"Whose side are you on, boy? You just told me you wouldn't marry Olivia if she were the last woman on Earth."

"That doesn't mean I want them punished for Eleanor's failures. Besides, I didn't know there was a side."

"There is, and you'd better stand with me."

"I don't think so, Father. I want nothing to do with something this dastardly. The marriage arrangement should stand. You shame me. I want you to give her the share of the mine that you promised. Then we'll be done with the Stewarts for good. We'll owe them nothing."

His father's mouth gaped and he stared. "I'll do no such thing."

Claude Bennett had never in his life done anything out of the goodness of his heart. When he came back from Africa with an agreement to turn over controlling shares in the diamond mine to Mrs. Stewart only if the two families were joined, Harrison was flummoxed. He had agreed to the engagement because he suspected his father had seized on Stewart's death as a means to gain complete possession of the mine. Harrison hadn't wanted the Stewart women left with no source of income. And the fact that the match would have benefited him too played a part. That engagement had been such a disaster that the mere suggestion of marrying Olivia in Eleanor's place was loathsome. He'd find another way to help the women if need be. Or manage to talk his father into it.

"We'll speak of this later." He turned toward the door. "I must call on Lady Devonworth. She suffered a sprained wrist a few days ago, and I wish to check on her."

"Tell her that I'd like to be introduced," his father called after him.

"Over my dead body," Harrison muttered under his breath. He stalked to the motorcar and climbed in. He started the engine and pulled away before he said anything more his father would try to make him regret. Having the man show up was going to be difficult. He'd push to be invited to the ball Lady Devonworth was planning. He'd play matchmaker at every turn and probably get Mother in on the efforts as well.

Harrison wished he could climb into his plane and fly off into the sunset. Never come back. See the world and see what else God had for him. Vistas beyond this small town and the climb to the top that his father wanted for him. When would he get to pursue his own dreams?

⌒✲⌒

Olivia's eyes were blurry from the hours of correspondence she'd done all morning. Her invitations to the Lightkeeper's Ball had gone out in the afternoon's mail. All that was left were the local people Addie had suggested. The florist had just left with an order for flowers, and Olivia had several people to interview for employment for the week leading up to the event.

Goldia stepped into the doorway. "Miss Olivia, Mr. Harrison is here."

Olivia put down her pen. "Very well, Goldia. Show him in."

"But, miss," Goldia hissed. "Your father's letter said to avoid him."

"I can hardly refuse to see him. He aided me when I was injured."

Her pulse pounded in her throat. She'd thought of nothing but Harrison in the days since she'd seen him. She hadn't wanted to remember the strength of his arms or the scent of his skin, but the sensations had plagued her sleep. In spite of her father's warning, she wanted to see him.

The dinner party at his mother's had been postponed due to Mrs. Bennett's illness. Olivia sat on the love seat and arranged her skirts around her. Pinching her cheeks, she wished for a mirror to check her hair. She had no reason to feel so nervous. He wouldn't harm her with all the servants here. Besides, he didn't know who she was. She told herself her jitters were only because of the danger and had nothing to do with the way she'd thought about him.

She heard his steps on the redwood floors and lifted her head to paste a welcoming smile on her face. When he appeared in the doorway, she swallowed hard. "Good afternoon, Mr. Bennett."

He bowed. "Lady Devonworth. How is your wrist? I trust you are recovered?"

"Completely, yes. The doctor called this morning and gave me free rein to do what I'd like."

"Any chance I could talk you into a flying lesson?"

Flying? Aware her mouth was agape, Olivia shut it. "You're serious?" His grin told her he knew how difficult she would find a refusal.

"Completely. I'm taking the plane up when I leave here."

She shouldn't be alone with him, but she was so tempted. The thought of soaring in the clouds mesmerized her. Perhaps she could find out more about his relationship with Eleanor. And hadn't she promised her mother that she would be open-minded to the thought of a match with Harrison? Without marrying money, the Stewarts' lives would change drastically. It was all riding on her. Besides, so far she'd found no evidence to link him to Eleanor's death.

But was that only because she no longer wanted him to be guilty? Her internal rationale fell flat when she remembered her father's warning. "Perhaps not just yet," she said, throwing away every contrary argument. "But might I watch?"

His white teeth flashed in his tanned face. "Of course. But I suspect you'll be sitting in the cockpit within fifteen minutes." He flicked a finger at the magazine that showed a Kewpie doll in a car. "I believe you're capable of more than mere wheels."

What was she made of? Sometimes she felt her only worth was in the prestige she could bring to a marriage. She didn't even know if she had any true gifts. She'd been trained to manage a household, be a complement to her husband, raise children, and be a wonderful hostess. The perfect Kewpie doll. Did life consist of more than that? Did anyone ever look below the surface? She was almost afraid to find out. It might make her discontented with her life. But with her mother's future riding on her choices, she was even more trapped.

"What time should I be ready for you to call?" she asked.

"As soon as you've changed."

She rose from her seat. "You mean *now*?"

His smile came and he nodded. "My mother was most disappointed to have to cancel tonight's dinner. She'd hoped to introduce you to my father." His tone turned ironic as she moved toward the stairs. "He wishes you to introduce us to your friends in New York. Expect a call from him. I tried to ward him off when he arrived today, but I'm not sure I was successful."

She froze with her hand on the banister. "Y-Your father is home?"

"He is indeed. He arrived this afternoon." He turned away from her. "You change, and I'll borrow some gear from Jerry."

No, no! Mr. Bennett would spoil everything. He would reveal that she was really Olivia Stewart. She fled up the stairs without a word.

SIXTEEN

THE STREETS OF Mercy Falls teemed with people. Men and women milled around the town square. Harrison frowned at the aura of unrest.

A red scarf around her hair and throat, Lady Devonworth leaned forward beside him in the motorcar. "Is something wrong?"

"I'm not sure." He guided the Cadillac to the sidewalk and hailed Mrs. Silvers, who worked at Oscar's Mercantile. "Mrs. Silvers, is there a problem?"

The woman wrung her hands. "Haven't you heard, Mr. Bennett? The news says we are definitely going to pass through the tail of Halley's Comet. We're all going to die in its poisonous gasses!"

The tail. Harrison's dream was about to come true. There had been some doubt about how close the tail would actually come. "I'm certain we'll all be fine," he said.

"We're all gathering at our churches to pray for God's mercy," she said, her voice rising. "You should join us."

"I'm sure God has this all under control," he said.

"It's just like the Revelation," she said. "This is the end of the world." She turned away and rushed down the street toward the brick church whose bell was tolling.

Lady Devonworth's eyes were wide. "Do you fear there is any truth to this rumor?" she asked.

He accelerated away from the sidewalk. "Most scientists believe we shall be fine," he said. "But I do know nothing about it will surprise God at all. That's enough."

She twisted her blue-and-white hanky in her hand. "You say that almost as though you know his thoughts."

"Isn't that what the Bible is for? So we know his thoughts and plans for us?"

Several blocks of tree-lined street went by before she answered. "In New York, church is the place where we meet our friends and show off our newest gowns. I have little experience with a God who cares what we do."

"He sees everything we do. And cares about it." He saw her eyes shutter. Did she not want God to see her?

"I try to do good to others," she said. "It makes me happy."

The society she moved in was foreign to him. An alien place where people thought their power and money would buy happiness. "Glad you can do what you like," he said, uncertain of how to respond.

Her large dark eyes caught his with their intensity. "What makes you think I can do what I like?"

"You just said . . ."

Her gloved hand waved in the air as though to brush off a fly. "I've been brought up to set the perfect table, to organize a party that's talked about for years, to take one look at a gown and know its worth."

He didn't glance away from the sorrow he saw in her eyes. "And this isn't what you want?"

"Would you be content with that?"

"There is more opportunity available to women now. Do something you long to try. You're going flying today. That's a start. God sees the woman inside. You can become that woman if you dare."

She laughed. "I hardly think my friends would understand. Their sole aim is pleasure and amusement. It didn't used to be that way. Mrs. Caroline Astor and others like her wanted to elevate art and American life for the good of the nation. The current set who have come behind her wish to use all the money at their disposal to impress others. They have no thought beyond the latest Newport party."

"Yet they are your friends."

She inclined her head. "They are. And Mrs. Alva Astor has been very kind to me, so it smacks of disrespect to speak like this. But there is a greed for power and status now in New York that is quite distressing. So many are self-serving in our culture."

"Are you seeing it only now that you're out of it?"

She turned toward him, her expression open. "Why yes, now that you mention it, I am. I'd like more from life."

"What would you do if you could?"

One dark brow lifted. He could watch her expressions forever. She was as complex as his aeroplane. More, really. He doubted he could ever fathom what went on behind that beautiful face.

Fiddling with her scarf, she stared out the windshield. "I would like to do something—worthy," she said, her voice a whisper. "My life seems so pointless. No one is my friend just because they like me."

Now was the time to ask her for money to back his dream of a seaplane. He could name it after her, and she'd leave a legacy of something worthwhile. But hearing the pathos in her final statement, he couldn't force the words past his lips. He liked her for who she was. He could almost wish she were penniless so he could woo her for herself alone.

He opened his mouth, then shut it again. The airfield came into sight. "We're here," he said.

Her shoulders straightened and she leaned forward. "It hardly looks able to fly. It's all cables and wires. Is it safe?"

He stared at it with fresh eyes. The thing looked like it was made of balsa wood and string. But it was strong, a good machine. "I've had it up several times."

She frowned. "What are those skis for?" She pointed at a pair of skis leaning against the building.

"They're for landing on the water. I'm going to attach them to the flying machine and try to land on a lake once I get the plane perfected."

"Planes can barely land on the ground. I must see it!" She was out of the car the moment it stopped. Her ribbons and lace fluttered in the air as she rushed to the skis. "These will allow it to land on water?" She glanced at the aeroplane.

The contraption had to appear strange to her. He ran a hand along a wire on the wing. "They will."

"But not today?" she asked, her voice tentative.

"The plane isn't ready for that yet. I haven't figured out how to attach the skis. I'll just take it up for a few minutes. I have to be back for dinner with my father."

Lady Devonworth's eyes lowered at his statement. She seemed to have little to say as Harrison pointed out the instruments and how the plane worked. Though she watched his every move, something changed. She became pale and withdrawn. Maybe her wrist still pained her. If so, this wasn't a good idea.

He got into the cockpit and started the engine. In minutes, the wind was rushing through his hair and he could see her waving her handkerchief far below. He kept it up for a few minutes, then made a flawless landing.

She rushed to the plane when it stopped rolling. Her cheeks were pink. "That was splendid!"

He grinned. "Ready to go up yourself?"

Her eyes sparkled and she nodded. "You're sure it's safe?"

"I wouldn't go up in it myself if it wasn't." He assisted her into the backseat of the aeroplane. "I think you'd better take off that scarf and put on this one." He held up a birdman's leather hat.

Her eyes widened and a genuine smile lifted her lips. "Oh, may I?" She reached for it.

"I don't think you can get it on with your hair up."

She nodded. Her slender fingers plucked the scarf from her head. When she pulled the pins from her hair, the dark tresses tumbled to her waist, and he had to shut his gaping mouth. He'd never seen such beautiful hair. Shot through with red and gold, it shone in the sun and held him mesmerized. Even when she jammed the leather hat over her head and down over her ears, her hair kept his attention.

He cleared his throat. "Your hair is going to tangle in the wind. Let's pull it back with this." Holding aloft a handkerchief, he approached her. "Allow me." Once he touched the softness of her hair, he wanted to plunge his fingers into those tresses. He wound the kerchief around as much of her hair as he could and tied it in a knot.

She'd fallen still the moment he approached. It was too much to hope that she felt the same attraction he did. She was difficult to read. He stepped back. "I think we're ready now."

The sunlight lit her face, revealing the curve of her cheeks and lips. He looked away and reminded himself to keep his attention on flying.

⸙

The flimsy contraption that seemed more wires than anything substantial began to move. Olivia's stomach did a cartwheel, but she wasn't sure if it was the fact she was about to leave terra firma or if it was because she was still digesting the news that Mr. Bennett was in town. The outing today only delayed the inevitable chore of facing the man—and revealing her identity to Harrison.

The aeroplane shuddered, and she bounced with it over the rough ground. The crashing ocean was just ahead. They had to lift above the meadow soon or they would land in the whitecaps. Ocean spray left a salty taste on her lips, and the wind tore at the leather cap pinning her hair in place. Her lips stretched in an inane grin as the wheels bumped one last time and the machine began to glide on the unseen air currents she'd read about.

She was flying! Her gown billowed in the air, and she had to keep grabbing at it and wrapping it around her legs in a most unseemly manner to keep it under control. Her gaze raked the countryside below as the contraption rose higher and higher. In moments they were skipping over the tops of the redwoods. Far below she could see boats rolling on the sea. She and Harrison were higher than the seagulls swooping down to grab crabs from the rocks.

Was that an eagle's nest on the rocky crest ahead of them? She squinted and saw a baby bird with its open beak poking from the nest. A rush of exhilaration left her light-headed. She twisted to look back at the meadow, but it was gone. All that was below them were trees and more trees. The landscape appeared unfamiliar now, and she had no idea where they were. She didn't even see any roads.

She leaned forward to speak in Harrison's ear. "Where are we?"

Though he was shouting, the wind nearly stole his words. "It's wilderness below us. We're a good twenty miles from Ferndale."

She sat back. So far so fast? It seemed impossible. Tipping back her head, she stared in fascination at the clouds in the sky. She didn't ever want to go down.

The plane banked and began to turn. She touched his shoulder "We're not going back, are we?" she shouted in his ear.

He nodded. "Have to! Only enough fuel for a short flight."

Before she could show her displeasure, the machine shuddered. Her heartbeat faltered with the engine's sputter. She tightened her grip on his shoulder. "What's happening?" she screamed as the plane sank toward the ground.

"Hang on!" He fought with the controls.

Olivia quivered as the wings almost seemed to flap with every shudder of the machine. She clenched her hands together and watched the trees draw nearer and nearer. They were going to die.

"Oh God, save us," she moaned. She pressed both palms flat against her cheeks and closed her eyes, unable to watch their doom draw closer. There was no break in that line of massive redwoods.

When Harrison yelled, "Watch out!" her eyes flew open and she saw the trees part slightly to reveal a tiny meadow. The plane began to hurtle toward the space.

Though she longed to close her eyes, her lids refused to shut. Her brain cataloged everything about the scene in front of her: the stream on the far side of the flat space, the size of the redwoods, the rocks jutting up through the grass in places, the lupines growing at the edge of the woods, and the sparrows that squawked and flew out of the way of the giant bird about to crash on their turf. The scene stamped itself into her memory.

Down, down they went. The moss was incredibly green, the rocks so glossy. It would be the last thing she saw in this life. The wheels touched down with a *thump* that jarred her spine. The machine bounced skyward again. She gripped the seat and held her breath as the plane shot toward the stream at the other end of the meadow. The wheels touched down again, and this time they stayed down. All around her the wires and plane parts groaned and screamed. She saw a wing fly off followed by a part she didn't recognize.

Something knocked hard by her feet. Harrison shouted out something unintelligible before he was catapulted from his seat. The next thing she knew she was flying through the air. She saw blue sky through the trees, then her attention turned to the mossy ground rising to meet her. She inhaled the feculent scent of decaying leaves and dirt, then hit the ground and went end over end.

SEVENTEEN

PLANE PARTS LITTERED the rocky ground. Harrison groaned and put his hand to his throbbing head. His fingers came away bloody. Lady Devonworth. Where was she? His head swimming, he staggered to his feet and looked around the clearing but didn't see her.

"Lady Devonworth," he called. Chirping birds answered him. He heard the sound of trickling water and realized how thirsty he was. There was no time for a drink though. She might be dying somewhere without help. The thought was unbearable. He called her name again and stepped past the strewn wreckage of his dream. There would be time to grieve the loss of his plane, but not now. He didn't dare allow himself to dwell on what this accident meant.

Stumbling over the rough ground, he stopped and peered under pieces of the plane. She had to be here somewhere. He double-checked what was left of the cockpit, then turned toward the trees. A flash of blue caught his attention. She was wearing blue. He ran toward the redwoods and found her half covered by a piece of the wing.

He dropped to his knees beside her. Twigs and moss were entwined in the long locks of hair unfettered by her cap.

"Lady Devonworth!" He touched her and nearly cringed at how cold she was. Was she dead? "Lady Devonworth?" He touched her cheek. When there was no response, he pressed his fingers to her neck and felt the strong pump of her pulse. "Thank you, God," he said.

Her legs were exposed. He averted his eyes and yanked her dress down over her limbs. When she didn't stir, he removed her leather cap and probed her head for cuts or lumps. All clear there. He didn't see any blood. Next he ran his hands down her arms. No broken bones. He needed to check her legs, but that felt much too intrusive with her unconscious and unable to give permission.

He rose and carried her leather cap to the stream, where he filled it with water. Back at her side, he dipped his fingers into the water and dribbled moisture onto her lips. Birds cawed overhead, and he heard the sounds of total isolation all around him in the absence of anything but nature. How far were they from help? In which direction did the closest town lie?

If Lady Devonworth couldn't walk, it might be days before they could get out. No one knew where they were, either. He'd told Eugene he was going up in the plane, but he hadn't mentioned which direction he was flying. At the time Harrison hadn't known himself. Eugene wouldn't know where to direct searchers when he failed to return. Goldia would be in the same predicament.

He dribbled water onto her lips again. "Lady Devonworth," he said softly. Her long lashes rested on her cheeks, but he thought he saw a flicker behind her eyelids. Touching her shoulder, he called her name again. Her eyes opened, and he was never so glad to see a glimmer of awareness as he was in the moment that he locked gazes with her.

"Harrison?" she said.

His name on her lips was so intimate he couldn't help but tighten his grip on her shoulder. "Does anything hurt?" he asked.

She shook her head, then winced. "My neck."

"Can you show me?"

She reached up to touch the base of her skull. "Here."

"May I?" he asked. She nodded and pressed his fingers on her neck at the hairline. "There's no cut. Perhaps you bumped it. Can you move your neck?"

"Yes." She rotated her neck. "Help me up."

"I . . . I didn't check your limbs. I fear you may have broken a bone."

She raised her head and reached toward him with her right hand. "I don't think so. I'm just bruised and sore."

He helped her sit. "Are you thirsty?"

"Very."

He held the leather cap to her mouth and she drank what water was left. "Let me get you more," he said.

"I'll come with you. I want to wash the mud off."

He helped her to her feet, but when she stepped onto her right foot, she cried out and fell against him. Cradling her against his chest, he supported her weight while she attempted to catch her balance. "Your ankle?"

"Yes," she said, her voice muffled against his shirt. "I fear I've sprained it."

"May I check it?"

She leaned away from him and nodded. "I suppose we'd better know how severely it's injured."

He helped her to a fallen tree at the edge of the woods. She extended her leg and he unlaced her boot. "I'm not going to take it off unless I have to. We might not be able to get it back on, and you'll need it if we expect to walk out of here."

"Very well." She bit her lip as he pressed on the flesh under the boot.

He detected no protrusion or dent that might be a broken bone, but he was no expert. If only a doctor were within walking distance. How was he going to get her out of here with a badly sprained ankle? Leaving her wasn't an option either. Not when a mountain lion or bear could happen along at any time. Or a wolf pack. The shadows were already lengthening. The redwoods would accelerate how quickly darkness fell.

"Is it broken?" she asked.

He realized the silence had gone on too long. "I don't believe so." He laced her shoe again. "Let's elevate your foot to alleviate the swelling."

She bit her lip and maneuvered to the moss, and he lifted her leg to the tree. "Wait here," he said. "I'll fetch you some water." He jogged back to the stream and filled the cap again. What about food? He had a small pack filled with sandwiches, but the food would be gone in one meal. There was no use in trying to keep some for tomorrow either. It was egg salad and would be spoiled without being kept cool. The ice block his cook had packed with it was bound to have melted by now.

They had no tent, no sleeping bags, no supplies. The moment they moved away from the stream they would have no water either. Searchers wouldn't have a trail to follow to this location. Their only hope was to walk out of here on their own two feet. When he returned with the water, he realized their situation was beginning to impress itself on her too. Her face was pale and her dark brows were drawn together.

"What happened? You said your plane was safe."

"It almost seemed as though we were out of gas, but there should have been plenty for our trip. I don't know for sure what happened. I shall investigate, though."

"You don't believe someone meant us harm, do you? After all, someone threw me off the boat."

He frowned. "I hadn't considered such a scheme."

"Did anyone know you meant to take me up in the plane?"

He thought back to his day. His father was aware of his plans. And Eugene was too. "A few people. I suppose someone might have mentioned it in town. But I'm sure our accident had nothing to do with you." He offered her another drink.

"We're stranded here, are we not?" she asked after taking a gulp of water.

She was too smart to swallow a rationalization, but he shrugged and forced a smile. "Just until your ankle heals a bit. With some rest, we should be able to make our way out."

"How far to the nearest town?"

"I haven't calculated that yet. I have a rough idea where we are, but I need to get my maps out and decide on the best course of action."

Her eyes widened enough for him to see the gold flecks in her dark brown eyes. She twisted a length of hair around her finger. "That means we shall be here overnight. Alone."

"Indeed. But I promise to be a perfect gentleman."

She glanced away, and a flush stained her cheeks. "I didn't doubt that for a moment. But people in town will talk."

"They may not even realize we're missing. I don't expect Eugene to raise a hue and cry."

"Goldia will," Lady Devonworth said, her voice trembling. "It will be all over the national news. My mother will see it. My friends."

"You can assure them nothing happened."

"It's not that easy," she said. "My reputation shall be ruined."

"Surely not!" Even as he protested, he knew how straitlaced New York society was. She would never again assume her previous social status so long as this hung over her head. "We can pray we are not newsworthy enough for the New York papers to pick this up."

She nodded but her eyes were shadowed, and he knew he'd failed to convince her. And with good reason. One whisper of this in the San Francisco paper and it would be all over the nation. The honorable thing to do would be to offer to marry her. He opened his mouth, then shut it again. Doing something so mad would only play into his father's plans at a time when Harrison was determined to forge his own path.

He rose and went toward the woods. "I'm going to gather some evergreen branches. We need bedding. Tomorrow I'll look for berries and anything else edible for breakfast. I have sandwiches for dinner.

Then we'll walk out of here first thing in the morning. With God's blessing, we'll reach a town by noon."

"Let's go tonight," she said. "If you fetch me a stick, I believe I can walk."

"I doubt you're able," he said. He stooped and grabbed a stout branch with a forked spot that he thought should hit her about right. Taking out his pocketknife, he whittled away the smaller branches on it and hacked it down to the right length. "Try that."

After he helped her to her feet, she fitted the forked spot under her arm and tried to step forward. Her awkward limp only lasted two steps before she collapsed. "I can't do it," she said.

"You'll be fine by morning," he said, helping her back to her spot by the fallen tree. But as he walked into the woods to look for supplies, he sensed everything was about to change.

Birds chirped around her as though they hadn't a care in the world. The throbbing in Olivia's ankle hadn't lessened, though it had been elevated for fifteen minutes. The forest seemed sinister, forbidding now that she was alone. The cool breeze through the redwoods made her shiver, and the mist that had begun to curl around the rough tree trunks and through the shrubs looked ominous. The picnic by the falls the other day marked the first time she'd ever been to the woods. Then, civilization was only a short walk away. Now, the wilderness pressed in on every side.

She strained to hear Harrison's return. *Harrison.* Heat blossomed in her cheeks as she suddenly remembered calling out his name when she awakened from the crash. Such familiarity must have shocked him. And made him wonder why she would think of him that way. He might read more into it than she was ready to deal with.

A rustle came to her ears and she sat up. "Mr. Bennett, is that you?" Aware her voice quivered, she tipped her chin up and pressed her lips together. She would *not* be afraid. If there was one thing she detested, it was a shrieking woman.

Harrison emerged from the shadows with boughs of evergreens in his arms. "It's just me. Were you frightened?"

The scent of pine enveloped her as he neared. "Not at all," she said, putting frost into her tone.

"What happened to 'Harrison'?" he asked, dropping the branches beside her.

"I beg your pardon?"

"You called me Harrison when you woke up. Why so formal now? If we're going to be spending all this time together, we might as well be friends enough to progress to first names."

She brushed a leaf from her skirt. "I hardly think we are friends, Mr. Bennett. Business acquaintances only."

"I've rescued a kitten on your behalf, seen you weeping at my fiancée's grave, and survived an aeroplane crash with you. We're about to spend the night alone in the forest together. I think that elevates us above acquaintances. What *is* your first name anyway?"

Tell him. She clamped her teeth against the words. With his inquisitive stare on her, she couldn't think how to deny his request without appearing rude. "I prefer you call me Lady Devonworth," she said.

The amused light in his eyes grew stronger. "Very well, Lady Devonworth, if you won't tell me, I shall have to make up one." He tipped his head to one side and regarded her. "With that dark hair and flashing brown eyes, you are a bit of a gypsy. I shall call you Esmeralda."

She had to laugh. "You've read *The Hunchback of Notre Dame*?"

"Several times."

"My mother thought it quite scandalous. She hates to catch me reading a novel."

He grinned. "It's going to be dark soon. I'll arrange the branches, then fetch our dinner."

His back was straight as the redwood beside her as he walked away. She hadn't wanted to offend him, but she couldn't bring herself to tell him. At least he'd made a joke of it.

The more the mist crept into their small camp, the more uneasy she became. It took him only a few minutes to arrange two beds of evergreen boughs and build a fire. There would be nothing to soften the prickle of the needles, and she planned to delay crawling into her bed for as long as possible. He left to scavenge the wreckage.

He returned with a wicker hamper. "Took me awhile to find it." He placed it beside her.

She opened the lid and found some sandwiches, pickles, and carrots. "This looks like a feast even if it is all squashed," she said to cover the way her tummy rumbled in a most unladylike way. She handed him some food and unwrapped her own sandwich from its covering of waxed paper. "It's still cold."

He settled beside her on the tree. "My cook knows how to pack a meal. I think there is cake in there too."

She nibbled on her sandwich and eyed him. When had she begun to like him, even trust him a little? "Maybe we should save it for breakfast. I didn't see any berries." Breakfast. The word reminded her she'd be spending the night with this man. Shivers made their way up her spine. It wasn't exactly *fear* she felt, but almost exhilaration.

When they got back to town, there would be repercussions. Her mother would ask what she thought she was doing to go off on a flight with this man. The society women would titter and talk behind their gloved hands. She could expect the invitations to balls and teas to dry up. The thought should fill her with horror, but she found she didn't care in this moment with the dying light slanting across the strong planes of Harrison's face. She watched his hands, so strong and capable, as he tossed his waxed paper into the hamper.

"I often have the oddest sensation that we've met before," he said.

"I've been to New York a time or two. My father has a house on Fifth Avenue. Have you met him? Claude Bennett?"

"Really, Mr. Bennett, we hardly run in the same circles," she said.

"True," he agreed, his tone mild. "There's something about the way you laugh." He gestured to the sky. "It's getting dark. I suggest we turn in before we are unable to find our way. It's cloudy. I suspect we'll have very little moonlight."

"Of course." She glanced at the woods. How on earth could she tell him she needed to make a trip into the trees alone?

He rose. "I think I'll take a little walk before bed. That way." He indicated the woods on the other side of the clearing. "Feel free to go the opposite direction if you like. Just don't get lost."

She watched him disappear into the mist, then struggled to her feet and grabbed her stick. He'd be back soon, so she'd better hurry.

EIGHTEEN

WHEN HARRISON RETURNED, he found the lady sitting on a log by the fire. The flicker of the flames threw shadows and light across her face. He stood under the concealing sweep of an evergreen and watched her for a moment.

The name Esmeralda suited her. Her dark brown hair cascaded down, obscuring her face. He couldn't decipher her. One minute he was sure she felt the attraction between them, and the next she was refusing to tell him her first name, as though he was beneath her.

He stepped into the clearing. "You should try to prop your ankle during the night."

"I will."

Darkness closed in fast, obscuring her features and the clearing. "Let me help you." He found her hand in the shadows. Her fingers closed around his, and he pulled her up, close enough for the scent of lilac to waft to his nose. He could have leaned down and pressed his lips against hers. For a crazy moment, he was tempted to do just that. What would she do if he did? Slap him? Scream? Probably. She considered him little more than a servant, and he didn't dare find out her response for fear of frightening her.

"This way," he said softly, leading her to the bed of boughs. The smell of crushed pine was sweet and pungent as he helped her onto the soft heap. "I'm sorry I haven't a covering for it."

"I shall be fine."

The branches rustled, but he couldn't see her expression. He dragged a log close. "Prop your ankle on this."

More rustling. "I can't find it," she said.

"Allow me." He patted the bed of pine until he found her foot, then guided it to the log. "Rest well. Things will appear much brighter in the morning." He moved to his own bed and lay down. The fragrance of pine enveloped him. Though he hadn't thought he could sleep, his eyelids grew heavy.

When he awakened, he wasn't sure at first where he was or what had alerted him. Sitting up, he strained to see in the darkness. The moon had come out from behind the clouds and made the mist curling through the clearing glow with an almost unearthly light. He glanced over at Lady Devonworth and saw her sitting up on her bed. Then the sound that must have awakened him came again. A snuffle and a scrape.

He scrambled from the branches. If only he had a gun or some kind of weapon. The noise was surely from an animal. Seizing the branch she had used for support, he whacked it onto the bed of pine so it made a crackling sound. "Get out of here!"

The animal roared. He realized he was facing a bear. With a stick. Lady Devonworth screamed, and he leaped between her and the beast. "Get out of here!" he shouted again, waving the stick in the air.

A hulking giant of an animal moved into a shaft of moonlight. A black bear. Harrison stood as tall as he could and waved his arms, shouting all the while. He debated about whacking the beast across the nose with the stick, but before he decided to escalate the encounter, the bear dropped to all fours and loped into the woods.

The arm holding the stick went weak, and he dropped it to his side. "It's gone," he said.

The next moment Lady Devonworth was in his arms with her face burrowed against his chest. "I was so frightened," she whispered. "I tried to call out to you but I couldn't speak."

Her hair was so soft under his hands as he smoothed her unruly locks. "We're going to be all right," he said, pitching his tone to a soothing murmur. He rested his chin on the top of her head as she trembled in his arms.

They stood entwined together for several long minutes. Harrison strained to hear any sound of the animal's return but heard only crickets and the hoot of an owl. When she finally drew away, he wanted to protest, but he let his arms drop instead.

He thrust his hands in his pockets to keep from reaching for her. "You should get some rest."

"What if it comes back?"

"I'll stand guard."

"You need sleep too."

"I'm wide-awake after hearing that bear roar." He forced a laugh, then grinned when her laughter tinkered out.

"Yelling at a bear." Her voice was amused. "I don't know what you thought that stick would do."

"I hoped it would make me look bigger than I was," he said.

"It appears you were successful." Her voice took on a husky quality. "I . . . I don't think I can sleep unless you are close."

"I'll be right here." He stepped past her and dragged the bundle of pine branches next to hers. "I'm not going to sleep though."

"You can at least rest. With the branch in your hand, of course." Her tone held a smile.

The boughs rustled as she settled back onto them. There was enough moonlight to see her face turned toward his. He sank onto his bed with the stick clutched in his hand.

She stretched out her arm, groping for his hand in the dark.

He grasped her cold fingers in a comforting clasp. "Are you chilled?"

"Yes. The mist is damp."

"Would you allow me to hold you, little Esmeralda? I promise to be a gentleman."

She laughed but didn't answer for a long moment, so he assumed the answer would be no, but she sighed and her fingers tightened on his. "Just a little while until I'm warmer. I'm so cold."

He crawled over closer to her and slipped his arm under her head. She rolled onto her side and snuggled against him as though she'd done it a thousand times. The tugging in the region of his heart was so strange. And unwelcome. She'd made it clear she had no romantic interest in him. Why then did he allow himself to hope they might have a future?

⌒⁀✻⁀⌒

For a moment, Olivia thought she was snug in her own bed. Then she felt the stick of pine needles and the sound of birdsong. The stream gurgled off to her right.

"Good morning, Essie."

She turned toward the voice. Harrison was sitting at the stream with a makeshift fishing rig. "Essie?"

"Short for Esmeralda."

She had to smile. "Good morning," she said, sitting up. "What time is it?"

He pulled his pocket watch out and opened it. "Nearly eight."

He was staring, and she pushed her hair out of her face. She must look a sight. She undoubtedly had pine twigs and dirt in her hair. "How long have you been up?"

"About an hour." He gestured to the fish on the bank. "I'm about to cook our breakfast. Hungry?"

Her stomach rumbled in answer. "Starving. Can I help?"

"Know how to clean fish?"

She grimaced. "No, and I'm not particularly keen on learning."

His laughter boomed out and echoed in the treetops. She smiled back at him, then stretched. He was charming, even with twigs in his hair. "Was there really a bear here last night?"

He sobered and stood with the fish in his hand. "I saw the tracks this morning. He was big. But there's no sign of him now."

A fire crackled in the center of the clearing. Stones surrounded it. Olivia tried to stand, but hot pain gripped her ankle. She grabbed for the branch beside her bed. Even propping herself on it only allowed her to hobble a few steps before she had to rest.

Harrison watched her with a grim expression. "I don't think we're going anywhere today."

She struggled to hold back the tears. "We can't spend another night here. People really *will* talk. And what if the bear comes back?"

"Don't borrow trouble. We'll get you well and get out of here." He stooped and lifted her in his arms.

As he carried her toward the fire, she remembered last night. His compassion and gentleness. His courage against the bear. It wouldn't do to dwell on that too much.

He set her on the log. "After breakfast I'm going to put your ankle in the cold running water. We need to get that swelling down."

How was she going to get through another day alone with him? She watched him prepare the fish. Before long, the aroma of sizzling food mingled with the scent of wildflowers and pine.

He handed her some fish on a shaved spit. "Sorry there isn't a better way to serve it. I had to make do with what we had."

She took the stick. "I'm impressed you know how to do this. Haven't you always lived in a city?"

He nodded. "But my uncle used to take me on wilderness treks. We lived off the land. You never forget that stuff."

She bit into the juicy fish. The smoky flavor filled her mouth. She chewed and swallowed. "That's the best fish I've ever eaten."

He grinned. "You were just hungry."

She devoured her portion of the trout, then licked the juice from her fingers in a most unladylike way. Out here under trees that touched the sky, she was a different person from the woman who walked the streets of New York. She became aware that Harrison was watching her. Her hair was on her shoulders, and she had no idea what had become of her combs and pins. It would have to stay unbound. There was an intimacy in that, making her throat dry when she met his gaze.

He stood. "Let's soak your ankle awhile." He lifted her again.

She curled an arm around his neck. Being so close to him was nearly unbearable, but she couldn't quite figure out why. He was just a man. She'd met many men. Though her head told her this was so, her heart seemed to be telling her something else. When he set her beside the stream, she leaned down to unlace her boot and hide the heat in her face. Her fingers fumbled over the laces, but she managed to get the boot off. She wasn't about to raise her skirt in his presence though.

"I'll leave you to soak it," he said. "I'm going to gather firewood for the night. Let me get your crutch in case you need it." He retreated to the fire, then returned with the stick. "I'll be back in about an hour."

When his steps faded, she eased up the hem of her skirt, took off her stocking, then put her throbbing foot into the stream and gasped as the icy water encased her ankle. If she could just get the swelling down enough to get out of here, she could endure anything. The cold soon numbed her skin. The sun was warm on her face as it came out from behind storm clouds. She leaned back and let herself feel the sensations. When had she last relaxed to this degree? In the city she was always rushing to the next appointment or concerned with answering the mail.

She was always trying to live up to expectations. Now her reputation was about to be in ruins. How would she ever get past that?

When she could stand the cold water no longer, she pulled her foot out, let it air dry, then put her stocking and boot back on. The swelling seemed to be better, but when she tried to stand again, the pain was just as intense. She'd never be able to walk out of here today.

With the help of her makeshift crutch, she hobbled back to the bed and eased onto it so she could elevate her foot. If she did everything right today, maybe they could get out of here tomorrow.

Leaves crackled to her left, and she saw Harrison emerge with his arms full of logs. He dropped his load by the embers of the morning's fire. "Any better?"

She shook her head. "Not really. I managed to get here, though."

"I thought about making a litter that I could drag. I'm just not sure how far we're going to have to trek to find people."

She shook her head. "I'm not convinced I could endure the bouncing. It throbs whenever it's not elevated."

He squatted beside her. "I think we need to move our camping spot. We are right by the stream, which is convenient, but there are bear tracks and mountain-lion tracks all around that stream. They'll be back."

Her chest tightened and she glanced at the dark forest. "But where can we go to be safe?"

"I found a dry cave a few yards that way." He pointed to their right. "It's still close enough that we can fetch water, but it's out of the animals' path to the stream. I've already tossed some pine boughs together for bedding. All I have to do is move us and our things over there."

"But what if it's a den for a mountain lion or bear?"

He shook his head. "I checked it out thoroughly. No spoor around, just some bat droppings."

Her skin prickled. *"Bat droppings?"*

He grinned. "No bats sleeping in there now. We'll be fine."

"Can we stay here for now?"

He glanced around. "Bears are active in the daytime too. I think we'd better move over. You wait here while I move our few things. I'm going to leave the food hamper here though. There's nothing of value left, and the smell might attract animals. That was probably what drew the bear last night."

She watched him rummage through the strewn debris. He took a piece of seat, some wire and metal, then disappeared into the trees. Every rustle in the trees made her tense. Every noise from a squirrel left her wary. When he finally returned to help her to their new lair, she was ready to feel safe.

As he leaned down to help her to her feet, she heard a whine in the air. Harrison shouted something and jumped on top of her. His breath was ragged in her ear. Her face pressed into pine needles as his body covered hers. The sun had left, and a few drops of rain fell. Then it came harder. Hard enough to obscure the landscape and blur her vision. The drone of it pattering onto leaves and vegetation grew louder.

"Are you hit?" he asked, his voice frantic.

She pulled her mouth free of the suffocating vegetation. "No, no, I'm fine. What happened?"

"Someone shot at us," he said.

"A hunter?" Her thoughts raced. Had it been another attempt on her life? But why here? No one knew where they were.

"Maybe. I'd stand up and shout, but the rain will muffle anything I might say." Harrison helped her up and they set off through the trees. Clinging to his arm, she hobbled as fast as she could. Rain sluiced over her face and plastered her hair. The cave wasn't far, but they were soaked by the time they reached it.

He glanced around the space. "I'll start a fire in the mouth of the cave. And fetch a club."

He sat on guard at the fire the rest of the day. It was only late in the night when she felt the branches shift as she lay dozing. She lifted an eyelid to see the fire blazing away, protecting them from intruders.

"Just going to take a catnap, Essie," he said, his voice slurred.

He slipped his arm around her, and she curled up next to his warmth without a thought to how inappropriate it was.

NINETEEN

WARMTH PERVADED EVERY pore. Olivia snuggled closer to the comfort of the body against hers. The heat made her feel protected. Until the male scent made her eyes fly open. She was entwined in Harrison's arms, inhaling the aroma of pine and masculinity. At the same time she heard male voices. Turning her head, she saw four men peering into the cave.

Rolling away, she sat up and frantically swiped at her hair. "You've found us," she said.

The men didn't look at her. They ranged in age from twenty to forty, and all of them had twigs on their clothing and mud on their boots.

The constable shifted from one foot to the other. "Your valet convinced Mr. Peers to take us up in his balloon. I saw the smoke from your fire, so I knew where to head."

Harrison rose from behind her. He brushed pine needles from his shirt. "Smart thinking, Constable. We thought we'd have to try to walk out of here today. Lady Devonworth has a sprained ankle, and we've been unable to make the trek."

Could Harrison not see these men had tried them both and found them guilty of fornication? Olivia saw it in the quick glances they shot between her and Harrison. In the way they shuffled, and in the unease on their faces. She curled her hands into fists.

Harrison fixed the man next to the constable with a stare. "Quinn,

I'll thank you to keep this out of the paper. There was nothing unsavory happening here."

A reporter. Olivia wanted to hide behind a giant redwood. This would be all over the country.

The man took off his bowler and wiped his forehead. Though clearly only in his twenties, he was already balding. "It's already in the morning paper, Harrison." His mouth turned down and he shrugged. "It's news, my friend."

Her face blossomed with heat. From the Mercy Falls news, it would hit the San Francisco papers. Then on to New York, Chicago, Boston. She was ruined. But maybe it would be a small article and missed by the bigger papers. Unless he ran a follow-up story. She would try to talk him out of it.

She opened her mouth, then shut it again. It was impossible to miss the gleam of avarice in Mr. Quinn's eyes. He had every intention of writing about what he saw when he stepped into the clearing. Nothing she could say would sway him. Could he be paid off? She meant to try at the first opportunity.

She managed a smile. "I'm glad you're here, gentlemen. I fear I shall still need some assistance, even after two days' rest."

"We had a bear appear our first night, so we took to this place, which I could defend with a fire," Harrison said, grabbing the walking stick. "I fear neither of us got much sleep."

Olivia caught the double meaning in his words and saw the men's faces change as well. The constable was the only one who didn't smirk. She grabbed the stick from Harrison's hand and thrust it into the ground to keep from whacking him with it.

"Shall we depart?" All she wanted was to get home and shut the door and fall onto her bed.

Harrison helped her from the cave. The men began to gather strewn belongings and put the items in bags they'd brought. They all went back to the clearing. Harrison directed them to the most important plane parts. The silence was as thick as last night's mist. By the time they headed into the woods, she wanted nothing more than never to see any of these men again—including Harrison Bennett.

The stick did little to alleviate the throbbing in her ankle. The constable strode ahead, forcing branches out of the way and tamping down weeds to allow her easier access. Bugs swarmed her damp skin, and every step was a misery. It was going to take hours of this torture to get to civilization.

She blinked against the stinging in her eyes. She would not cry. It would take every ounce of fortitude she possessed to get through the next few days. The physical pain of walking out of here was nothing compared to the emotional anguish that awaited her. Surely there was a way to salvage this.

I could marry him.

The stray thought made her stumble, and only the stick prevented her from tumbling into the bushes. What of her initial suspicion of him? The only clue she had indicating his guilt was her father's letter telling Eleanor that the Bennetts were dangerous. But Harrison had rescued her from the sea, and he could have disposed of her out here in the wilderness. He'd been so gentlemanly, so concerned for her. He'd withstood a bear for her.

She didn't believe he was capable of murder, but that didn't mean she was ready to marry him.

❧

Olivia had never been so glad to see a truck in her life. Harrison assisted her onto the black leather seat next to Mr. Quinn, who would drive them out of here, then went around to climb in the back with the rest of the men.

Mr. Quinn glanced at her from the corner of his eye. The smirk in his eyes made her want to squirm, but she held her chin up and looked straight ahead. The interior of the truck smelled like oil or grease, but getting her dress stained was the least of her worries.

"I'm glad you appear to be unharmed, Miss Stewart," Mr. Quinn said, his voice smooth.

She started to thank him, then froze when she realized he'd used her real name. When she turned her head to look at him, he glanced back and his smirk widened.

"How do you know my name?" she managed to ask without her voice trembling.

"I know quite a lot about you. But I have to wonder why you are using some title instead of your given name of Olivia Stewart."

She had to convince him to stay quiet until she had a chance to reveal the truth herself. "It's very simple. I wanted to find out what happened to my sister."

One eyebrow rose, and the truck jerked to the right as he glanced at her. "You doubt that she drowned?"

"If I promise to give you the full story when I get to the bottom of the situation, would you promise not to print my name until my investigation is concluded?"

He pursed his lips. "I'd get your full cooperation to run the full story?"

She felt no qualms about promising that. The murderer would be behind bars. "Yes."

"It's a deal. So what makes you doubt she drowned?"

"I don't doubt she drowned. I just don't believe she willingly went swimming."

"Suicide?"

"She feared the water. If she were going t-to do away with herself, she wouldn't choose drowning."

His eyes gleamed. "So that leaves foul play."

She clutched the seat as the truck careened around a corner. "I fear so."

"Do you suspect anyone?"

A few days ago she would have been forced to admit she suspected Harrison. But that was no longer true. She shook her head. "I'm looking into some acquaintances she made while she was here."

"Like Frederick Fosberg?"

"How do you know about him?"

"She seemed to be making a fool of herself over him at a party I attended."

"Do you know the man?"

"Not well. I'm planning on doing a piece on him and the new business he's opening. Say, how about the two of us work together? I'll help you get to the bottom of this."

The last thing she wanted was this man poking into her business, but what choice did she have? "Thank you," she said, resigning herself to the inevitable.

⚜

Harrison bounced on the wheel well when the truck hit a pothole. The constable sat beside him on the floorboards.

"How much talk in town?" Harrison asked Brown once they were underway.

"The town is abuzz with it. It's the only thing discussed at the soda shop and the mercantile. There is much speculation that perhaps the two of you ran off together instead of crashed."

As he'd suspected. "So the lady's reputation is ruined, is it not? Even if you tell of the wreckage you saw, people love a juicy rumor instead of truth."

Brown inclined his head. "I fear so."

Harrison turned to look at the steeples and rooftops of Mercy Falls in the distance. The lady had a high position to maintain. The only way to salvage her good name was for them to be married. This was his fault. He'd taken her up in the flying machine without a thought for her reputation. At the first opportunity, he would ask for her hand.

His mouth went dry at the thought. It was too much to even hope that she would say yes. He had money but no title. Her family would forbid such a marriage. And she'd been open about her friendship with Eleanor. He'd have to tell her the truth.

The truck rumbled into town. People turned to stare. He saw the women begin to talk at once. Some even turned their backs on the vehicle. All but one rubbernecker frowned. Addie's bright smile was like sunlight breaking through the trees. He waved and she hurried toward the truck with Edward and the dog Gideon in tow. When the truck stopped, she rushed to greet them.

"Thank God you're all right!" She peered past him. "But where is Lady Devonworth?"

He leaped to the pavement. "Her ankle was sprained in the crash. She's in the cab."

"Oh that poor girl." She went around the back of the truck and up to the door of the cab where Lady Devonworth sat.

Harrison followed her. When Addie opened the door, he reached past her with his hand extended. "Allow me, Es—I mean, Lady Devonworth."

She took his hand. When she emerged into the sunlight, he noticed she appeared pale and tired. "My house is just down the block. May I offer you rest there first? I'll take you home after tea."

"I'll come along," Addie added, glancing at the group of women staring at them.

"I'm so weary," Lady Devonworth said.

He slipped his fingers under her elbow and turned her toward his house. "A pain powder would help, I'm sure. I'll have my father summon the doctor."

She stopped. "Your father is at your house?"

"He's across the street in his own house, but I'll call him."

She smoothed her windblown hair. "I-I think I'd rather go home. We can summon the doctor from there, can we not?"

She was likely uncertain about meeting his parents in her present state. Besides, her departure would give him the opportunity to explain the situation to them without an audience. "As you wish."

He backtracked to the truck where the men still milled around. "Could I trouble you to take the lady to Stewart Hall, Quinn?"

"I'd be happy to." He tossed a cigarette to the ground and went to the cab.

Harrison assisted Lady Devonworth inside. "There's room for you, Addie. I can have Edward and Gideon ride in the back with me."

She took Edward's hand. "We'll just walk. It's only a few blocks. I'll stop along the way and fetch the doctor."

"Thanks." He leaped into the back of the bed, and the truck started off with a jerk.

With every bump along the street, his stomach tightened. How could he go about making this right without offending her? Surely she must be sick with worry about what this situation was going to do to her life. At least she could sort out the trouble here. Mercy Falls residents would be quicker to forgive this transgression than her friends in New York.

The truck turned into the tree-lined driveway of the Stewart home. A few gardeners lifted their heads when the truck pulled to a stop, then they went back to their work. A maid beat rugs over a line in the side yard. The running of the house had continued even though Lady Devonworth had gone missing. Did none of the servants realize the danger she'd been in?

As soon as the truck stopped, he leaped out. When he opened the vehicle's door, he found her drooping with exhaustion. Dark circles bruised the skin under her eyes. Without asking permission, he put his arm around her waist and helped her up the steps. She didn't even protest.

"Open the door!" He banged the front door with his foot.

Moments later Goldia opened the door. "Mr. Bennett! Oh no, is she hurt?"

He brushed past her with Lady Devonworth stumbling beside him. "The doctor is on his way." He went down the hall to the parlor and sat her on the sofa, then raised her boots onto the cushions.

"We must get your boot off," he told her. He glanced back at the maid, who stood behind him wringing her hands. "Would you help me?" He stepped away and allowed her to kneel by her mistress. "Careful of her ankle."

She unlaced Lady Devonworth's boots, then wiggled the right one. "It's not coming off."

He grabbed the boot heel and gave a tug. Lady Devonworth winced. "I think it's severely swollen," he said. "If you'd hold her calf, I'll try to get it off." Lady Devonworth gritted her teeth and gripped the cushions.

Goldia nodded and grasped the lady's leg under the skirt. He began to work the boot off her foot. When it popped free, he stepped back again. "Roll her stocking down."

Goldia nodded and worked the sock off Lady Devonworth's foot. She gasped. "Oh, sir, it looks terrible."

He winced when he saw the purple bulging flesh at the ankle and down the foot. When he glanced back at Lady Devonworth, she lay with her eyes closed. She'd probably fainted from pain. "Fetch some tea. She hasn't eaten much today either. Some toast perhaps?"

Goldia nodded and rushed from the room. Harrison pulled a chair close to the sofa and sat on it to wait for Addie and the doctor. He took her hand and studied the face of the woman he intended to make his bride. If only there was time to properly woo her, he believed he could actually love her.

TWENTY

OLIVIA GRITTED HER teeth against the pain in her leg. It radiated from her foot all the way to her knee. She groaned and flung out her arm. It hit something soft. She opened her eyes and became aware that she was lying on the sofa. In her house. A pillow cushioned her head, and light slanted through the curtains at the window.

Opening her eyes fully, she realized someone held her hand captive. She turned her head and stared into Harrison's face. Her heart thumped against her ribs at his intense expression.

"How did I get in here?" she asked. "I don't remember."

"I half dragged you." His smile was gentle. "How do you feel?"

"Like an elephant stepped on my foot."

He had flecks of mud and debris on his trousers. He continued to stare at her. "It's badly sprained. Maybe even broken. Addie should be here shortly with the doctor."

She became aware that he wasn't just holding her hand, he was rubbing his thumb across her palm in a most distracting way. If it wasn't so pleasant, she would snatch her hand away. His touch reached a place inside and made her feel warm and cherished in a most delicious way. Which was quite ridiculous, of course.

She struggled to sit up, but he shook his head. "Lie still. You need to keep that foot elevated. Besides, I need to talk to you."

His tone and expression were so grave that her pulse increased to a rapid pounding in her chest. "I-Is it my father? He's been found?"

When he frowned, she realized he knew nothing of her search for her father. Or who she was. Her secret was still safe. "Never mind. What is it you wish to say?"

His eyes grew more somber. "You saw the reaction in town to our return." When she nodded, he reached to the coffee table with his free hand and grabbed a newspaper. "This is the morning paper." He turned the front page around to face her.

She read the headline: HARRISON BENNETT AND LADY DEVONWORTH MISSING FOR TWO DAYS. She squinted at the print below it. "What does it say in the article?"

"It suggests we might have had a tryst and faked a plane crash to cover it up."

Her head swam. Exactly what she'd feared would happen. "We can refute it. Take a photographer to the site of the crash. And Mr. Quinn will print no more stories."

"Four men saw us there. Sleeping side by side."

Heat rushed to her cheeks and she flashed back to that moment. Had she ever felt as content as these past two mornings when she'd awakened in his arms? "There's no way to prove our innocence?" she asked.

He shook his head. "None. And there's more. Goldia told me she has fielded several calls from the papers. The San Francisco news ran the story in the evening paper." He pressed her hand harder. "I'm sorry, Essie. This is my fault."

By the utmost exercise of her will, she managed to keep down the bile that rose in her throat. This couldn't be happening. Her life and reputation couldn't be swept away so quickly. Her mother would hear this news and fear the worst. "I must call home," she murmured. She could only hope the New York papers missed it.

"There's time for that later," he said. "We must decide some things before the doctor arrives."

"What things?" She jerked her hand from his grasp and struggled to a seated position. He gently took her ankles and lifted her feet to the coffee table. Even that gentle motion made her ankle throb.

"Tell me," she said when he sat back in his chair.

"There is only one way to save your reputation," he said.

Though she wanted to shake her head at what she knew was coming, she couldn't move. He was right. Marriage was the only thing that could save her reputation now.

He took her hand again. "If we marry, no one will say anything. I will arrange for a private ceremony at once. We can announce that we were privately wed, and the kinder members of society will allow our prevarication to stand."

She shook her head. "I don't know what to say."

"If you prefer a more elaborate ceremony, I can arrange that too. We would suffer a bit more gossip, but it would be forgotten soon enough." His eyes became veiled and his mouth hardened. "Unless you fear it is more scandalous to marry beneath you."

Tell him the truth. She opened her mouth to tell him everything, but the doorbell rang and he rose. "There's the doctor." He moved his chair back from the sofa. "We'll discuss this later."

Addie rushed into the room with Dr. Lambertson on her heels. "How are you feeling, my dear?"

"I shall be fine," Olivia assured her.

The doctor moved to her side and began to press on her ankle. "It's quite a bad sprain, Lady Devonworth. It's going to take some time for you to recover." He nodded to Goldia, who stood hovering in the doorway with a tray of tea and cookies in her hands. "Fetch me some hot water and soap. I shall wash and wrap it."

Goldia handed the tray to Addie, then hurried from the room. When her eyes fell on the food, Olivia was suddenly ravenous and thirsty. "I'll take some tea," she said.

"Let me help you," Addie said.

While her friend poured out the tea, Olivia glanced at Harrison and found him staring at her. Her nerves fluttered at his expression. Her head began to ache. If only she hadn't gotten into that plane! This labyrinth was too complicated for her to find the way out.

Society would crucify her.

⌒⁂⌒

Once the doctor finished wrapping Lady Devonworth's ankle and departed, Harrison walked with him to the door. "You don't believe the bone is broken?" he asked.

Dr. Lambertson shook his head. "She will need to stay off it for at least a week though. It's badly sprained. She should not have been allowed to walk on it for as long as she did."

Harrison nodded. "It's my fault. I crashed the aeroplane and we had no choice but to walk out of the forest."

"You should have made a litter for her and carried her out once help arrived."

"She was quite adamant about walking," Harrison said. "Thank you, doctor." He followed Dr. Lambertson out to the porch, where he saw a car roll to a stop in the driveway.

"Your father is back in town," the doctor remarked as he went down the steps.

Harrison watched the two men speak, then his father strode up the driveway. His bowler was perched perfectly on his head, and he swirled his gold-tipped cane as he came. His smile was full of confidence.

Harrison shook his hand. "Father, what are you doing here?"

"I had to see if my son had survived, of course," he said loudly. He leaned forward and whispered in Harrison's ear, "I forbid you to marry that woman. I did some checking. No one I spoke to has heard of the Devonworths. She's certainly not on par with Olivia Stewart."

"The crash was an accident."

His father grimaced. "Of course it was. I'd like to meet this scheming woman."

Harrison took a step back and crossed his arms over his chest. "She's indisposed."

"I'll only stay a moment. Your mother says the lady has a mind of her own but is quite beautiful. She must be to have you so enthralled."

Harrison barred the hall. "Please leave for now, Father. This is not the appropriate time."

The older man huffed, then stepped away. "Very well. Convey my regards." He jammed his bowler onto his head and stalked off the porch.

"Who was that?" Lady Devonworth asked when he returned to the parlor.

"My father. I must warn you that he will be most opposed to our marriage. He has his heart set on Olivia Stewart as my wife. I told him this was not the best time to make your acquaintance."

She paled and bit her lip. "Thank you. I should like to be at my best when I meet him."

"I suspect that will be at least a week."

She nodded and sat up straighter on the cushions. "Someone shot at us in the clearing," she said. "I can't help but wonder if the man could be the same one who threw me from the boat."

He frowned, realizing he hadn't even thought of the attempt on her life the day they met. "We've never really talked about that incident. Do you have enemies?"

"I didn't think so. But after our escapade in the wilderness, I began to wonder. Do you know why the plane went down? Could it have been sabotaged?"

"I never considered the possibility. I'll make a trek out to the site and check it out." He studied her downcast eyes and pale cheeks. "If what you say is true, perhaps the shooter meant to harm me." He shrugged. "Or it might still have been just a hunter."

Her eyes widened. "I hadn't thought it might be connected to you. Eleanor's death. Might she have been killed by someone who hated you?"

"Whoa, where did that come from? Eleanor has nothing to do with this."

"You must admit it was most strange. She feared the water. So why would she have gone swimming?"

The information made him flinch. "Eleanor feared the water? Did anyone mention this to the constable?"

"I don't know."

"You told me Eleanor's mother asked you to look into the circumstances of her death. So is that the real reason you're here?"

She looked down and didn't meet his gaze.

His lips twisted. "So now you think I'm safe? Because I let you walk out of the forest alive?"

"Yes."

"A more pressing matter is in front of you," he said. "Or do you want to ignore what happened today?"

"I can only tell the truth and say the plane went down."

There was still only one choice that he could see. "I believe you know better, Lady Devonworth. At least let us announce our engagement and explain why you accompanied me without a chaperone. We can break the engagement at a later date after everyone has forgotten this incident."

"I must speak with my mother. Perhaps the gossip hasn't reached New York. If so, this will soon die down."

"Don't wait too long. We don't have long to salvage your reputation." He found the thought of her reluctance quite unbearable.

TWENTY-ONE

PAPERS COVERED THE rosewood desk's polished surface. Tiger sat in Olivia's lap kneading her leg. The invitations to the Lightkeeper's Ball had all been sent out before the aeroplane accident, but Olivia was beginning to wish she'd never offered to hold the ball. Would anyone even come now?

She pulled a vellum sheet toward her, dipped her pen into ink, and began to list pieces of this strange puzzle that now preoccupied her.

> *Father's death*
> *Eleanor's death*
> *Eleanor's fearful letter to me*
> *The attack on the boat*
> *The mysterious voice in the speaking tube*
> *The letter from Father*
> *The shot in the forest*
> *The plane crash*

How did they all tie together? Was it possible these events were related to Harrison's family and not her own? She didn't see how it was likely. The kitten mewed when she quit petting him and jumped down. Olivia opened the drawer in the desk and lifted her father's letter from it. The cheap paper's creases were already becoming thin from the number of times she'd reread it. Her father's warning against

Mr. Bennett *and* Harrison couldn't be plainer. *If only Father would show himself and explain.* She didn't understand why he continued to allow the world to believe him dead.

She heard the doorbell ring and lifted her head. Was that a man's voice?

Goldia appeared in the doorway. "Mr. Frederick Fosberg is here, miss. With his mother, Mrs. Martha Fosberg."

"Show them in." She swept everything into the drawer, then shut and locked it. By the time she'd thrust the key into her pocket and maneuvered to the sofa on her crutches, Goldia was leading them into the room.

Mrs. Fosberg rushed toward her. "My dear Lady Devonworth, I'm so sorry to hear of your misfortune."

Olivia smiled. "Thank you, Mrs. Fosberg. Have a seat. Goldia, will you tell the cook to prepare some refreshments?"

No one else in town had called this morning. Well, hadn't she expected the cold shoulders? "Thank you for coming." These two were to be commended for braving the town's censure.

"I'd like to introduce you to my son, Frederick," Mrs. Fosberg said.

"I'm honored, Lady Devonworth," he said.

She studied the man who had seemingly mesmerized her sister. He had blond hair slicked back with pomade and a pencil-thin mustache. His sack coat was the height of fashion. It had narrow lapels and was fitted at the waist. The slight flare at the bottom gave him an athletic appearance. His trousers had an impeccable line. This was a man who took fashion very seriously. His blue eyes looked her over as well, and she didn't know if she cared for the amused glint in his eyes.

She inclined her head and repeated her planned story. "Mr. Fosberg, it's good of you to come. I'm in need of some advice on a sum of money left to me by my father. I'd like to invest it." He didn't have to know it was a paltry amount.

"I'm happy to assist you. My office is well known for guiding clients to good investments. May I ask how you heard of my services?"

"From Eleanor Stewart," she said, watching him closely. When wariness replaced the amusement in his eyes, she knew he was hiding something.

"You knew Miss Stewart?" he asked.

"Quite well. We grew up together. I heard she was quite taken with you."

The last of his smile evaporated. "I am happy to assist anyone in need of my services."

She would have to switch tactics. "I'm holding a ball to raise money for the lighthouse. I'll make sure you get an invitation."

His smile came almost too quickly. "Thank you for that, Lady Devonworth. I'm most honored you would think of me."

His set might be the only ones who would attend her ball after her fall from grace. "I shall save you a spot on my dance card," she said, putting on her best smile.

His eyes crinkled at the corners as he smiled back. "I should like that very much," he said, his voice soft.

"Did you meet Eleanor before she came here? I found a dance card for an event and noticed you danced with her quite often."

He sat back in the chair. "Lady Devonworth, is there something you are trying to ask me?"

What would he say if she told him the truth? "Her mother asked me to look into her death. When did you see her last?"

"The day before she died." He crossed his arms over his chest.

She didn't care if he didn't like being questioned. "How did she seem to you? Distraught?"

"She was fine. A little edgy. She kept looking out the windows."

His mother had been fidgeting. "Lady Devonworth, I don't understand why your questions are so pointed. The poor girl drowned. Are you suggesting she had a liaison with Frederick?"

Olivia's ankle throbbed, her head hurt, and she desperately wanted to talk to a friendly face about her troubles. "I don't know, Mrs. Fosberg. Eleanor's family is not convinced the drowning was accidental. I am trying to bring some closure to the situation."

The older woman smiled. "I understand, my dear. But Frederick hardly knew the woman."

"That's not exactly true, Mother," he said. "I will admit to my own doubts about how she died. She feared water. I don't understand how she came to be drowned in that manner."

Aware her mouth was open, Olivia snapped it shut. Goldia brought in refreshments and placed them on the table. She passed around blue-and-white teacups, then backed out of the room. When her maid was out of the room, Olivia took a sip of her tea and asked, "What can you tell me, Mr. Fosberg?"

He stared into the teacup balanced on his pinstriped pants. "I loved her," he said.

His mother gasped. So did Olivia. "How did she feel about you?" she asked.

"She was going to break her engagement to Bennett. I suspect he killed her when she did."

TWENTY-TWO

HARRISON TOOK AN appreciative sniff of the cool forest air. Pine, decaying bark, and leaf mold hung in the air. He'd needed to stretch his legs this morning after fielding questions all evening from his parents, so he took Eugene with him to collect the dismembered plane parts. The blue bowl of sky played hide-and-seek with them behind the towering redwoods as they hiked back to the site of the crash. He inhaled again and exhaled his worries.

Eugene paused to wipe perspiration from his brow. The normally immaculate valet had flecks of mud on his trousers and wide rings of moisture under his arms. "Are you sure this is wise, sir?"

"I need to see those plane parts. I want to check for sabotage."

Eugene lifted a brow. "Sabotage? How would you ever know? And for what purpose?"

Harrison couldn't explain his obsession. Everything had changed when he discovered Lady Devonworth believed Eleanor had been murdered. There was too much to explain away: the attempt on her life, the crash, the man shooting at them. He had no idea how they all fit together, but he wanted to find out.

"The clearing is just ahead," he said, pointing to where the path veered to the right. Ferns the size of trees grew in the shadow of the redwoods. A glint caught his eye, and he paused to stare at a crushed patch of weeds.

"What is it, sir?"

"I'm not sure." He knelt and picked away twigs and moss to reveal several shell casings. "I believe our shooter stood here." The shells were cool and hard in his palm. He pocketed all four of them. "I shall show them to the constable."

The men continued on toward the sound of rushing water. Harrison's spirits plunged when he saw the debris of his beloved aeroplane strewn around the open field. There was no putting it back together. He would have to start anew. At least he had some modifications in mind. There should have been plenty of gas in the tank, yet the plane had faltered as though it had no fuel.

Eugene stood beside him with his hands in his pockets. "Do we seek anything in particular?"

"The engine and fuel system," Harrison said.

"Righto, sir." His valet wandered off in the direction of the stream.

Harrison picked up pieces of plane and discarded them as he went. Finding what he sought would be difficult. Flies buzzed around his head, and his boots sank into the boggy ground. It was best not to dwell on his time here with Essie. Tossing and turning on his bed last night, he'd remembered the scent of her hair and the way she fit into his arms.

He tore his attention from the evergreen boughs. There was one last patch of scattered debris to examine. He lifted a wing and found the prize. The fuel tank. The damp ground soaked the knees of his trousers as he knelt and uncapped the tank. The interior was too dark to make out the level of liquid inside. He grabbed a nearby stick and stuck it into the tank. When it clanged against the bottom, he withdrew it. The end of the stick was dry. Empty.

"Did you find something?" Eugene's voice came from behind him.

"An empty tank." Harrison rolled the container over and followed the lines out. "I'm looking for a leak. See what you can find."

Eugene knelt beside him and dug through parts as well. "There's this, sir," he said, holding out a long end of fuel line.

Harrison almost didn't want to see it. If he found clear evidence of tampering, then what? He ran his fingers over the length of line. His forefinger snagged on a rough edge on the side away from him. When he turned it over, he found a hole. The edges went inside. Sabotage.

"It appears someone put a nail through this," he said, showing it to Eugene.

"Perhaps it happened when the plane crashed."

He shook his head. "There were no nails. This was deliberate."

His valet raised stricken eyes to his. "You think someone wanted you dead?"

"It appears so. No one knew I was taking Lady Devonworth up in the machine. It was a spontaneous decision."

Had someone killed Eleanor to get to him? And how did the attack on Lady Devonworth play into the killer's plan? Had someone gotten wind of her intention to investigate? Perhaps the attempt on her life was to deter her from being too nosy. He rubbed his head. None of this made sense. He needed to tell Lady Devonworth, though, warn her to be on guard.

"Let's go," he told Eugene.

"What about these parts?"

"I'll show the fuel line to the constable and ask him to investigate Eleanor's death as well."

"Sir? Miss Eleanor drowned."

"I discovered she was afraid of the water, Eugene. Lady Devonworth is a friend of the Stewart family, and they believe she would never have gone swimming."

The men left the gurgling brook behind and tromped out of the forest.

⌖

Olivia didn't want to believe Frederick Fosberg, but his blue eyes were full of truth. If only she had spoken with Eleanor before her death.

There were too many contradictions to know what to do. Whom to believe.

Eleanor had been happy to marry Harrison. She liked nice things and pretty dresses, and Mr. Bennett's promise that she would be the star of Mercy Falls had certainly had an impact on her. While Mr. Fosberg was attractive, Olivia doubted he had the money that Harrison had. Could Eleanor have actually fallen in love with Fosberg? Even if she had, that didn't explain her death. It was clear to Olivia that Harrison hadn't been consumed with a passion for Eleanor. He had merely been dutiful in a sensible arrangement. He would have bowed to her request to break the engagement, if in fact she'd made one.

Olivia prided herself on her ability to see past appearances and discover truth, but her abilities had failed her ever since she came here. "Do you know if she broke her engagement?" she asked Fosberg.

"When we last spoke, she was expecting him to call on her. She intended to tell him then that the two of us planned to wed."

Mrs. Fosberg sat wringing her hands. "You never breathed a word of this to me, Frederick!" She turned to Olivia. "My dear, I'm so sorry."

"I needed to know the truth." Olivia barely managed to speak past the constriction in her throat.

She didn't want to believe Harrison had harmed Eleanor. Maybe there was another explanation. Pain throbbed behind her eyes. Only decorum kept her from asking the pair to leave. She needed time to think this through, to analyze all the ramifications of what this new information meant.

Silence fell with the lengthening shadows. The Fosbergs drank their tea in a hurried manner as though they sensed Olivia's desire for solitude.

"Thank you for your candor," she said as the mother and son took their leave. "Do call again." When she heard the front door shut, she slumped onto the sofa and put her foot on the pillow.

She had reached for her tea when the doorbell rang again. Who would be calling when she was an outcast?

"Olivia!" a woman's voice called out from the hall.

Olivia bolted upright. "Mother?"

The sound of running feet came down the hall, and her mother burst into the parlor. Olivia had never seen her mother rush or show any indecorum. The older woman's cheeks were flushed, but her attire was impeccable, as though she had just left her house on Fifth Avenue.

"My dear girl," she cried, holding out her arms. She rushed to the sofa and embraced Olivia.

Olivia inhaled her mother's delicate rosewater scent and relished the tight squeeze of the maternal embrace. "I didn't expect you for another week," she murmured against her silk dress.

"I told you I would come at once."

Olivia pulled away and smiled up at her mother. "'At once' usually means after days of packing."

Her mother unpinned her hat and placed it on the table. "Not when you call with such momentous news. And when I arrived, I found you had been in an aeroplane accident! Really, Olivia, what were you thinking to go off with a man unchaperoned in such a hoydenish way?" She draped herself elegantly on the Queen Anne chair by the fireplace.

Olivia sat up and smoothed her hair. Though her ankle throbbed, she didn't raise it to the coffee table, an act her mother would find most uncomely. "I am trying to discover what happened to Eleanor," she said. "I've been spending as much time with Harrison as possible so that I can question him."

"Well, this is going too far!" Her mother nodded to the teapot on the silver tray. "Is that fresh?" When Olivia shook her head, her mother rang for the maid. When the girl appeared in the doorway, she requested fresh tea and cake before turning to Olivia with more questions. "I saw the newspaper, Olivia. You were alone with that man for two nights."

"Nothing happened, Mother."

"Of course nothing happened. I've raised you to know better than that." Her mother smoothed her dress.

Olivia clutched her hands together. "I'm told the news was in the San Francisco papers."

Her mother gasped and put her hand to her mouth. "Olivia, no!" She moaned and put her hands on her cheeks. "You're ruined." She fanned herself. "And I shudder to think what my friends will say if word of this reaches New York."

"I know, Mother."

Olivia had spent her life trying to be the perfect daughter, to make her parents proud of her. In one careless act of thoughtlessness, she'd thrown it all away. Harrison had said she could be the woman God saw inside if she had the courage. What if she used this opportunity to be herself?

"He offered to announce our engagement," she blurted out. "Should I allow it?"

Her mother's expression went from stricken to calculating. "Harrison offered to marry you?"

"He did. He said we could break the engagement after the furor died down."

The maid arrived with fresh tea and white cake squares. Silver clinked against china as she served them then slipped back out of the room. Even when they were again alone, her mother said nothing.

"Mother? What should I do?" Olivia asked.

Her mother sipped her tea and stared at her with thoughtful eyes. She put her cup and saucer on the table beside her. "It's tempting. But you realize we would be playing into Mr. Bennett's hands if we allow this? If your father's letter is to be believed, both men are dangerous. Perhaps they have been working all along to force you into this position. Whose idea was it to go in that plane?"

Olivia bit her lip. "Harrison's," she admitted. "But he knew I'd been longing to experience it."

"Ah." Her mother pressed her lips together. "Just as I expected." She sighed and took up her tea again. "'Harrison,' is it? I must say it would solve our financial pressures. I would insist Mr. Bennett make the financial arrangements at the announcement. I'll not wait until a wedding that may never happen."

"He would delay until the marriage, I'm sure."

Her mother smiled. "I could tell him I know his son planned to ruin you to force this engagement. He would not want that leaked. Then when we have the money, you could break the engagement. I'll take you to Europe to find you a man with money *and* a title."

Olivia stared at the smug expression on her mother's face. Had she always been so manipulative? "Mother, that's not honorable!"

Her mother sipped her tea before answering. "The pair killed your sister."

"I no longer believe Harrison guilty of anything like that."

The cup rattled on the other woman's saucer. "Your father believed otherwise."

"Besides, Harrison doesn't know I'm Olivia Stewart. You must say nothing to his father until I tell him."

"When do you plan to inform him?"

"As soon as possible." She dreaded it though. He didn't seem the type to tolerate deceit.

"Very well. Let's not speak of unpleasant things. What of this ball you are planning?"

"The lighthouse was destroyed in a storm, and there have been several ships lost already without its light. It must be rebuilt. The invitations have been sent."

Her mother sniffed. "I would imagine you'll be receiving refusals after the news of your disgrace gets out."

Olivia caught her breath. Katie and Will were depending on the success of this ball. If her naivety had destroyed it, she couldn't face Katie with the news. "It must be a success! What can I do?"

"Announce your engagement, I suppose. Your friends in New York will be curious to meet him. The ball could be an engagement ball as well. And a masquerade, you said?"

Harrison in a costume. She wanted to see that. "True. I would have to call them all, since the invitations have already gone. I never gave Harrison an answer to his proposal other than that I would speak with you about it."

"I don't see that you have much choice at the moment. Agree for now. You don't have to go through with it."

"But if I give him my word . . ."

"Don't be tiresome, Olivia. Now ring for the maid. My head is beginning to pound and I want Goldia to rub it with rosewater."

"Yes, Mother." The respite would give her a chance to consider all her options. She needed to sort through her emotions after learning from Fosberg that Eleanor was in love with him and planned to break her engagement to Harrison.

Twenty-three

WITH HER MOTHER upstairs resting, Olivia finished a letter to her cousin back in New York, then hopped on her crutches out to the garden with a journal. She always thought better when surrounded by nature. Her list of ominous events was tucked into the front cover.

She sank onto a stone bench by the topiary and dropped her crutches to the ground. The breeze brought her favorite aroma of freesia to her nose. This area of the garden held only white flowers, which lifted her spirits. A pond full of koi added the only touch of color to the area.

Opening her journal, she perused the list she'd started, then added Mr. Fosberg's accusation about Harrison, much as it pained her. Bees droned a sleepy song in her ears, but she was much too energized to think about a nap. She was missing an important piece of the puzzle, something that tied all these things together, but what?

A car door shut and she lifted her head from her journal. Peeking over the shrubs, she saw Frederick Fosberg striding toward the pillared porch. What was he doing back so quickly?

Hanging on to one crutch, she rose and hailed him. "Mr. Fosberg, I'm here."

His confident stride faltered, and he changed direction to join her in the side yard. "I'm sorry to disturb you again, Lady Devonworth. There were some things I wished to inform you of that I didn't want to mention in front of my mother. They are of a most confidential nature."

She settled back onto the bench, and he joined her. "Confidential?"

He swatted away a bee. "Indeed. This matter involves Eleanor's mother. It was for this reason I first met Eleanor. I wished to get a message to Mrs. Stewart."

She studied his earnest blue eyes, the determined jut of his jaw. "What message?"

He leaned forward. "As you know, I work for a large law firm based in San Francisco. Our headquarters building was demolished in the Great Fire that followed the earthquake. Fortunes were lost in that fire."

She knew it well. Her own family had suffered some financial setbacks, but her father had quickly recouped with wise investments. Or so they'd thought. "The news was full of it."

"We sold the lot recently. The new owner began excavation and discovered our vault, still untouched, under the ruins."

She had no idea where this was going, but she nodded. "Go on."

"I was sent to examine the contents. One of the safety-deposit boxes belonged to Eleanor's father."

She sat up straighter. "You found money? Stocks?"

He shook his head. "A will."

She waved her hand. "The way I understand it from the family, Mr. Stewart's will was on file with his attorney in New York. Odd that he had a copy with a San Francisco lawyer."

"When was it written?"

"Ten years ago."

"I have another will in my possession, Lady Devonworth. Newer than that. Written in 1906."

Four years ago. She couldn't contain a gasp. "And you told Eleanor this? Why did you not contact Mrs. Stewart directly?"

"I tried but was unable to get her address. I contacted Mr. Stewart's business partner, Mr. Bennett, but he told me it was of no matter. He claimed there was an even newer will on file."

"He lied to you?" It hardly surprised her. She didn't trust Mr.

Bennett. "But that still doesn't explain why you took this matter to Eleanor."

"When Bennett refused to let me talk to Mrs. Stewart, let's just say I became suspicious. The man has a reputation in the city that is less than savory. When I learned that a member of the Stewart family was in residence, I decided it would be too good an opportunity to pass up. I showed the will to Eleanor."

"I fail to see where you are going with this, Mr. Fosberg. What difference does the will's date make? Mr. Stewart is hardly likely to leave his estate to anyone but his wife and daughters."

He held her gaze. "It seems there was an heir that the family knew nothing about." He hesitated and cast his gaze to the brick path, then stared at her again. "This heir made a difference to the execution of the will."

She didn't care for the somber expression in his eyes. "An heir?"

"A son."

"Mr. Stewart had no son."

He glanced away. "It's a delicate matter to discuss with you, Lady Devonworth."

She realized her hands were clenching her skirt, and she forced herself to loosen her fists. "You mean an illegitimate son?" Her voice trembled. Her father had always wanted a son.

"Indeed."

"Did Eleanor discuss this discovery with Mrs. Stewart?" She knew there had been no such discussion. Her mother would have been prostrate with the news. It would have been impossible to keep from Olivia.

"She did not. She asked my help in investigating the matter further."

"What is this son's name?"

"Richard Pixton. But I suspect he's changed his name." He reached into his pocket and pulled out a sheaf of papers. "We managed to track him to San Francisco, where he boarded a steamer bound for Eureka four years ago. That ship reached port, but no one by that name has emerged in this area."

She studied the passenger list in his hand and found the man's name. "So you think he's here—in Mercy Falls—but under an assumed name?"

"I do."

"For what reason?"

He shrugged. "I have no idea."

"Do you think he came here to confront Mr. Stewart? I believe Mr. Stewart first began his trips to Mercy Falls about that time."

"I thought of that. I even wondered if Mr. Pixton killed him."

"What would that gain him?"

"A fine inheritance."

"Which he has never claimed," she pointed out.

"True enough. Eleanor wondered if he wanted more of the money. The will states that if Mr. Stewart's other heirs are dead, Mr. Pixton would inherit all of it."

The attempt on my life. "He must be here then. He must be the one who has been stalking me since I arrived. It was only by luck that I survived the murderous attempts."

He frowned. "Why would anyone wish to harm you?" He stared at her. "*You* are Miss Olivia, are you not? There is somewhat of a resemblance to Eleanor in the tilt of your eyes. It makes sense now why you would be investigating Eleanor's death."

Mr. Fosberg's stare was still drilling into Olivia. His question hung in the air between them. There was no way to get out of this without a flat-out lie, something she wasn't willing to do.

"I am Olivia Stewart," she said. "Please don't reveal it to anyone else. I need anonymity to find out who killed my sister."

His lips twisted and he opened his mouth.

She held up her hand. "However, I'm not ready to believe it was

Harrison Bennett who did it." She bit her lip. A week ago she was just as convinced he'd murdered Eleanor. *But that was before I spent so much time with him.*

Mr. Fosberg scowled, then stood and paced across the grass. "I'm sure he murdered her," he said, his voice hard.

She thought through her own misgivings. "Just because she broke their engagement is no reason to assume he is a murderer."

"He could have hired it done."

"Harrison doesn't know my identity even now. If he'd hired someone, he would have needed to obtain a recent picture of me to pass on to his henchman. So he would have recognized me immediately." Her arguments against Harrison being the killer gained strength the more she puzzled it out. Mr. Fosberg's dislike of Harrison added fuel to her determination to defend him. "I think it has to be someone else. Who else did Eleanor see when she was here?"

His jaw jutted and his eyes narrowed. "No one. You're as taken with the man as she was when she first came here."

She could see the complete dislike on his face. "Did you convince her he was untrustworthy? What do you have against him?"

He shrugged. "I can see you'll have to discover his true character for yourself. I'll take my leave now, Miss Olivia."

"Lady Devonworth," she corrected.

"As you wish." He put his bowler back on his head and headed to his car.

Would he keep her secret? It was all going to come out very soon. The moment Mr. Bennett saw her, he would reveal her identity. She had to tell Harrison, but it was going to take the right moment.

Mr. Fosberg brushed past a young maid carrying rugs and a rug beater toward the line. The maid sent him a smile that quickly faded when he didn't speak. Olivia watched him slam the car door. The automobile rattled back down the drive.

Something about the young woman's reaction intrigued her as the girl stood looking forlornly after the departing automobile. Olivia beckoned to the maid. "I'd like to speak with you a moment."

The girl dropped her burden and wiped her hands on her white apron as she approached Olivia's bench. "Yes, ma'am? Can I fetch you some tea or lemonade?"

Olivia shook her head. "Do you know Mr. Fosberg?"

The young woman was about nineteen with a fresh complexion, blond hair, and vivid green eyes. She took a step back, and her eyes grew wide. "I didn't do nothing wrong, miss. I just smiled at him."

"I'm not accusing you of anything," Olivia soothed. "What's your name?"

"Molly Chambers."

Olivia sent her a reassuring smile. "I'm told he spent quite a lot of time with Miss Eleanor. I'm wondering if his influence on her was of the highest nature."

The alarm in Molly's face ebbed and she glanced behind her, then took a step closer. "Mr. Fosberg is said to have a way with the ladies, miss."

Olivia remembered the way the girl had smiled. "Has he paid you undue attention, Molly?"

Quick color rushed to the girl's cheeks, and she didn't hold Olivia's gaze. "I'd rather not say, miss."

The girl had probably entered service by age fifteen. Had she been here the whole time or perhaps worked for the Fosbergs? "How long have you been employed by the Stewarts?" Olivia asked.

The girl's eyes went wide again. "You wouldn't let me go, miss!"

"No, no," Olivia said. "But I think you know more about Mr. Fosberg than you are willing to admit. Where did you work before you came here?"

Molly looked away and her lips turned sullen. "I was at Eaton Hall," she said.

"The consumption hospital Mrs. Fosberg runs."

"Yes, miss."

"You saw Mr. Fosberg there quite frequently."

Molly nodded but didn't look up from her perusal of the flowers.

Olivia pressed her lips together. How could she get the girl to tell what she knew? "Did Miss Eleanor know you had a relationship with Mr. Fosberg?"

Molly's gaze came up then, wide-eyed. "Oh no, miss!" She clapped her hand over her mouth.

"So you did have a relationship."

"Please don't make me leave," Molly said, tears in her eyes. "I love working here."

"I wouldn't do that," Olivia assured her. "How long did the liaison go on?"

Molly wrung her hands. "Until he decided he had a chance to marry Miss Eleanor. He warned me to say nothing to her."

"Are you still seeing him?"

Molly shook her head with vigor. "No, miss."

"Would you say his words are trustworthy?"

The maid twisted her hands again. "Oh, miss, don't make me talk anymore," she whispered. "I still love him."

The poor girl. Olivia could read between the lines. She'd best verify anything Mr. Fosberg told her. And also take anything this girl said with a grain of salt. It was possible she wanted Mr. Fosberg for herself and was seeing things through that filter.

TWENTY-FOUR

THERE WAS NO mistaking Fosberg's flashy automobile as it whizzed past Harrison's Cadillac. Or the fact that the man had been at Stewart Hall. It was the only residence out this way. Harrison slowed the vehicle and puttered out the macadam road to the Stewarts' house by the sea. As he parked and got out of his car, a swell rolled in with the sharp tang of kelp on the wind.

He rang the bell, but the butler told him Lady Devonworth was out back in the garden. He went around the side of the mansion to the labyrinth of garden paths. The scent of honeysuckle and the drone of bees hovered in the air.

A sound floated on the wind and he paused to listen. A sweet voice sang, "Come, Josephine, in My Flying Machine." He listened a moment and smiled when he heard, "Up, up, a little bit higher. Oh! My! The moon is on fire." The moon had seemed ablaze the night he'd lain in the clearing with her head cradled on his shoulder. Or maybe his emotions had affected his eyes. Right now the attraction he felt toward her was tangled up.

He squared his shoulders and walked toward her voice.

"'I'm a sky kid,'" she sang. Her voice faltered when he stepped into her view from behind the arbor. Color flooded her cheeks and her dark eyes flashed gypsy fire at him. "What are you doing skulking around?" she demanded.

His lips twitched. "One trip in an aeroplane and you're a sky kid, Essie?"

Her cheeks grew rosier and she tipped her chin up. "That's a ridiculous name! Did you just come to mock me?"

"No." He indicated the bench. "Mind if I join you?"

"Of course not." She scooted over, but her expression stayed remote.

He had no idea how she really felt about him. The iron bench was hard under his thighs. Nearly as hard as the line of her mouth. She hadn't been so cold when he last saw her. What had changed? Eyeing her expression, he doubted she would tell him.

With her fingers laced in her lap, she appeared to be a demure young woman who never did the unexpected, but he knew better. Something was brewing behind that beautiful face, but he suspected she'd only share what it was if he made her angry enough.

He cleared his throat. "Do you want to tell me why you're so angry with me?"

Her eyes narrowed. "When were you going to tell me that Eleanor broke off her engagement to you?"

He grabbed the tail of his temper as it attempted to escape. "Where did you hear that?"

"Does it matter?" she asked, a note of challenge in her voice. "It's true, isn't it?"

How much should he tell her? All of it or only enough to distract her? He thought he caught a glimpse of something in her eyes, a longing to be wrong. Or was it his foolish hope instead? "Do you really want to know the truth?" he asked in a quiet voice.

"I do," she said. Her voice trembled a little, but she put her hand over his.

He took heart from her impulsive gesture and placed his other hand over hers, then regretted it when she quickly pulled back. "I'll hold nothing back. But listen quietly and don't ask any questions until I'm finished. Agreed?"

"Agreed."

"She didn't break her engagement to me. I broke it." When she gasped and opened her mouth, he held up his hand. "Remember your promise. I'm not done." She shut her lips and he stared at her, willing her to believe him. "I know this isn't pleasant to hear, but I caught her and Fosberg in a . . . a compromising position."

She opened her mouth, then shut it again at his warning glance. She shuddered, and he realized how hard this was for her. She'd loved Eleanor. But he didn't think she knew her friend very well.

A toad hopped across the grass by his feet. He watched it go and tried to think of an easier way to tell her the story. There was nothing easy about such an unsavory tale. "I'll just say it," he said, his voice harsh. "She spent the night at his cottage two miles up the coast. I received a tip that I'd find them there. I didn't care enough about Eleanor to be upset, but I refused to be made a cuckold. His valet tried to dissuade me from entering, but I forced my way in and found the two of them in bed together."

She gasped. Or was it a moan? He wished he could take her hand but forced himself not to touch her. Her head was down and her shoulders drooped. "I'm sorry. I wish I could spare you this, but there's more. When they saw me, Fosberg leaped from the bed in his nightdress. Eleanor clutched the covers to her neck and screamed at me to get out. I told her I was leaving and that our engagement was at an end. By the end of the next day she was dead. So, yes, I do feel some guilt about her death. Perhaps she feared I would tell what I'd seen, but I had no intention of humiliating her."

"I-I can hardly believe it of Eleanor."

"I've told no one. Not even my father, though I'm going to have to tell him. He has a crazy idea to marry me off to Olivia Stewart. I wouldn't marry a Stewart if she were the last woman on Earth." He spat the name Stewart from his mouth.

Lady Devonworth went white and still. "So is that why you wish to marry me? To foil your father's plans?"

"No." He wasn't ready to tell her his feelings. "Have you spoken with your mother about my proposal?"

"I have. She believes it the proper thing to do."

"Is that a yes then?"

She nodded her head without looking at him. "I fear I have no choice." She raised teary eyes to his. "So she really did kill herself?"

He hesitated. "I don't know," he said. "She didn't seem the type to do harm to herself. I believe Fosberg would have been willing to marry her. He seemed quite besotted."

She nodded. "He said they were going to be married," she said, looking away.

He saw the guilt in her eyes before it was hidden from him. "What else did he say?"

"That she broke her engagement to you and that you killed her."

"I didn't kill her!" he said. When she didn't answer, his chest constricted. "Do you believe him?" *Please say no.* He held his breath and waited for her answer. Her hand crept across the metal to grasp his. He squeezed her fingers.

Her head came up and her eyes met his. "No," she said. "I don't think you're capable of murder."

He wanted to sweep her into his arms and press his lips to hers, but he restrained himself. There was time to win her. And he would.

❧

Gaslight chandeliers cast shadows in the cavernous dining room as Olivia pulled a chair out to sit by her mother, who was at the head of the table. Delicious aromas filled the air: barley soup, roast duck with cranberry sauce, and chateau potatoes.

Her stomach objected to the thought of food, but she took up her napkin and smiled at her mother. "Dinner smells heavenly."

Her mother gave her a sharp glance. "Whatever is the matter, Olivia? You look like you've lost your best friend. And where are your friends, by the way?" She leaned back so the footman could lay the napkin in her lap. "And I thought I saw your young man out there."

"I saw Katie in the upstairs hall. She and Will will be down shortly." She put her napkin in her lap. "Harrison was here, Mother, and I agreed to marry him. But there is a wrinkle in that plan. He is quite opposed to marrying Olivia Stewart."

Her mother shot her a startled glance. "What do you mean?"

"There were some problems between him and Eleanor. He said Olivia Stewart would be the last person he would ever marry." She bit her lip. "I could hardly tell him my name then."

Her mother shrugged. "An engagement will suffice for now to restore your reputation. You can break it in your own time and tell him the truth." She glanced at the mantel clock. "I like to dine precisely at eight. It's five after."

"Katie said to extend her apologies. Jennie was crying and upset, and they read her a bedtime story. She's been having nightmares since the storm destroyed the lighthouse."

Her mother's expression softened. "Poor child." She motioned to the other footmen hovering in the doorways. "You may serve the hors d'oeuvres." The men jumped to do her bidding and went to the serving tables, where canapés were arranged with caviar, cheese, foie gras, and liver pâté. Her mother selected the caviar only, took a bite, then dabbed at her lips with the linen napkin. "So you still haven't told me what is wrong."

Olivia glanced at the clock. She likely had ten minutes before their guests joined them. The subject was hardly dinner conversation, but her mother would never let it go until she pried out the information.

She sipped her water, then put down the crystal goblet. "Mr. Fosberg returned this afternoon. He told me a most distressing tale."

Her mother paused with a canapé halfway to her mouth. She put it down on her saucer. "About Eleanor?"

"It's about Father."

Her mother smiled. "He's located your father?" Her voice was as animated as a girl's, and a flush lit her skin.

A pang struck in Olivia's midsection. Her mother genuinely loved the man. Olivia wasn't sure how she herself felt. Her father had been like a king or nobility to her. She'd worshipped him and tried everything in her power to make him proud of her, to make him utter one word of praise. The discovery that he had feet of clay was a blow she wasn't sure she could recover from.

"No, Mother. H-He says he has a valid will that Father executed. It was discovered in a safe that was buried in debris during the Great Fire. It was written in 1906."

Her mother's eager smile faded. "Your somber expression tells me this is somehow bad news. You know how I detest it when you dance around information, Olivia. Out with it."

Olivia toyed with her spoon and stirred sugar into tea. "According to the will, Father has another heir. A son." She glanced up to see how her mother received the surprise.

The words seemed to echo in the high-ceilinged room. It was her mother's greatest shame that she'd never given her husband a son. If only she hadn't had to tell her mother this news.

Her mother's eyes grew wider as the words sank in. Her high color faded to a sallow yellow. Her throat clicked as she swallowed. "I don't understand, Olivia."

The facts. Stick to the facts in a neutral tone of voice that might calm Mother. Olivia somehow managed to speak in an even tone. "Father had an illegitimate son, Mother. The son was traced here to Mercy Falls but evidently changed his name, and Mr. Fosberg was unable to track him down."

"What is his name?"

"Richard Pixton."

Her mother's hands curled into fists, and she banged them onto the table so hard that Olivia's water glass toppled. "Pixton!" She swallowed again, and a single tear ran down her cheek.

"You know the name?" Olivia asked.

"Lulu Pixton was my personal maid. She threw herself at your father, and I dismissed her at once. I thought she went to live with her sister in San Francisco."

"That's where Richard was born." The older woman moaned at Olivia's words, an eerie sound that raised the hair on the back of Olivia's neck. Olivia reached over and took her mother's hand. "I'm sure Father didn't love her, Mother. I'm sure he was just trying to do the right thing. He was always careful to attend to his responsibilities."

"His responsibility was to me, his wife! And to his own children." Her mother rose so quickly that her chair tipped over. "I'm going to my room. I have a most dreadful headache. Give my regards to our guests." She rushed from the room.

Olivia dabbed the spilled water with her napkin. She motioned for the footmen to remove her mother's utensils and to repair the table. Her chest was tight, and she ached for her mother's pain. And where was Father? They needed him now.

TWENTY-FIVE

HARRISON SLID HIS arms into the vest Eugene held out. "I don't feel like eating dinner tonight, Eugene." Nealy looked up at Harrison's words as if to check that his master was all right.

Tonight he was to attend a celebratory dinner hosted by the owner of the business Harrison had just acquired. He was surprised his father had agreed to attend, given his displeasure over the price Harrison had paid.

"Yes, sir. Would you like me to make your apologies?"

"No, I have to go. Who knows what my father would say to Mr. Riley if I'm not there." He buttoned the vest, then grabbed the jacket from the form by the window. "I hope I'm not seated next to Fosberg. It's going to be all I can do not to throttle him."

He didn't expect an answer from his valet, and sure enough, Eugene simply took the clothes brush and went over Harrison's suit one last time. The valet was a great sounding board but seldom offered advice. He knew his place, though Harrison thought of him more as a peer than a personal servant.

"I think I love her," Harrison said. "How did that happen?"

Eugene knelt and gave the toes of his shoes one last buff. "I imagine it's the usual way, sir. She's very beautiful."

"Yes, she is. And I like her spirit. The way she analyzes everything. She takes something you say and hears what you're really saying underneath. How does she do that?"

"Women are most incomprehensible," his valet said. Eugene stood and stepped back. "I believe you'll pass muster and not put me to shame."

Harrison grinned. "I'll try to do you proud." He clapped a hand on Eugene's shoulder. "Have you ever been in love, Eugene?"

"No, sir. When would I have time?"

"We've had some attractive chambermaids. There was that pretty lady's maid my mother had a couple of years ago. What was her name?"

"Lucy."

Harrison tugged on his cravat. "Ah, yes, Lucy. Whatever happened to her?"

"She married the butler."

"That's right." He dropped his arm when Eugene gently pushed it out of the way to fix the blasted tie. "But I'm sure you've had ample opportunity to find a wife."

"A wife would demand more time than I can give her."

Harrison had already turned toward the door but veered back at Eugene's words. "Are you happy here?"

He studied his valet. Eugene was what, about twenty-five? Average height and slim build. Pleasant enough features. Brown eyes and a trim mustache. Harrison paid him well too, so Eugene should have been appealing to the opposite sex.

Eugene smiled. "I've been with you for four years, sir. I hope I may be so bold as to say I look up to you. You have been very good to me. My life is full."

"I realize that every important decision I've ever made, I've discussed with you. Though you never tell me what to do, talking it out has always helped. So what should I do about Lady Devonworth?"

"There isn't a woman alive who could resist you when you put your mind to wooing her, sir."

"Spoken like a true friend. So I just woo her? I've already proposed, but I'm sure she has no idea of my true feelings. She just thinks I merely want to do the right thing. I'm not sure how to go about letting her know how I feel."

"She's quite taken with your aeroplane," Eugene pointed out.

Harrison scowled. "Which is now strewn across half of California."

"You have the new model nearly completed. Ask her to go up in it again."

"I intend to have it finished by the time the comet's tail arrives in two weeks. But I need to be assured there will be no more sabotage." He glanced at Nealy. "Perhaps I will put Nealy to watching it."

Eugene stepped past Harrison and opened the door, then stood aside. "Has the constable discovered who was behind your accident?"

Harrison went past him into the hall. "I doubt he will. There are no clues. He's asked at the pubs and cafes, but there has been nothing for him to follow up on. I need to be especially vigilant before taking up the new plane."

He paused partway down the hall, then turned to see Eugene following five paces behind. "Take the night off, Eugene. Take a girl to dinner."

His valet's teeth gleamed as he grinned. "I'll see what I can do, sir. Though it would never do for both of us to be in love. Someone around here needs to have his brain engaged."

Harrison laughed. "You might have a point. Good night."

"Thanks."

Harrison jogged down the hall to the stairs and out the door to his car. He had instructed his driver to bring it around, but the Riley home was only a few blocks away and it was a beautiful night, so he decided to walk and waved the driver back to the carriage house. It took only five minutes to stroll to the Rileys'. When he stepped into the foyer, he could hear the tinkle of glassware and the murmur of laughter and conversation. The last thing he wanted to do was to make small talk when he could be working on his aeroplane.

He found the guests milling through the massive dining room.

Everyone was talking about the Lightkeeper's Ball, and the level of excitement about it was high, though the chatter stilled when he entered and he intercepted a few sly glances. Nothing like this had ever been done in Mercy Falls, and people would be unlikely to refuse to attend in spite of the scandal that had just erupted. Lady Devonworth's New York friends were another matter, however.

After chatting with the host and his wife, he found his way to the food. Tall linen-covered tables held hors d'oeuvres of every type. Footmen served glasses of champagne and wine. He greeted neighbors and customers as he made his way through the crowd to where his mother was talking to Addie and John North.

"There you are, Harrison," his mother said when he brushed his lips across her powdered cheek. "I was beginning to think I'd have to come drag you from your house."

"Just running a little late." He shook hands with John.

"We're celebrating," John said, his grin widening. Addie blushed and glanced away. John's grin told the story.

Harrison's mother rapped her fan on Harrison's arm. "They're going to be adding to their family."

"Congratulations." Harrison meant it. The Norths had been childless since their marriage two years ago and had hoped to give a sibling to Edward, John's son by a previous marriage.

A warm sensation enveloped him when he saw the way the Norths looked at one another. If only Lady Devonworth would look on him with that kind of love in her eyes.

Still smiling, he turned toward the door and froze. Fosberg had arrived.

❧

Firelight flickered in the huge stone fireplace. Olivia sipped her after-dinner tea and stared at the crackling flames. Her father's letter to

Eleanor lay in her lap. Will and Katie were playing checkers at the game table, and their banter flowed around her, but she paid little attention to what they said.

The Jespersons' game ended. "I'm going to peek in on Jennie," Will said.

Katie joined Olivia on the sofa. "You're very pensive," she said. "This news about a missing half brother has rocked you, has it not?"

"Very much," Olivia admitted. "I thought my father an honorable man. Aloof, but a good man."

"You seem nearly to idolize him. Was he home much?"

Olivia shook her head. "His businesses took him away quite often. Africa, California, Europe. When he was home, the world revolved around him. He often hurt me with his comments about how disappointed he was that I wasn't the son he wanted."

Katie wrinkled her nose. "I hate to hear that. I'm sure he loved you very much."

"I always felt I had to earn his attention. You know what I thought of first when I'd heard he died in that cave-in? That I would never hear him say, 'I love you.'"

Her friend squeezed her hand. "I'm sorry, my dear."

"So am I. But now there is another chance. I don't understand why there has been no communication from him since this." She lifted his letter off her lap. "Why hasn't he shown himself?"

Katie hesitated. "Are you sure it's not your wishful thinking? How can he be alive and here in town without being seen?"

"I've wondered the same thing. But I have to find him if he's alive," she said. "He's the only one who can straighten all this out."

"Are you sure that's his handwriting?" Katie asked.

"It certainly appears to be his."

"Will's brother is a private investigator. You could try to have him track your father."

Olivia shuddered. "I hate to involve someone like that in our private affairs."

"He wouldn't have to know the reason. You could simply say you suspect your father is still alive. And he'd be very discreet."

"Perhaps." Olivia stared at the letter. "I need to see the will that's in Mr. Fosberg's possession."

"He didn't show it to you?"

Olivia shook her head. "At the time I didn't think much about it. But after speaking with Molly, I wonder why he did not reveal it. I suspect his motives."

A smile tugged at Katie's lips. "You really don't want to believe anything bad of Harrison, do you?"

"I believe Harrison is honorable."

"Your attitude about him has turned around completely. When we first met, you suspected he murdered Eleanor. Now you are his staunch defender."

Olivia heard the amusement in her friend's voice and had to smile herself. "I know him better now. Or do you think I'm deceiving myself?"

Katie selected a trifle from the dessert tray. "I've never believed him capable of murder. He's been a friend to Will and me for years. I don't care much for his father, but Mr. Bennett's actions are hardly Harrison's fault." She nibbled on a chocolate éclair, then eyed Olivia. "You said Harrison offered to announce your engagement. What are you going to do?"

Olivia had thought of little else. "I agreed to the engagement. The ball will be an engagement ball as well."

Katie clasped her hands together. "Olivia, that's wonderful!"

"Don't rejoice too much just yet. He'll break the engagement when I tell him I'm Olivia Stewart."

Katie's smile faded. "What do you mean?"

Olivia held her gaze. "Eleanor was not . . . true to him. He is rather bitter about the Stewart family and told me that his father is insistent that he marry Olivia. But he said he would never do such a thing."

"I believe he cares for you, Olivia."

She wished she could hold such a happy view of the situation. "Mother sees nothing wrong with stringing him along until the scandal dies down."

"What does she have planned for you if you do break your engagement?"

"She intends to haul me to Europe. She has it in her head that Bennett and Harrison are responsible for Eleanor's death." She held up her hand when Katie smiled. "I know, I believed the same thing a few days ago. I'll convince her when I get to the truth."

"So what happens when you get to Europe?"

"Mother hopes to marry me to someone more suitable." Her spirits dipped just repeating her mother's plans. She didn't want to be married for status. Not to Harrison or to anyone else. "Sometimes I wish I were a common person, just a milliner or a dressmaker. It's dreadful to be sought after for what you possess."

"You should be careful what you wish for," Katie said.

"Oh, I realize how fortunate I am. And I'm grateful." She realized she sounded anything but grateful.

"God has you right where he wants you," Katie said. "He provides for our needs no matter how much money we have. Any money you have is from his hand."

Olivia had never really considered that God had given her family their money. Her father had been quick to take credit for their family's astute business sense. "I think I shall call on Mr. Fosberg tomorrow and ask to see the will."

"Do you want Will or me to go with you?"

Olivia shook her head. "I can handle Mr. Fosberg. I shall take Mother with me. He can't deny our right to see the document." She yawned. "I'm exhausted. It's been a grueling day. I think I shall ring for Jerry to carry me upstairs."

"I'm going up too. Jennie must be awake, or Will would have joined us."

Katie rang for Jerry, and the footman carried her up to her bedroom. "I can make it from here, Jerry. Thank you," she told him at the bedroom door. He put her down on the end of the bed and laid the crutches beside her, then left her alone.

If only she could shut her thoughts off. And her feelings. She wanted to talk to Harrison. Tonight. Right now. She rang the bell for Goldia.

Goldia stepped into the room. "There you are, miss. I have your nightdress laid out."

Olivia stood and balanced herself on the bedpost, turning her back to her maid. She allowed Goldia to undo the buttons and help her step out of the dress. She stood shivering as Goldia dropped the nightdress over her head, then sat in front of the dresser as the maid released her hair from its pins and began to brush it. The rhythmic touch of the bristles through her hair eased the tension in her shoulders.

"I thought I saw your father today," Goldia said.

Olivia tensed and turned to face the girl. "Father? Where?"

"At the general store. I was buying some ribbons for your new hat and saw him through the window. I ran out, but he was gone."

"Do you think it was really him? In broad daylight where he might be recognized?"

Goldia resumed brushing. "I only caught a glimpse so I can't be sure. But the walk was so familiar."

Olivia's heart lightened. "Perhaps he will be in touch with us soon." Maybe she would do as Katie suggested if he didn't show himself. A detective would track him down in no time. She thanked Goldia, then hobbled to bed and crawled under the covers after her maid pulled them back. Goldia extinguished the gaslight at the door, then exited, plunging the room into darkness.

Olivia snuggled under the sheet and her eyelids drooped. It seemed only moments later when her eyes popped open, but the moonless night told her at least an hour had passed. It was likely about eleven. She bolted upright in bed as a voice came from the speaking tube beside her again.

"Olivia. I need to talk to you. Come to the kitchen."

She grabbed the speaking tube. "Who is this?"

"Don't you recognize your own father, Olivia? Come to the kitchen. Now."

The imperious voice was clearly her father's. Without another thought, she reached for her dressing gown, belted it around her, then hobbled to the door on her crutches.

TWENTY-SIX

HARRISON MANAGED TO avoid Fosberg until the party began to disperse about eleven. It was difficult to keep smiling and talking to guests when he wanted to take the man by the collar and toss him into the street. He chatted with the Norths until he thought Fosberg was gone, then walked them to the door and said good night. When he turned to go back to the parlor, however, he spotted the man still inside. Fosberg stood talking to Harrison's parents by the fireplace.

Harrison stopped in the doorway and turned to exit, but his mother called to him. He turned back and approached the three. "I believe I'll say good night now."

His father clapped his hand on Fosberg's shoulder. "Good news, Harrison. Mr. Fosberg is leasing the building on Main and Sunset."

Their premier leasehold. Harrison looked at Fosberg's smug face. "I'm not leasing anything to him."

His father's smile faded. "Well, I am."

"Then you'll do it without me. I'm not signing any paperwork for it. The man has publicly accused me of murder."

His father stared from Fosberg to Harrison. "What are you babbling about?" he snapped.

"Ask him."

Fosberg was stone-faced. "You're speaking nonsense."

"Lady Devonworth told me of your belief that I killed Eleanor."

"I don't have to stay and listen to such nonsense." Fosberg brushed past Harrison.

Harrison followed him. "Do you deny your accusation? And you didn't even tell her the full story."

His father was on their heels. "Harrison, that's enough. I've already accepted Mr. Fosberg's offer. I have his check in my pocket."

"Then you have my resignation. I'll have nothing to do with helping him get established in this town." Harrison strode past Fosberg and slammed the door behind him. He heard his father bellow his name, but he ignored it and stalked down the driveway and down the street to his own house.

Now what? He had some money in the bank, but it would only pay his expenses for a few months. Though finances would be tight, he could devote all his energy now to researching flight. He could look for investors without being hampered by his father's expectations and the responsibility he felt toward the family business.

Now was his chance to follow his dream. Fosberg had just done him a favor.

When Harrison stepped into the hall, Eugene met him at the door. "Your mother is on the telephone," he said, taking Harrison's jacket.

Harrison's gut tightened. He went to the hall where the telephone was and picked up the earpiece. "Hello, Mother."

"Your father is quite upset, Harrison. Come over and talk this out."

Her tearful voice got past his defenses. "I can't. There is nothing to talk out. I'm not going to lease Frederick Fosberg anything."

"Your father says he's paying a good sum. It's just business, after all."

"And I've found such business practices aren't for me." He inhaled and hoped to gather courage. "This has been coming a long time. You know where my heart lies. I want to spend time on my aeroplane."

"Son, you have a God-given gift for numbers and business. How can you throw that away?"

Her reminder made him sag against the wall. It was the one thing he hadn't thought through. The gift. Was he throwing away something God intended him to use? He thought of the way he felt when he was working on a new acquisition. Getting the new business on a solid financial footing, finding its strengths and bolstering its weaknesses. He was usually able to focus and be involved, yes, but his mind often wandered to the design of his machine. So which was God-given?

"Harrison, are you there?" his mother asked.

"I'm here." He rubbed his forehead. "I don't know what to tell you, Mother. I'm not signing any lease with that man."

"What did you mean about his accusation?"

"He suggested to Lady Devonworth that Eleanor broke our engagement and I killed her in a rage." He'd told no one about what he'd seen at the cottage. No one but Lady Devonworth.

His mother gasped. "Surely the woman misunderstood him."

"She did not," he said.

"*Did* Eleanor break the engagement?" his mother asked.

"No. I did. But I don't wish to discuss the reasons." He exhaled heavily. "It's late, Mother. We're all tired. I'm going to bed."

"At least pray about this," his mother pleaded.

"I shall do that. But I think God has been leading me in this direction for a long time."

"Mr. Fosberg might have been upset about something. I'm sure his words were not as serious as you are making out."

"And I'm sure they were. Good night, Mother." He hung up the phone and went upstairs where Eugene waited.

His valet helped him off with his vest, then hung it up with his coat. "I quit Bennett and Bennett tonight."

Eugene paused in his brushing lint off the jacket and vest on the form. "Totally quit? For good, sir?"

"Yes. And it feels great. Tomorrow I'm going to go to the club and see about finding some investors to rebuild the aeroplane."

"I'm not sure it will be easy. Not after crashing the last machine."

"I have a great new design that I want to work on. I want to land it on water and prove it can be done."

"Should I look for another position, sir?"

Harrison stared at his valet. "Of course not, Eugene. I'm going to make a go of this. And I have enough savings to see us through for a while. You're indispensable to me."

But the reminder that others depended on his decisions tempered his elation. His entire staff looked to him for their support. He had to make this work. He looked at the bed, then grabbed casual clothes.

"I'm going for a walk," he told Eugene. He called to Nealy and stepped into the night air.

Olivia nearly slipped on the slick surface of the stairs. Little moonlight came through the windows, and the servants had extinguished all the lamps. Holding on to the banister, she made her way down to the first floor by scooting on her bottom with her crutches in one hand. In the hall, she got the crutches under her arms, then lit the gaslight in the hall. Its hiss was nearly as comforting as the warm yellow glow it cast.

She moved through the labyrinth of rooms to the kitchen, a room she wasn't sure she'd ever been in. The cook was usually jealous of his domain, and she tended to leave him to his territory. She thought it was through this hallway, but she found herself in a place that dead-ended at a servants' bathroom.

Retracing her steps, she went down another hall. This time she saw a sliver of light under a closed door. She pushed the heavy door, and it opened into a large kitchen lined with cupboards, a mammoth stove, and a large chopping table. A small lamp only barely illuminated the space, but there were lots of shadowy corners that left her uneasy.

The room was empty. It held a lingering scent of garlic and cinnamon. "Hello?"

She stepped into the room, and the door swung shut behind her. She jumped and whirled when the latch clicked. Stepping back, she turned the knob and it opened easily. When she peered into the hall, there was no one there. The window in the back door drew her. She peered out into the sprawling yard, but it was too dark to see past the first two feet.

She turned back to the seemingly empty room. "Father?" she called softly. No one answered.

Where was the speaking tube he'd used? She glanced around the room and saw it by the door. There was a similar apparatus in most rooms in the house. Could he have used one in the parlor and intended to get here before she did? Pulling out a chair by the battered table against the wall, she sat down to wait.

Though it was late, all thoughts of sleep had fled. Where was he? She didn't know how long she waited. At least fifteen minutes. Toying with a fork, she listened for any sounds in the quiet house.

"I might as well go back to bed," she said aloud. She rose and pushed the chair back in. As it scraped against the floor, she heard something.

"Olivia," the voice called from outside. It was right outside the back door. Or so it seemed.

She limped toward the door, then paused with her hand on the doorknob. Why would her father want to talk outside in the dark? Was it even him?

"Olivia, come here," the man said again.

She listened closely to the voice. It *was* her father. She unlocked the door and hobbled with her crutches onto the back stoop. The ocean waves crashed in the distance, and she smelled the tang of salt in the air. "Father?" The dew drenched her cloth slippers as soon as she stepped onto the grass.

She moved farther into the yard. "Father?" The darkness was complete, and she couldn't see more than a foot in front of her face. If only she had a lamp. A bench should be to her right, so she moved in that direction.

A sound came from behind her. Before she could turn, a cloth covered her nose and mouth, and a sickeningly sweet smell made her cough and gag. She fought the strong arms that held her tight as the man dragged her backward. She was dizzy, so dizzy. She fought to stay conscious. She was dimly aware he was dragging her toward the cliff. Was this how Eleanor had died? Drugged and thrown into the sea right outside the house?

With renewed vigor, she dug her nails into her attacker's skin and heard him swear under his breath. Even now he sounded a bit like her father, but she knew he couldn't possibly be. Whipping her head back and forth, she managed to catch a fresh breath of clean air that cleared her mind. She tore into his skin with her nails again and wished she could sink her teeth into his wrist, but the cloth still partially covered her mouth.

His grip loosened, and she ripped free of his hands. The cloth fell away from her mouth. She screamed but all that came out was a choked cry. The chemical he'd used on the cloth had tightened her throat and dried her lips. She stumbled toward the house, but he was on her again before she'd gone two steps.

"You little hellion," he muttered in her ear.

That voice wasn't her father's. The cloth came toward her mouth again and she screamed. This time the sound was a little louder, but she didn't think anyone in the house would hear her.

"Harrison!" The suffocating smell enveloped her again, and the strength drained out of her legs. She sagged, and the man dragged her back toward the drop-off again.

She wasn't ready to die. It was her last thought before he pitched her over the edge.

TWENTY-SEVEN

THE MOON WAS out, illuminating the shrubs and flowers along Pacific Way. Harrison hadn't intended to walk this far. And he especially had no intention of walking past the mansion where Lady Devonworth slept behind the stone walls. He paused at the driveway to the Stewart estate. No lights winked in the windows. The only movement was the wind through the live oak tree branches.

What was he doing here? He'd thought a walk would clear his head, but it only made him more confused about what the future held. The night was silent, broken only by the distant sound of the surf on the rocks and the click of Nealy's nails on the sidewalk beside him. There was no voice from God telling him what he should do now. He didn't have much to offer a lady. No security, only his dream of building a flying machine that would make a difference.

It was only when he turned to retrace his steps that a troubling sound broke the night air. He paused, listening. A cat in distress? Had her dratted kitten gotten into trouble again? Shrugging, he took another step toward home, but Nealy whined and went a few feet closer to the house.

"Come on, Nealy," Harrison said, continuing to walk away.

He'd gone only three feet when he heard a woman cry out. The utterance sounded like *his* name. Nealy barked and ran toward the manor. Harrison whirled and looked toward the house to see if Lady Devonworth had spotted him and wanted to talk. The house was still dark and motionless. Now that he thought about it, the cry had been distant, apart from the house.

Though aware he was trespassing, he jogged around the side of the mansion to the backyard. The gardens were extensive. Shrubs and trees blocked his vision as he stared. "Lady Devonworth?" His voice seemed loud in the dark. "Are you back here?"

Nealy barked, a ferocious sound. The dog raced off into the night.

He heard a man yell, "Let go of me!"

Harrison raced toward the sound. A dark figure bowled him over, then darted away, leaving a whiff of chloroform in his wake. Harrison jumped back to his feet. His inclination was to give chase, but what if Lady Devonworth was hurt? His chest tightened.

He turned back toward the sea and rushed on. "Lady Devonworth!" he yelled. The scent of chloroform increased his anxiety.

He followed Nealy's barking and found the dog at the edge of the cliff. The dog peered over the edge and howled. Harrison stared down into the water. The whitecaps caught the gleam of moonlight as they rolled to the rocks. He scoured the water, praying not to see a person in that treacherous riptide.

Nealy continued to whine even though Harrison commanded him to be quiet several times. His eyes narrowed. Was that an arm thrown above the waves? He dropped to one knee and leaned over the edge. His gut clenched when it came again. A person struggled in the rough seas below.

"Essie!"

Leaping to his feet, he kicked off his boots and tore the coat from his back, then dived over the cliff. He attempted to miss the rocks by timing his headlong entrance into the water to match the breaking waves. The wind rushed by his face and nearly took his breath away as he plummeted toward the salty spray. Seconds later the cold water closed over his head. His knee struck a rock, and pain encased his leg.

He kicked out with his good leg. His face broke the surface of the water and he drew a breath into his burning lungs. "Essie!" He jerked around wildly for any sight of her. Striking off in the direction where he'd last seen her, he swam several feet, then treaded water while he searched the waves for her.

Had he been mistaken? Maybe he had seen a piece of flotsam. The undertow pulled at him, trying to drag him out to sea. He let it carry him awhile, praying it would take him to her. The current turned and rolled him parallel to the coast.

"Where are you?" he screamed over the sound of the waves. If she'd been drugged, how could she fight the heavy surf? A splash sounded beside him, and he saw his dog swimming with determination to his right. A surge lifted Harrison high. As he crested the top and began to fall into the trough, he spotted a white face in the water. "Dear God, help me."

He began to swim toward her, but Nealy reached her first. The dog seized the collar on her dress in his teeth and began to paddle toward the shore. Harrison kicked closer to them, then dived to prevent a wave from washing him past her. Reaching out, he managed to grab hold of something. As his head broke the surface, he realized he had hold of her hair. With his other hand he grabbed hold of her arm and pulled her closer. Her eyes were closed and he couldn't tell if she was breathing.

"Good dog, Nealy," he crooned. "I've got her now."

The dog released her and swam alongside Harrison. Harrison pulled her close but still couldn't tell if she lived. He had to get her to land. The undertow took a tighter hold and tried to take him under, but he kicked out and managed to break its grip. Swimming at an angle to the shore, he fought the waves to keep her head out of the water. Inch by inch he drew closer to the rocks. At first he saw no place for a suitable landing. His strength was fading fast. His clothes dragged him down. His kicks were taking more and more energy, especially with his knee screaming with pain.

His head went under and he came up sputtering. Somehow he

managed to keep her nose out of the water. He willed her chest to move, for him to see some sign of life. Another wave lifted them and carried them toward the rocks. Just as he thought they were both about to be crushed against the teeth of the shore, he heard Nealy barking. The dog had reached a flat spot and pulled himself onto a smooth stone. Harrison thought they might be able to land. He struck out for it. The surge ended just shy of the cliffs, and his feet touched the bottom.

Half carrying and half dragging her, he staggered ashore and collapsed onto the sand. Panting, he rolled her onto her stomach across his legs and pushed on her back. Seawater came from her mouth. He pushed again, but she lay inert. He laid her face up on the rocks and patted her cheek.

"Get help, Nealy," he told the panting collie. The dog barked and ran away.

Harrison touched her again. "Don't die," he whispered. "I love you."

❧

She was cold, so cold. Olivia coughed at the burning in her lungs and tasted salt and kelp. She gradually became aware of hard rock under her cheek and the warmth of a hand on her back.

"Esmeralda, you're alive."

Even half-drowned, she recognized the relief in Harrison's voice as he called her that ridiculous name. What was he doing here?

I love you.

The words in Harrison's voice reverberated in her head. What a strange dream she was having. She coughed and the harsh sound brought her fully to her senses. This was no dream. The Pacific roared off to her right, and its foam struck her in the face when she struggled to sit up. The black rocks cut into her palms, and salt stung her cut lips.

She coughed again. "What happened?"

Harrison supported her back. "Easy now. How much do you remember?"

She tensed. "A man. He put a cloth over my nose and it choked me. I think he threw me over the cliff."

He pulled her closer against his chest when she shivered. "He nearly knocked me down running away."

She managed to get her eyes to focus. "You're wet too. You saved me?"

"Nealy helped. God made sure we were in the right place at the right time."

He brushed his lips over her forehead, and she turned her face into his wet shirt. His arms held her close. The moment seared her with its intimacy. And those words continued to reverberate in her heart.

I love you.

Why did she hear them in her head? Her teeth began to chatter. "I'm so cold," she muttered.

"I've got to get you to the house and fetch the doctor."

He helped her up and turned her toward the black cliffs that glistened with moisture in the moonlight. There appeared to be no clear path to the top. She had little strength to climb, and her ankle throbbed. They walked a few feet, and she realized he was limping as well.

She paused and looked up at him. "Are you injured?"

"Just a bruised knee." His face was tipped up as he studied the formidable barrier in front of them. "I think there's a path around the point, but it's a little distance. Can you make it?"

"I don't have a choice."

They set off on the rocks slippery with kelp and seaweed. Her breath came hard through her burning chest. She realized she'd nearly drowned in the same manner as Eleanor. "I-I have to rest," she gasped. She sank onto a boulder.

He sat beside her, and his breathing was as labored as hers. "I'd go on to get help, but I'm not sure it's safe to leave you. Do you know who tried to kill you?"

She remembered the hard hands, the overpowering odor of the chemical-laden cloth. "I don't know. It was too dark to see." Staring up the rock face, she shuddered. "I think this is how Eleanor died. Was she found here?"

"Yes."

She shivered and clasped her arms around her. "I would have drowned if you hadn't saved me."

When her hand touched his, he grasped it and raised it to his lips. "I'm thankful God brought me out for a walk."

She remembered her panicked flailing when she struck the water. The way she'd prayed for God to save her. Had he seen her struggles in the water? Had he really provided a hero for her tonight, or had it all been coincidence? In the cold blackness of the sea, she'd felt alone and abandoned. Addie said God saw everything. Maybe she was right.

"Are you ready to try again?" he asked when she shivered once more.

"Yes." She hoisted herself up and clung to his arm along the slippery rocks. The wet nightdress hampered her every move and was heavy enough to slow her progress.

I love you.

Was that God talking to her? The voice had sounded like Harrison to her. Or maybe it was all a dream. Glancing at him out of the corner of her eye, she wished she had the courage to ask him.

"You're looking at me in a most odd way," he said. "Is there something wrong?"

"D-Did you speak to me before I awakened?" He glanced away, and she wished she hadn't said anything.

"I feared you were dead."

He wasn't going to tell her what he'd said. Were words of love on his tongue only her wishful thinking?

TWENTY-EIGHT

HAD SHE HEARD him? Harrison's lungs burned as he labored up the slope with his arm around Lady Devonworth's waist. Her ankle was still swollen, but she moved along better than he'd imagined she could. There was something in her manner that made him think she'd heard his declaration. He tried to tell himself he hadn't meant it—that only the extreme stress of the moment had prompted those words.

The truth was that she had entangled herself in his heart in a mysterious way. But then he'd never been in love before, so it was all new and amazing. He thanked God that she was alive. But the attacker was bold. He'd come right into her own yard and taken her from the presence of several people.

They crested the hill and limped toward the house. Lights glared from the windows, and servants ran to and fro in the yard. Nealy was barking frantically as if to try to get someone to listen to him. An older woman stood on the back stoop wringing her hands and weeping. She glanced up and squinted in the dark toward Harrison. Lady Devonworth was sagging with fatigue, so he swept her into his arms and started toward the manor. His knee felt like a spike was rammed into it, but he ignored the pain.

The woman started down the steps toward them. "Is she alive?"

"She's fine," he called. Nealy ran to greet them, his tired tail wagging.

"She's soaking wet. What happened?" She narrowed a glare at Harrison as if this were all his fault.

"He saved me," Essie murmured, reaching toward her. "I nearly drowned." Her hand drifted down to the dog. "Nealy too. Good dog." Nealy wiggled all over with pleasure as her hand grazed his ears.

"And what were you doing out in the middle of the night?"

"She'll explain later," he said. "She needs dry clothes. And a doctor." He brushed past the agitated older woman and onto the stoop. "Someone get the door and call the constable."

The butler sprang to yank open the door. "Stay, Nealy," Harrison told the dog on the porch. Goldia met him in the kitchen. "Show me to her room," he told her.

She opened the door to the hall. "This way."

The back stairs took them to the second floor. Her bedroom was four doors down. Goldia flung back the covers, and he deposited Lady Devonworth on the bed.

"Get her dry and warm," he said. "I'll get the doctor."

He backed out of the room and rushed down the staircase. He met the older lady in the hall. The woman probably wouldn't stoop so low as to use the servants' stairs. The icy glare she sent his way pained him as much as his knee.

"Have you phoned for the doctor?" he asked.

"He's on his way. And who are you?"

"I'm Harrison Bennett. Who are you?"

"Harrison." Her smile was weak. "I didn't recognize you, dear boy." She drew herself up. "I'm Mrs. Stewart, owner of this house. I should like to know what you were doing w-with Lady Devonworth in the middle of the night."

Eleanor's mother. He studied her cold expression. No wonder she'd raised a daughter who had little use for faithfulness.

"Saving her from a murderer," he said. When she gasped and put her hand to her mouth, he wished he hadn't been so blunt. "Someone chloroformed her and threw her over the cliff."

"Oh, that dear girl," Mrs. Stewart said, tears springing to her eyes. "Is she going to be all right?"

"I think so. She's cold and fatigued, but she was coherent and able to hobble up the hill." Or at least partway up.

Her smile faded and she looked him over. "How did you happen by, Mr. Bennett?"

"I was out for a walk. I heard her call my name. I ran to the back-yard, and the man nearly trampled me as he rushed away. I got to the cliff and saw her in the water. If you look at the back of the lot, you'll see my boots and jacket."

"Indeed, the servants discovered your garments," she said. "A thank-you is in order."

"It was only by God's grace that I was able to get us both to shore. Your daughter wasn't the first person to die on those rocks."

She blanched and fell silent. His words were brutal, but he needed to be blunt to make her realize the gravity of the situation.

The doorbell rang, and the butler rushed to usher in the doctor. In the hubbub of the moment, he slipped out to the portico. Lady Devonworth wasn't going to want to see him again tonight.

✧✦✧

Harrison paused long enough to let Mrs. Lindrum know he would be in the carriage house until lunch. His knee still ached but he ignored it as he set out across the backyard to the building that housed his aeroplane. Nealy was on his heels. A voice hailed him and he turned to see Constable Brown waving to him. He paused under a live oak tree outside the carriage house.

"Saw you as I rounded the corner," Brown said. "I wanted to get your version of last night's events." He patted the dog's ears.

The man's brown eyes were friendly enough, but Harrison thought he saw a glint of suspicion. "I was in the right place at the right time." He explained what he'd heard and done.

Brown jotted in his notebook. "Can you describe this man who knocked you down?"

"It was too dark to see him. I smelled chloroform."

"Lady Devonworth said he drugged her. She thinks she scratched him."

"She didn't mention the scratches to me. That's surely a clue to look for. Did she say where the scratches were?"

"His arms. Which may not help us much unless the man rolls up his sleeves." Brown raised a graying brow. "Might I see *your* arms, Harrison?"

Harrison stared at him, then took off his jacket and rolled up his shirtsleeves to reveal unmarked skin. "Satisfied?"

"I had to check. Can you explain why you were there?"

He studied Brown's expression. The lawman had always been fair. "Do you remember when you first realized you loved your wife, Constable?"

The man grinned and took out a cigar. "Quite well, Harrison. I think I'm beginning to understand."

"I went for a walk with no intention of going past the manor. It was most fortuitous that I did, but there is no good explanation for it other than that I subconsciously hoped to catch a glimpse of Lady Devonworth."

"So the rumors of an impending announcement are true?"

"Yes," Harrison said. There was no reason to mention that his only ammunition was that the engagement would save her reputation.

"Miss Eleanor drowned in circumstances very similar to what Lady Devonworth faced last night. Only she was not so fortunate."

Harrison clenched his fists. "As I told you after the plane crash, I fear her death was no suicide. And someone fired on the lady and me in the clearing after the accident. After last night, Lady Devonworth's fears that she was the intended target don't seem so far-fetched."

"I shall continue to discuss this matter with Lady Devonworth."

He knew he should tell Brown about Eleanor's affair with Fosberg, but it felt very unsportsmanlike. Still, the man could help them find Eleanor's killer. He needed to know. "I would suggest you speak to Fosberg. He and Eleanor were . . . close."

"How close?"

"I'll leave him to tell you. Suffice it to say that I broke off our engagement."

"I will investigate the matter." Brown turned back toward the house.

"One moment, Constable." Brown turned around to face him. Harrison gestured to the carriage house. "I'm working on a new aeroplane, but I'm reluctant to try it out until I find out about the sabotage on my other machine. Have you uncovered anything about that?"

The constable shook his head. "A hole in a fuel line is too vague to trace. I questioned your neighbors and those who might have seen anything out at the airfield. I've turned up nothing."

It was as Harrison suspected. His new machine would have to stay under guard constantly. At least until his enemy revealed himself. And he would eventually. If Harrison had arrived at Stewart Hall a little earlier last night, the man would have been exposed and caught. He thanked the constable and headed out to his machine.

When he reached the door, he dug out his key and started to fit it into the lock. It took a moment for him to realize the lock dangled open. Strange that Nealy hadn't alerted him. Harrison clearly remembered locking the building two nights ago before going to bed. He nearly went to try to catch Brown, but if he left now, any intruder would escape. He pushed open the door and stepped into the space. Dust motes danced in a shaft of sunlight. The building was empty. His flying machine was gone.

Not a muscle could move. He stood gawking at the empty space. A thousand thoughts fought for supremacy, but uppermost was how the thief had managed to snatch the machine out from under Harrison's nose.

Something shuffled behind him. With his fists at the ready, he whirled only to see his father step from the shadows. Harrison's arms sagged to his side. "My flying machine. It's gone."

His father nodded. "I disposed of it. It was taking up too much of your time. I had it taken away yesterday afternoon."

His father's effrontery took his breath away. Harrison reminded himself that he was to honor his father even when the man did something this unfathomable. "I want it back. Where is it?"

His father advanced toward him. "Be reasonable, son. Let loose of this ridiculous dream. You have a bright future ahead of you in business. Don't let this hobby distract you. My father was like you. I went hungry many nights because he cared more about playing pool than about feeding his children."

Harrison had never heard the pleading note in his father's voice. Nor had he shared this information about his growing-up years. It explained a lot—why his father was so driven to succeed, why recognition mattered to him.

He fought the pity that might have excused his father's incredible behavior. "I'm not changing my mind. I'm done at Bennett and Bennett. Where is my machine?"

His father's coaxing smile faded. "In the scrap heap."

A crushing weight came down on Harrison's chest. He nearly couldn't breathe past the pressure. "I'll just rebuild it." He turned to the door before he could say something he might regret. John North had several carriage houses. He'd see if his friend would allow him the use of one.

TWENTY-NINE

THE SUNLIGHT WARMED Olivia. She stretched, then groaned as every muscle protested. She'd lain abed all day yesterday, but she was not going to stay down today. Even her ankle felt better. She sat up and rang the bell for Goldia. Breakfast would fortify her for the day ahead.

Harrison had left the other night without a word. She tried not to let his departure bother her. He knew she was going to be all right, so why should she have expected him to dance attendance on her until dawn?

Katie poked her head through the doorway. "I heard the bell so I thought you must be awake. How are you feeling this morning?"

"Nearly human again." She smiled to dispel the dark reminder of what had happened. "Has Harrison called this morning?"

Katie stepped into the room. "I haven't heard the telephone ring."

Her mother came through the door in time to hear Katie's last words. "I met that young man, Olivia. He's quite a handsome devil." Her mother handed her the dressing gown from the foot of the bed. "We've received an invitation to a ball at Buckingham Palace. There will be no shortage of wealthy nobility looking for brides. Once your engagement to Harrison is at an end, we shall find you a husband who deserves to marry into the Stewart family."

Olivia winced as she got out of bed and shrugged into the dressing gown. "I want more from life than that."

"Your father and I were married because it was the wise thing to do. And our life together was quite lovely," her mother said, her voice firm.

She'd thought her parents doted on each other, though her father was often off on his adventures to Africa while her mother made frequent excursions to Europe. But that matter of her father's infidelity changed all her perceptions. Her mother seemed to have forgotten that. Olivia wanted a marriage like Katie's. It was clear her husband wanted to be with her more than he wanted to be gone.

"I'm going to wear the blue silk today," she told Goldia.

"Are you going out?" her mother asked.

"I'm going to go see that will." Olivia sat in front of the dressing table and began to undo the plaits in her hair. Goldia picked up the silver brush and began to brush out the strands before styling it atop Olivia's head.

"Should I accompany you?"

Olivia could tell by her mother's tone that she'd rather step in dog dung. "I believe you need to come with me. You have more right to see it than anyone. But I will do the speaking."

"What if Mr. Fosberg refuses to let us read it?"

"Then I shall call our attorney and he can handle it."

"In that case, perhaps we should let Mr. Grayson take care of it all. No need to sully our hands."

Olivia turned to face her mother. "Don't you want to know what is going on, Mother? I know I do. If we have to involve our attorney, it could take weeks, months."

"There is that," her mother agreed. "Very well. I shall be in the parlor."

Freed of her mother's nervous energy, Olivia quickly finished her toilette. With her hat firmly pinned in place and the new dress swathing her slim figure, she sailed forth to do battle. Or as well as she could manage with every muscle aching from her adventure. Her mother had already called for the limo. The chauffeur drove them to town.

Olivia planned out her strategy as the automobile navigated the narrow streets. As the motorcar passed Harrison's house, she strained for a glimpse of him. How was his knee faring?

She had the driver stop for a moment at Oscar's Mercantile while she ran inside for some stationery. Mrs. Silvers's face lit when she saw Olivia.

"My dear Lady Devonworth, how are you? I was quite distressed to hear of your accident the other night."

"I'm fine, thank you. A little sore, but that is all."

"Thanks to Mr. Harrison." Mrs. Silvers pressed her hand to her bosom. "So romantic, the way he saved you."

She suppressed a smile. "Indeed."

"The whole town is buzzing about the ball! How good of you to invite all of us. I've always wanted to see inside Stewart Hall."

"I'll be honored to show you around," Olivia said, smiling. Though the ball was turning into even more work than she'd anticipated, for once she was planning something that was of greater value than showing off the newest dress.

The car pulled up in front of the Fosberg residence. "Wait here and I'll see if they'll receive us," she told her mother when the chauffeur opened the back door of the limo and helped her out.

With her card in hand, as well as her mother's, she rang the doorbell of the modest two-story home. On a tree-lined street in a nice neighborhood, it wasn't as grand as Olivia had expected. A middle-aged woman opened the door, and Olivia stated her business and dropped her cards into the silver tray.

"One moment, Lady Devonworth." The maid ushered her into the narrow foyer, then went down the hall.

A few moments later Mrs. Fosberg rushed out of the door on the right with her arms outstretched. "My dear Lady Devonworth, how kind of you to call! And your mother too?"

"She's in the car. Let me summon her. Is your son at home?"

His mother beamed. "He is indeed! I'll call him while you fetch your mother."

For an instant, Olivia had hoped he might be gone. She hated confrontation. But this was a discussion that had to be held.

ᶜ⌒ᵗ✦ᵗ⌒ᵕ

Olivia sipped her tea and waited for a lull in Mrs. Fosberg's stream of conversation. Mr. Fosberg leaned against the wall by the window as he listened, but she sensed a watchfulness in the set of his shoulders and the reserved smile in his eyes. He knew they were here for a purpose.

When Mrs. Fosberg paused to draw a breath, Olivia jumped in. "Mr. Fosberg, I wonder if I might have a word with you in private?"

He straightened. "Of course."

"Mother, I'll be right back." She saw the relief in her mother's face as she followed Mr. Fosberg to the library. Her mother could be the backup if he refused to hand over the will.

He sat behind the polished desk and indicated the chair on the opposite side. "Please, make yourself comfortable."

She settled onto the creaking leather and clasped her gloved hands together. "I've come to take a look at my father's will."

He regarded her over the top of his steepled fingers. "I suspected as much."

"I admit I'm surprised you didn't show it to me right away."

"I thought it best to have your mother present. In fact, I think she should be here for this now." He rose. "Let me escort her in, and I'll read the will."

Olivia nodded, and he left the room. Perhaps she should have called their attorney and waited for him to come from New York so he could be present for this. She glanced around the room and took in the leather-bound books and certificate from Harvard. Several moving boxes were strewn about as well.

He entered the room with her mother in tow. Shutting the door behind them, he seated Mrs. Stewart beside Olivia, then went to the desk and opened the top drawer. He removed an envelope and slid a sheaf of papers from it. "This is the will."

Olivia nearly asked to read it herself, then decided against it. She could always ask to peruse it when he was done. She glanced at her mother, who was biting her lip. There was no real reason for them both to be so nervous, but she couldn't still the shiver that ran up her back.

Fosberg cleared his throat. "This is the last will and testament of Marshall Stewart. I'm not going to read every provision. You can read it for yourself shortly. However, I want to bring your attention to the part that will be the most contentious." He trailed a finger down the page, then laid it aside and went on to the next. "Here it is. You and your daughters have been designated a yearly stipend of ten thousand dollars. He goes on to say, 'To my son, Richard Pixton, I leave the rest of my estate and ask that he take care of my wife and daughters with any additional needs as long as they are living.'"

Olivia sat with her hands together. Her father had stripped them of nearly everything. Ten thousand dollars a year wouldn't begin to cover her mother's normal expenses.

Mrs. Stewart wetted her lips. "You can't be serious."

"I'm afraid so. You can see why I've been torn over how to proceed."

Torn? Olivia saw no remorse on his face. Would he be happy to see them impoverished? Did he have some personal stake in this?

"And where is this mysterious Mr. Pixton?" her mother demanded.

"I have been unable to locate him."

Her mother waved a dismissive hand in the air. "Then this changes nothing."

"I'm afraid it does. The estate will have to be transferred to his name. My firm has been designated to oversee the funds, which we will do until he can be found. I'll need you to submit a list of your living expenses so we can draw up a suitable budget."

Her mother rose. "You're telling me that we are now beggars? That our money will have to be funneled through your office?"

"Not beggars, ma'am. But, yes, any monies will need to be approved. We are trustees until Mr. Pixton is found. Then he will take over that duty."

Olivia found her voice. "We shall contest this, of course. Our attorney will be in touch. The money is still in our bank, and it will stay there. I fear you are only involved to earn the executor fees."

Fosberg's expression turned grim. "You would fight your father's wishes?"

"I am not convinced it is even his will."

He held out the paper. "Do you wish to see it?"

"I do." She snatched the will and scanned to the signature. It appeared to be her father's handwriting, but she didn't trust this smooth man. How much her opinion had changed in a few days.

"There are three copies in my possession," he said. "You are welcome to keep that one and show it to your attorney. I'm sure he will tell you that it is perfectly in order."

She tucked it into her handbag. "We shall see. Come along, Mother. I want to call our solicitor immediately."

Her mother rose as though her bones hurt. Her eyes were wide and frightened. Olivia refused to allow herself to believe the situation might come to pass. Her father couldn't possibly have wanted this to happen.

THIRTY

THE JUNKYARD HAD not yet disposed of his flying machine. Harrison arranged for it to be taken to the Norths' carriage house this morning, and he stopped to tell John it was coming. The Norths were outside. Addie wore gardening gloves and was puttering in the flower bed by the porch. John was playing baseball with Edward while Gideon ran barking between them. Nealy leaped out of the motorcar and ran to join Gideon.

Addie stood with a smile. A smear of dirt smudged one cheek. "Harrison, how good to see you! Have you time for refreshments? Lunch will be ready in fifteen minutes."

"I wouldn't turn it down," he said, returning her smile. "If you're sure I'm not too much trouble."

"Never! I'll tell the cook to lay a place for one more." She hurried to the door and went inside.

John tossed the baseball to Edward. "Play with Gideon and Nealy for a while, son." He joined Harrison at the porch.

"My aeroplane will be here this afternoon," Harrison told him. "I can't thank you enough for allowing me to store it here."

"My pleasure. I talked it over with Addie, and we want to invest in your new company too," John said. "We both believe the flying machines are going to be our future mode of transportation. I'd like to be a full partner if you're willing."

His friends' faith in him made a lump form in Harrison's throat. If only his own family had that kind of trust. "I could use a partner with your kind of business savvy," he said.

John clapped him on the shoulder. "We can talk about it after lunch. I have several other possible investors I would like to discuss with you. And a location for a factory to build our aeroplanes. We have much to do before the air show in a couple of months."

A factory. He hadn't dared dream that big. "Thank you," he said, his voice hoarse.

The rumble of an engine came from behind him, and he turned to see the Stewart limo stop in the driveway. He saw Lady Devonworth and Katie Jesperson in the backseat. Essie's smile was tentative, and he stepped off the porch to open the door for her.

She took his hand. "I didn't know you were invited for lunch. Perhaps Addie is matchmaking."

"I just stopped by. Addie didn't tell me she was having a party." He released her hand and helped Katie out as well.

"It's just us, not a party," Katie said, smiling up at him. She moved past, leaving him alone with Lady Devonworth.

She seemed tongue-tied and didn't look at him. He offered her his arm and she took it. They moved toward the house. "All recovered today?"

"A little sore. I see you are still limping a bit." Her tone indicated she was asking only as a courtesy.

Had her mother convinced her he'd played some part in the attack on her? Her eyes were shadowed and her mouth was strained. "You look as though you're still in shock," he said.

Her gaze met his then, and her eyes were filled with anguish. "I'm quite recovered from the other night. Th-The Stewarts received distressing news this morning."

They reached the foot of the steps. Katie and the others had already gone inside. He pressed her hand. "Can I help?"

She rubbed her head. "Mrs. Stewart doesn't know what to do. She discovered her husband has left his entire fortune to an illegitimate child. At least according to Mr. Fosberg."

"Fosberg told her this?" He shook his head. "I don't trust that man."

"I don't either, but I saw the will that he produced. It is supposedly a newer will than the one in the possession of the Stewarts' solicitor." She hesitated, and her fingers tightened on his arm. "There's more, Harrison. I'm not even sure Mr. Stewart is dead. I found a note sent to Eleanor just before her death. Mrs. Stewart is sure it's his handwriting."

He liked hearing his name on her lips. "This is almost too much to take in. I would do nothing about the money yet. It's still in Mrs. Stewart's possession, is it not?"

"Yes, but Mr. Fosberg is planning to take control of it."

"This seems entirely too convenient. Could Fosberg have forged the will? And the note to Eleanor from her father? What did it say?"

She glanced away from him, and he could tell she didn't want him to know the note's contents. "Tell me, Essie."

She sighed. "It warned her to run from you and your father. That you meant the Stewarts harm."

He pressed his lips together. "And you believed it?"

"At first," she admitted. "I know you better now."

Why would Mr. Stewart be hiding somewhere and allowing this to go on? "We need to find the man if he's alive. Unless this is all a forgery. Does Fosberg know you found the note to Eleanor?"

"No, I don't believe so."

"It's possible he warned her away from us Bennetts because he wanted her for himself."

The tightness in her mouth eased as they talked. "Katie is going to have Will's brother look into it." She glanced at the door. "I have to tell Katie and Addie that we might as well call off the ball. My friends won't come under the present circumstances, and I doubt we can raise enough money with only the townspeople in attendance."

He pressed her hand again. "What if we announce our engagement today? Would they come then?"

Her eyes filled with hope. "Maybe. Unless they hear that the Stewarts have lost all their money."

"I don't like your friends. They are fair-weather ones only."

"I never realized that until now." Her dark eyes studied him. "You're still willing to do this?"

Words of love hovered on his tongue, but he reminded himself this was an arrangement to save her reputation. She'd shown no indication she thought of him warmly.

He nodded. "Shall we tell our friends first? Then we can call the newspaper and put in an announcement. I'll call the New York and San Francisco papers as well. That will put an end to the gossip and, hopefully, your friends will be happy to attend the ball."

"We can call it an engagement ball as well. They will have even more motivation to attend." Her eyes sparkled. "It's a masquerade ball. I find I'm most interested in what you will wear."

"I'll have to give that some thought. And what about you? How shall you be dressed?"

"Perhaps Juliet. You can come as Romeo. It seems suitable for an engagement ball, does it not?"

She would need suitable jewelry for that, and he knew just where to buy it. And the exact piece.

❧

Still warm from the congratulations of her friends, Olivia rode with Harrison in his motorcar to tell her mother what they had done. Though the dog was in the backseat, she was no longer afraid of him. Nealy had saved her twice now.

Before they left the Norths' home, Harrison had telephoned Mr.

Quinn to arrange an interview. They'd scheduled a photography session as well. Everything was about to change.

She glanced at the handsome man beside her. What would it be like if he'd actually said the words she'd dreamed as she was gaining consciousness? How would it feel to be loved for herself and not for her pedigree? She had to tell him the truth. Now.

He parked at the manor. "Ready?" His eyes were warm and kind.

Kindness was important to her. She'd seen too many dictator-type husbands.

He turned off the engine. "Before we go in, there is something I need to say."

She held her breath. Was he going to declare his love? Something squeezed in her chest, and she recalled the words she once dreamed he spoke to her. *I love you.* She should interrupt him and tell him who she was first, but she lacked the courage to do so.

"Go on," she said when he paused.

"The news will be out soon. I broke ties with my father and the family business. He is going to lease our premier property to Fosberg. We had words and I quit."

"Y-You quit? But you have such a good head for business. What are you going to do?"

"Build flying machines. John and I."

Her pulse jumped. "Oh, how grand, Harrison! Truly. You'll be part of a new era."

He raised a brow. "You're not asking how I intend to support a wife. Mrs. Stewart will ask, I'm sure. I have to tell her the truth and say I have some savings, but this venture is a gamble. I believe in it though."

She put her hand on his. "I believe in *you*, Harrison. Anything you put your hand to will be a success." The warmth in his eyes intensified. She knew she should snatch her hand away, but she left it in his, forward though the action was.

He squeezed her fingers, then raised them to his lips. When he turned it over and kissed her palm, her skin burned even through the glove she wore. What did her response to him mean? She'd never experienced this kind of reaction.

Tell him. No, she couldn't. Not now, with his eyes so tender. The moment he found out she was Olivia Stewart, those warm eyes would go cold.

"We should go in," she whispered.

"I suppose we should," he agreed, though he made no move to release her hand. "But first I—"

Someone touched her shoulder, and Olivia turned to see Goldia outside.

"Mrs. Stewart wants to see you, miss," she said.

Olivia pulled her hand out of Harrison's grip. "We'll be right in." What had he been about to say? She was afraid to imagine.

He climbed out of the car and came around to escort her inside. She liked being on his arm, fancied the way her head came only to his shoulder, admired the feel of his muscles flexing under her fingers where they lay on his arm.

"Take courage," he said under his breath when they stepped inside the parlor where her mother waited. "She's not your family. You don't have to answer to her, not really."

What would he do when he found out? She feared her deception would prove he should never trust a Stewart.

"There you are, my dear," her mother said. "You've been gone quite a long time." Her curious gaze touched Harrison's face.

Harrison stiffened beside Olivia. It was a stark reminder of how he felt about her family. How was she ever going to tell him the truth?

She clasped her hands together. "We have something to tell you, Mrs. Stewart. I've accepted Harrison's kind offer of marriage. It will be in tomorrow's paper." *Act surprised,* she mentally begged her mother.

Her mother stared, then nodded. "Quite fitting. Though you are not in her social standing, of course, Mr. Bennett. I applaud you for doing the right thing."

He gave a stiff bow. "I understand I'm not worthy of Lady Devonworth. But I can tell you that I will treasure her."

Treasure her. The words filled Olivia's heart. If only Harrison meant them. If only this wasn't a role he'd chosen to play to protect her honor. His restraint when dealing with her mother was admirable, especially considering the contempt he felt.

Olivia glanced at her mother's writing desk and saw the morning's post on it. A pile of letters was neatly stacked. From her mother's New York friends, no doubt. They would all be asking questions about the scandal. An engagement would polish her mother's tarnished crown as well.

"We have an appointment with the newspaper in a few minutes," Olivia said, brushing her lips across her mother's powdered cheek. "Mr. Bennett insisted we tell you first."

"Come back as soon as you can," her mother said as they moved toward the door. "We have much to discuss, my dear."

"We should be back by dinner. Mr. Bennett wants to talk to his mother. His father has departed until next month." Olivia took Harrison's arm again and they stepped out into the hall. "That went smoothly," she whispered.

He opened the door for her. "I managed to hold my tongue. It was clear she thought I was far beneath her family and yours."

The censure in his voice made her chest squeeze. How would she ever tell him she was a Stewart?

Harrison had little more to say on the way to the newspaper office. She tried not to care that he didn't bring up what he'd started to say before Goldia had interrupted. She wanted to ask him if he meant what he'd said about treasuring her. Maybe they could forget about canceling the engagement after the gossip died down.

She wasn't ready to show her heart to him. Not until she knew more about his feelings.

⌘

The small newspaper office smelled of ink and dust. Olivia wanted to jiggle her foot, but she forced herself to be composed and calm. If Quinn leaked a hint of who she was . . . She pasted on a smile when he stepped into the room.

"Ah, right on time," he said, going around to his chair behind the desk. "Where is your fiancé?"

"In the men's room. I must ask you to remember your promise to me."

His eyebrows rose. "You haven't told him you are Olivia Stewart?"

She held his gaze. "That's my business only."

He looked away. "I've done some digging into Eleanor's death. And into Fosberg." He pulled a file toward him and opened it. "Fosberg and she had a tryst two days before she died."

"I know about that," she said.

His lips tightened. "I thought we were working together."

"I was trying to protect my sister's reputation. I don't want that in any article."

"You promised me the full story."

She should have known better than to think she could evade him. "I meant the full story about who murdered her. I don't want her besmirched."

"She did that all by herself." He thumbed through his file. "Her body was found by a fisherman. Fully clothed right down to her shoes. She didn't go out for a pleasant swim."

Olivia shook her head. "Of course not. She was terrified of the water."

He nodded. "Makes sense. The constable was never satisfied that it was a simple drowning, by the way. He suspected your lover boy."

She sagged against the wooden back of the chair. "Why would he suspect Harrison?"

"Don't be a dunce. He had to have figured out his fiancée was playing footsie with Fosberg."

"He didn't harm her," Olivia said, her lips trembling. "I'm sure of it. What about Fosberg?"

"He's got a reputation with the ladies, but it appears he deserted his normal lady friends after he met Eleanor. The two seemed very close. One of his friends called him 'besotted.'"

"With Eleanor or the name Stewart?"

The reporter shrugged. "Who knows? Maybe both. He told his partner he was going to marry her out from under Bennett's nose. Almost like he had a personal vendetta against Harrison."

That was a new wrinkle. Olivia tried to recall if Harrison had acted like he knew Fosberg, but she thought he'd claimed not to before returning from Africa. "I shall have to ask Harrison about his relationship with the Fosbergs."

He leaned forward. "And that brings up something else. Fosberg's mother seems to have had a relationship with your father."

"What?" She restrained herself from leaping from the chair. "What kind of relationship?"

"I've been told it was romantic. She often invited him to dinner at her home whenever he was in town. He sent her flowers on two occasions."

Olivia shouldn't have been so rocked by the news now that she knew about the illegitimate son. Still, the revelation left her gasping. Had he been unfaithful his entire marriage?

THIRTY-ONE

THE COUPLE STOOD on the Bennetts' front porch. "News of our engagement should be in tomorrow morning's papers," Harrison said. "I need to tell my mother tonight."

Lady Devonworth hung back. "Do you think your mother will be displeased? Your tone suggests it. I assumed she would be happy."

She was probably picking up on his reluctance to open the front door. "My parents will be entirely *too* pleased," he said. "Especially my father. His desire was always for me to marry one of the Four Hundred. At least I won't have to see his smug face just yet." He forced himself to open the door. "Hello?"

"Harrison?" His mother's voice floated from the library. "I'm in here."

He took Olivia's hand and led her to the last door on the left. The library was his mother's favorite room. She had read every one of the eighteen hundred volumes in the cavernous room, many of them more than once. His mother sat in her wheelchair by the window with a book in her hand.

"My dear Lady Devonworth! I didn't realize you were with Harrison." She held out her hand. "Forgive me for greeting you in such a disheveled state."

"You look lovely, Mrs. Bennett," Lady Devonworth said, her voice shy.

The women clasped hands, and his mother pulled her down for a hug.

"We wanted to tell you some good news," Harrison said. "Lady Devonworth has agreed to become my wife. Our engagement will be announced in the newspaper tomorrow."

His mother squealed. "Oh, my dear boy, what tremendous news!" She held out her arms and he leaned down for her to embrace him. "We shall be most delighted to welcome you to the family, Lady Devonworth."

"That's most kind."

"This calls for a celebration!" his mother said, releasing her. "We must plan a party."

"The Lightkeeper's Ball is coming up," his fiancée said. "We thought we'd make it an engagement party too."

His mother beamed. "Of course, of course. I'm proud to tell the world." She sent a questioning glance at Harrison. "I suspect you and your father need to talk. You could call him in San Francisco."

"My plans have not changed, Mother," Harrison said. "John North is joining me in my new business."

His mother sat back in her chair. "It's much too risky for you to try this now. Not with a family to care for."

"I'm fully in support of this venture," Lady Devonworth said. "I want to learn to fly myself."

"You're just trying to find your way," his mother said to Harrison. "Your father did the same thing at your age. I don't believe you'll throw away a gift God has given you."

"I believe God has been leading me this direction all along, Mother. Passion shows the heart. I love aeroplanes. I'm better at designing them than I am at pushing pencils. Anyone can tally a row of numbers. God has given me a passion for my new work, and I'm going to follow it."

"You'll have a family to support, son. Please think about this."

"We must be going," he said instead of answering her. "Mrs. Stewart expects us for dinner shortly."

His mother motioned for him to roll her to the door with them. "How are plans for the ball coming, my dear?" she asked. "Is there anything I can do to help?"

They reached the door. Lady Devonworth smiled down at his mother. "Thank you, Mrs. Bennett. I'm sure I shall need your assistance as the day gets closer."

"Oh, do call me Mother, my dear." His mother's eyes were misty. "I've always wanted a daughter. This is a happy, happy day for me."

Harrison's gaze met Lady Devonworth's over his mother's head. Did she feel as much guilt at their deception as he did? He wished with all his heart that their engagement was real and that a wedding ceremony loomed in their future. He would do all he could to see that it happened.

He stopped. "Is something wrong?"

"I'm just thinking about the Stewarts' troubles. I realize we can believe little Fosberg says, but he told me that when he tried to contact your father about the newer will, Mr. Bennett brushed him off. Wouldn't your father have wanted to see it?"

"I would think so." His sigh came, heavy and full of frustration. "He's so driven about forcing his way into society. I could see him fighting to maintain his power, his chance to be one of the accepted set."

She stared at his dear face. How could she even tell him her other fears? She wetted her lips. "Harrison, what if your father arranged for Mr. Stewart to be in that cave-in?"

He stiffened. "My father is many things, but he's no murderer."

"It is so convenient that he would announce Mr. Stewart's death and at the same time present an agreement between the two families that no one knew about."

He shook his head. "What of your belief that Mr. Stewart may still be alive?"

She took his hand, needing human contact. Needing his comfort. "I don't know what to think about that. Why wouldn't he show himself? It's cruel to leave his family in this limbo."

He slipped his other hand around her and pulled her to his chest. His chin rested on her hair. "My dear, I fear someone is playing a vicious joke on you. Whoever it is knew you would come outside if you thought Mr. Stewart was there. And you did just that."

"Why would anyone want to harm me?"

He sighed. "I don't know. It makes no sense. If you were a Stewart, I could understand it. It could be this Pixton wants to eliminate the Stewart family so he can inherit the entire estate. Or maybe it's whoever killed Eleanor. He thinks you know more than you do."

She wetted her lips. Now was the time to tell him, but once she did, he would be too angry to listen to her concerns. "About your father and that agreement. Our attorney, Mr. Grayson, has managed the Stewart money for years. After your father came back, he said the old diamond mine was played out, but that he and Mr. Stewart had agreed to a partnership of the new black-diamond mine if the two families were joined. Mr. Grayson wondered if your father was hiding some shady dealings and trying to force the merger."

"Did Grayson get a chance to look at any of the diamond-mine books?"

At least he wasn't taking offense. She shook her head.

"Father had the agreement in his possession?" he asked. "I thought your attorney had it."

She tried to remember exactly how it had been revealed. "I'm sure Mr. Grayson said he had never seen the agreement before your father came home. The solicitor urged Mrs. Stewart to ask for an audit of the books, but she didn't want to upset you or your father when the two families were about to be joined."

"I wouldn't have been angry."

His words soothed her, but not as much as his touch. She leaned into his embrace and felt the pump of his heart under her ear. "Mr. Stewart lost a great deal of his money. The Stewarts no longer have the wealth of a generation ago. They have only their pedigree. Your father has a great deal of money. I'm sure that affected Mrs. Stewart's decision." She slumped against him. "It is quite dreadful to be auctioned off to the highest bidder. That's what was happening to me in New York. Before I met you."

Did his lips brush her brow? The touch was so light she couldn't tell. She closed her eyes and heard his voice again in her head. *I love you.* Why did that linger so when it had to have been the result of the trauma she'd suffered?

"God sees who you are inside, Essie. So do I. Your worth has nothing to do with your pedigree."

She raised her head and stared into his face. "The same could be said for you, Harrison. God sees how much imagination and passion you have for your aeroplanes. I heard the way your mother tried to manipulate you."

His lips twisted in a rueful grin. "Both of my parents are good at it. I usually find myself doing what my father wants. My mother's question affected me today more than his manipulation."

"When she asked if you were throwing away God's gift?" When he nodded, she patted his cheek. "If we have a passion for something and the ability to do it, surely that comes from him."

"I'm becoming more and more sure of that. God sees my ability. My ideas don't come from sheer human imagination."

His words tugged at her heart. God surely gave her the wit and intelligence she possessed. She knew she was more than a Kewpie doll to be posed for the most advantage. If she dared, she could make a difference in the world, just as a man could.

This would take some thought. "We should go."

"Of course." He released her.

Her name was all she had. Did she dare risk it by stepping outside what was expected of her? She thought she'd have the courage if Harrison were by her side.

THIRTY-TWO

THE HIGH-CEILINGED DINING room felt warmer and happier than usual to Olivia. It had nothing to do with the heat from the fireplace spilling into the damp evening. It was all about Harrison's presence at the head of the table over dinner. She barely noticed her mother and her friends at the table, only Harrison. Their hands touched when they both reached into the basket of dinner rolls at the same time. His eyes warmed her more than the fire. She liked having him here.

After dinner he walked Olivia to the library door. "I'll be happy to make the call to your attorney if you wish," he said.

His presence gave her strength and courage. How was that even possible when she'd disliked him so intensely in the past? "I need to do it myself, but thank you," she said. She left him outside the library and closed the door before she picked up the earpiece and told the operator she needed to make a long-distance call to New York. She gave the woman the number, then hung up to wait to be called back after the connection was completed.

She could almost feel Harrison's presence outside, and she remembered that word *treasure* again. Was there any hope at all that he might come to feel that way, or would all hope be lost the moment he discovered she was a Stewart? She turned to the bookshelves so she wouldn't run to the door and rush into his arms. She perused the titles but didn't really see them.

The telephone rang and she answered it. "I have your party on the line," the operator said in a nasal voice. "His wife gave me the number where he could be reached in San Francisco. Go ahead."

"Mr. Grayson," Olivia said. "I'm sorry to disturb you at night, but we have an emergency out here. It's quite fortuitous that you are in San Francisco."

"Miss Stewart, I'm always at your disposal," he said. "How can I assist you?"

His gruff voice had calmed her fears all of her life. Mr. Grayson had been their solicitor since before Olivia's birth. She could trust him implicitly. She launched into the latest claim on her father's estate. "What is our next step?" she asked.

"I need to see this so-called will," he said.

She glanced at the safe. "I have a copy in my possession."

"I'll be on the next packet ship to Mercy Falls in the morning. I'll be there by early afternoon. Will that be suitable?"

"We'll be here." All of her questions couldn't wait until then. "What if it's legitimate?"

"I find it difficult to believe your father would leave your future completely in the hands of an unknown man. He was most meticulous about his desire to assure himself of your future. I suspect a forgery."

"How would we find out if the document is forged?"

"There are experts who can determine that."

She hated all the *ifs* the situation left dangling. "And if it's real? Can we contest it?"

"We will indeed contest it if that is the ruling."

"One disturbing detail is that this unknown half brother of mine has not come forward. Until he does, our money would be in the control of Mr. Fosberg. Do you know him?"

"I do." It was clear Mr. Grayson was picking his words carefully. "Let me simply say I would not willingly allow him to oversee my money. What of Miss Eleanor's fate? Have you been able to discover anything?"

"I believe someone killed her, but I don't know who. However, I just became engaged to Harrison Bennett. So Mother's future will be secure when she receives part ownership of the black-diamond mine."

"Your father had great hopes for the first diamond mine, but the income from it has been less than stellar of late."

"Less than stellar?" Harrison was estranged from his father. Would he be disinherited? She shook her head. Mrs. Bennett had been delighted by the engagement. At least a marriage would give Mr. Bennett what he wanted. Perhaps she could negotiate a settlement for her mother.

If anything came of her feelings for Harrison. The stray thought hit hard. She'd tried to deny she felt anything for him, but she did. She always had.

"Miss Stewart, are you there?"

"I'm here, Mr. Grayson," she said, collecting her composure.

"I have not seen the will yet, and it has not yet been submitted to a probate judge, so right now you and your mother can do as you wish."

"There's another matter. It's possible my father isn't even dead." She told him about the note to Eleanor.

"I will want to see that note as well and have it evaluated for forgery."

"So you don't think it likely Father is still alive?"

"I knew your father for thirty years, Miss Olivia. He could be somewhat self-absorbed, but I don't believe he would cause you this kind of pain. Nor would he leave you to face danger alone. I'm quite certain if he were alive, he would show himself."

The more she'd turned the situation around and looked at it, the more she'd come to that conclusion as well, but the confirmation from her father's longtime friend flooded her eyes with tears. It was almost like receiving the news of her father's death again. She'd clung to that thin sliver of hope, ridiculous as it was.

"Thank you for your candor," she said, her voice choked.

"I wish it were otherwise."

"So do I."

"Good night."

"Good night," she echoed. She replaced the earpiece and opened the door to Harrison. He stepped inside with his hands in his pockets. "You reached him?"

"I did. It appears he too thinks the will might be a forgery. He claims to have experts who can determine that."

He withdrew his hands and stepped closer. He thumbed away the moisture from her cheek. "Why are you crying, darling?"

Darling. She loved hearing that word in his deep tones. His voice was so tender, so filled with what seemed to be genuine caring. She was afraid to trust it now that she was facing her own feelings.

"He thinks the note from Mr. Stewart is a forgery too. I hate to tell Mrs. Stewart."

Her mother's voice spoke from the doorway. "Come to the fire. I have the maid bringing in mulled cider. You can tell me what Mr. Grayson had to say."

Harrison's hand squeezed hers, then dropped away. Olivia sighed and followed her mother.

❧

The manor was quiet once Harrison left and the Jespersons went to bed. With Goldia following, Olivia tiptoed to the attic stairs and glanced into the yard before going up them. The guard Harrison had insisted on patrolled the property below. Not that Olivia would be unwise enough to obey a message sent through the speaking tube again.

She reached the attic floor. The lights were dim but cast enough illumination for her to make out the trunks pushed against the walls and the shelves stacked with wooden crates. She sneezed at the dust in the air and moved toward the trunk by the small attic window. Through the glass she could see the moon on the water—the sea that had nearly claimed her life twice. She shuddered and turned back to the task at hand.

Goldia clutched herself and rubbed her palms on her arms. "Miss Olivia, it's cold up here. Can we go?"

"We just got here, Goldia. I haven't even looked for them yet."

"Your mama will be mad if she knows you're snooping through her stuff."

"She doesn't have to know. If she'd just tell me what I need to know, I wouldn't have to snoop." Olivia opened the nearest trunk and sneezed again at the musty scent of old clothes.

"How do you know it's even here? Your mama has never been here."

"She was looking for her journals last summer and realized Father had taken the wrong trunk when he shipped out some books."

Though she raked her hands through the soft pile, she found nothing more than dresses from the 1850s. No journals. For as long as she could remember, her mother had kept a household journal where she listed daily events and jotted personal notes as well. Olivia wanted to find out more about Lulu Pixton. It wasn't a subject her mother was willing to discuss.

Closing the trunk, she moved to the next. Every trunk she checked had clothing. She glanced at Goldia. "Anything?"

"There are a bunch of books in this crate," her maid said.

Olivia joined her. "Recipe books. But we must be getting close." She replaced the lid and dusted off her hands before prying open the lid on the next one. "Here they are!" She lifted the journal on top and flipped it open.

"What are you doing up here?"

Olivia turned to see her mother at the top of the stairs. She was in her nightdress and dressing gown, and her mouth was tight.

Her mother glanced at the journal in Olivia's hand. "Those are private, Olivia." She approached with her hand held out.

Olivia passed it over. "I need to know about Lulu, Mother."

"That's in the past. I don't like to think about it."

"The past just caught us. We have to think about it. I need to be prepared for what's coming. Did the woman teach her son to hate us? Will he make our lives miserable when he shows up?"

Her mother turned the book over in her hands, then glanced inside. "This isn't even the right journal."

"Talk to me," Olivia begged. "This affects all of us."

"Come down to the parlor. I won't have this discussion in such an unsavory place."

Her mother retreated to the steps, and Olivia followed after dismissing Goldia. At last she might find some answers. She was possessed of a deep curiosity about her half brother. And what if *he* was the voice on the speaking tube? It wasn't unheard of for a son to resemble his father in voice and stature.

When they reached the bottom of the stairs, Tiger entwined himself around Olivia's ankles, and she picked him up. His gentle purr would help her endure what she had to hear. On her way to the parlor, she heard the doorbell. It was after ten, hardly the time for a social call. The butler went to the door, and she heard Harrison's deep voice. When he stepped through the door, his tie was cocked and he was hatless.

"What's wrong?" he asked as soon as he saw her. "I saw the light in the attic."

"Were you watching the house?"

He shrugged and his grin was shamefaced. "I know you have a guard, but I just wanted to make sure there was no other attack."

Warmth spread through her. "It's quite good of you to care."

"Oh, I care," he said in a quiet voice as her mother joined them. He reached over and brushed at her hair. "A cobweb," he said, a teasing light in his eyes.

"Mr. Bennett, do you realize the time?" her mother demanded.

"I'm sorry, Mrs. Stewart. When I saw the lights, I feared an intruder was afoot."

Her mother's expression softened. "Very well. Since you're helping my dear Lady Devonworth with this mystery, join us in the parlor for a discussion. I'll ring for cocoa." She sailed down the hall to the parlor.

Olivia exchanged a glance with Harrison. He raised a brow and she shrugged as they followed her mother. "Were you planning on watching the house all night?" she whispered before they entered the room.

"Just until I was sure you wouldn't be answering any summons by speaking tube."

His grin enveloped her with its easy intimacy. When his hand touched her back at the door, she wanted to lean into him and brush her lips across the faint stubble on his chin. Shocking. She moved quickly to sit by her mother on the sofa while he took the chair.

"This is most distasteful," her mother said after the maid left cocoa for them on the table. "I quite dislike remembering this time, my dear."

"I know." She waited to see if her mother would continue or if she would go to her room with another headache.

Her mother rubbed her head. "I have the most dreadful headache coming on." She sighed and stirred her cocoa. "I thought I could trust that girl. She'd been with me for so long."

"When was this? I don't even know how old Richard would be," Olivia asked.

Mrs. Stewart cast a wary eye upon Harrison. "It was right after my daughter was born. I nearly died after her birth. The woman took advantage of my infirmity to entice my husband into a relationship."

Olivia had heard the stories of how her mother hadn't left her bed for several months following her birth. "How did you discover it?"

"My mother told me about it, of all things. She caught them in the kitchen." The older woman shuddered and sipped her tea.

"Did you confront Lulu and . . . your husband?"

Olivia winced at the mental image of a pregnant young woman

"I said nothing to him. He went away on business and I dismissed her at once. Actually, my mother handled it for me." She put down her cup. "It was quite distasteful. Lulu came crying to me, asking for me to reconsider my decision."

"Did you?" Harrison asked, his voice gentle.

"Of course not! I couldn't have a viper in my bosom. I had the servants remove her."

Olivia winced at the mental image of a pregnant young woman alone and friendless. "Did she have family in the area?"

"She sometimes visited a sister. I don't remember her name. It will come to me though."

"At least she had someone then."

Her mother frowned. "You sound sympathetic to her."

"I was just imagining myself in her situation."

Her mother fixed her with a stare. "You would never be so unwise."

"Of course not."

"Do you think she would be vindictive now?" Harrison asked.

"She wasn't that kind. She would have taken in every stray cat in the neighborhood if I would have let her."

Harrison leaned forward. "So Richard would be a few months younger than your daughter. Which one? Olivia?"

Olivia's mother nodded. "That's right. How do we even know if he's still alive? He hasn't come forward to claim anything."

Something about the situation had bothered Olivia, and she finally figured out what it was. "Mr. Stewart knew his name. He mentioned him by name in the will. So he had to have been in contact with Lulu after she went to San Francisco. Can we check bank records and see if he supported her in any way?"

Her mother blanched. "You're right. I hadn't thought it through." She rubbed her head and moaned. "That woman. I can't believe she would have been bold enough to contact him. And knowing my husband, he probably *did* give her money."

"We might be able to trace Richard that way," Harrison said, leaning forward in his chair. "With your permission, I'll get on it."

"Our solicitor will be here tomorrow. He can handle it," her mother said.

Olivia saw Harrison sit back in his chair. "I'd like you to be here when we talk to our attorney, Harrison," she said. "If you don't mind."

He straightened. "I would welcome the chance to help."

"M-Mrs. Stewart, you seem to blame Lulu for the entire situation. What of your husband's role?"

The older woman gave her a cold glance. "Men will always be men, my dear. You'll learn that soon enough." She rose. "We must get to bed. Lady Devonworth, you can see Mr. Bennett out." Her tone made it clear her daughter was not to dawdle.

THIRTY-THREE

OLIVIA WALKED WITH Harrison to the front door and stepped out onto the porch with him. She wished she dared ask him what he had started to say several times. The gaslight by her head hissed and danced in the faint breeze off the ocean.

She took his hand. "Thank you for looking out for me tonight, Harrison. I want you to go home now. I'm going to bed and I promise I won't answer any summons."

He raised her fingers to his lips. "I'd rather stay awhile. Want to take a walk in the moonlight?"

She hesitated. Maybe she could get up the courage to tell him her name. "Is it safe?"

"I'll protect you," he said, smiling. "I'll have the guard walk a few feet behind us."

"I'd love to," she said.

"Need a wrap?"

"I'm fine." Just being around him warmed her more than any shawl. She took his arm and they strolled down the drive.

"I think we'd better stick to the sidewalk," he said, guiding her toward the street. "The gardens could hide an intruder."

They passed the guard, and Harrison told him to keep an eye on them. She liked the way he slowed his steps to match hers and the tender way he helped her down the curb. It seemed so much more than mere courtesy. Was it? The path was dark except for the occasional open arc lamp. Every time they stepped into the shadows, she wished he would stop, take her in his arms, and kiss her until she was breathless—which wouldn't take much, because she already had to force herself to drag in air whenever she was in his presence.

Was this love?

They walked in silence to the end of the block, then turned to go back the way they'd come. Olivia saw a movement near the shrubbery and paused. The glow from the arc light illuminated the figure of a man hiding in the bushes. Her fingers clamped onto Harrison's arm.

"There's a man watching us," she said.

"I see him. Wait here." He walked toward the shrubbery. "You there! Show yourself."

The leaves erupted and the figure raced off the other way. Olivia stared. There was something about the shape of his head, the way he held his shoulders. She started to shout, "Father," then choked back the word. Harrison gave chase to the fellow and she ran after them. The guard rushed past her and pursued the men as well.

The men vanished around the corner, and she paused to catch her breath. Her chest burned with the exertion, but she forced herself to break into a jog again. She turned the corner and saw Harrison coming back toward her.

"I lost him," he said when he reached her.

She seized his arm. "Oh, Harrison, I think it was Mr. Stewart."

He frowned. "Honey, are you sure? You thought the man who called you to the backyard was Stewart too. The lighting is poor. How could you tell? I couldn't make out anything but a dark shape."

She liked hearing the word *honey* on his lips. His doubt rattled her, though, made her question what she'd seen. "I can't explain it, but I think it was him. Something about the shape of his head. But why wouldn't he reveal himself to us?"

"We keep going round and round about that. Was he in any kind of trouble when he disappeared?"

She shook her head.

"Did he gamble?"

She stared down the street, willing the man to reappear. "He hates gambling. He says gamblers are fools."

She remembered the tilt of his head. "Could it be Richard? Maybe he looks like Mr. Stewart."

"I don't know. I suppose it's possible." He turned her back toward the house. "I want to get you safely inside. I should never have brought you out in the night."

The guard joined them and hustled them back to the manor. She kept glancing back for another glimpse of the man, but all she saw were shadows and shrubs.

❧

Silver chinked at the luncheon table on the terrace and mingled with the birdsong in the background. Lady Devonworth had insisted Harrison stay the night at Stewart Hall, and he'd been happy to oblige to ensure there were no more attacks. Though he hadn't done much to prevent last night's stalker. Harrison had tried to push the events from his mind by talking about aeroplanes with Will during the meal, but his thoughts kept going back to what had happened.

Mrs. Stewart's mouth was pursed and her eyes went distant every time she looked at him. He knew she blamed him for last night's near miss. And rightly so. He should never have taken his fiancée from the premises. He still shuddered when he thought about what might have happened. The man might have had a gun.

"Did you see this man Lady Devonworth claimed was Marshall?" Mrs. Stewart asked. She stared out the window.

"Only from the back. I thought he looked too slim to be Mr. Stewart." He raised an apologetic glance Lady Devonworth's way.

"I was probably mistaken," Lady Devonworth said.

How much of what Lady Devonworth saw was wishful thinking? If that man last night had been Mr. Stewart, he would have spoken to her. It was dark. No one was around. There was no reason for him to hide.

"What I don't understand is that if it really *is* Mr. Stewart, why would he want to harm you, honey?" he asked her.

She blanched. "Harm me?"

"He threw you over a cliff into the sea," he reminded her.

"That wasn't him. That man's voice was huskier than Mr. Stewart's, younger somehow too. I believe Mr. Stewart had left, and the attacker took advantage of the opportunity."

"You heard him call your name just before you went outside."

She bit her lip. "True. That lends more credence to the possibility that it's Richard Pixton." She stared at him, then at Mrs. Stewart. "But I'd thought he was trying to protect me," she said.

"Who, dear?" Mrs. Stewart speared a section of orange.

"Mr. Stewart. He saw us leave the premises and was watching to protect me. When we saw him, he had to run."

Harrison stared at her, not sure how her mind worked. "How do you reason that out?" Not that he totally disbelieved it, but it seemed a leap in logic.

"I keep seeing him just before danger strikes. I think he's doing the best he can for me."

Mrs. Stewart banged down her fork. "Oh, for heaven's sake! If my husband is out there, he would let us know. He's not a cruel man, and letting me mourn him if he's not dead is the height of cruelty."

Lady Devonworth's lips flattened. "I didn't mean to offend, Mrs. Stewart."

The doorbell rang. Who would call right at lunchtime?

"I imagine it's my brother Philip," Will said, scooting back his chair. "That lad pays no attention to time." He darted through the door to the dining room, leaving the door open behind him.

Harrison heard backslapping and boisterous greetings between the brothers. It appeared they had been separated for several months. Will returned to the terrace with two men in tow. Harrison appraised the younger of the two, Philip. Very young and a snappy dresser. But Will had said he was good at his job. The older, portly gentleman must be the attorney, Mr. Grayson. His hunch was confirmed when Lady Devonworth and Mrs. Stewart leaped up to greet him.

"Have you had luncheon, gentlemen?" Mrs. Stewart asked.

To his credit, Philip flushed. "No, ma'am, I came straight here from my boat."

"Nor I," Grayson said. "But don't trouble yourself. I can eat in town."

"Nonsense," Mrs. Stewart said. "I'll have two more plates brought. Sit here by me, Mr. Grayson." She indicated the chair to her right.

A hummingbird sat on the back of the chair, and it darted away when Philip approached. When he sat down beside Lady Devonworth, he eyed Mrs. Stewart as though he wasn't sure whether she would snarl or smile.

"Will tells me you have some experience in tracing missing men," Lady Devonworth said.

"It's my passion," Philip said. "How can I help you? Will was very vague."

Under the table, Harrison took her hand. She squeezed his fingers and a smile lifted her lips. Did she sense his feelings? Every time he tried to tell her, something interrupted. He was unsure if God was warning him off or if it was coincidence.

Mrs. Stewart dabbed her lips with the napkin. "My husband was reported dead after a diamond mine he was examining caved in."

Philip took a notebook from the inside pocket of his jacket and began to write. "Where did this occur?"

"At a black-diamond mine in Africa."

Will whistled. "I hadn't heard that. Black diamonds. I've never seen one."

"Marshall was most excited about the acquisition of that mine," Mrs. Stewart said. "The explosion buried fifty men. Their bodies were never recovered."

"Who informed you of this accident?"

"I received a telegram from Mr. Bennett. He'd been on the scene and was able to give us the details of what happened. Apparently, Marshall was there when a new lode was discovered. In the excitement, he wanted to see it for himself. Mr. Bennett was ill and stayed behind." She shot a narrowed glare at Harrison.

Lady Devonworth's grip on Harrison's hand had made his fingers numb.

"Do you suspect foul play?" Philip asked.

Mrs. Stewart played with her fork. "I didn't. Now I don't know." Her voice faltered. "Lady Devonworth here found a letter he sent to Eleanor. According to this letter—in Marshall's handwriting—he isn't dead. And he warns her against the Bennetts."

"Have you found any evidence this is true?"

Mrs. Stewart glanced at Lady Devonworth, who stared down at the table and said, "I heard a voice in the speaking tube that claimed to be Mr. Stewart. After I went down to meet him, I was attacked and thrown into the sea after being rendered unconscious by chloroform. And last night Harrison and I saw a man who resembled Mr. Stewart."

"Last night, you say? Where?" Philip put down his pencil.

"Just down the block." She described the man they'd seen. "I don't believe it could possibly be Mr. Stewart, though. He would never harm me."

"If he's here in town, someone has seen him."

"And no one has," Mrs. Stewart said.

"That's not exactly true," Lady Devonworth said. "Goldia thought she saw him in town."

"That girl is a flibbertigibbet. You can't believe anything she says."

Mrs. Stewart glanced at the attorney. "You need to find out if these documents are forged."

"I'll take them back to San Francisco with me. I have plenty of genuine examples of your husband's handwriting," Grayson said. "We shall soon root out the truth of the matter."

Glancing at Lady Devonworth's hopeful face, Harrison hoped she wasn't about to be hurt.

❧

The next two weeks passed in a whirlwind. Harrison had to go to San Francisco to talk to investors about his aeroplane. Olivia made personal long-distance calls to her friends but was not able to coax anyone to come to her Lightkeeper's Ball. All of them were distant and aloof. They'd seen the article about her being in the wilderness with Harrison, though none would have said so to her. Olivia ended the calls with a sense of disquiet.

Did she have any true friends? People who cared about her for herself and not her name or her money? Now what? She called Katie and Addie, and they helped her make calls to local people. Harrison's mother and some of the women from the church helped too, and by the end of the week, the butler was bringing in a flood of acceptances every afternoon.

Mr. Grayson had called with news that the signature on the will appeared genuine, and the news put her mother into a funk for two days, even though Olivia encouraged her with the reminder that Richard Pixton had not been found, and Mr. Grayson was filing to contest the will. Not even Will's brother had succeeded in locating her half brother. Nothing was going right.

Thursday morning she put on her hat and called for the car. She had to find out if what Mr. Quinn had mentioned about her father and Mrs. Fosberg could possibly be true. The driver took her by the Fosberg house first, and a gardener told her Mrs. Fosberg was inside.

Olivia instructed the driver to wait and went to the door, where she was escorted to the parlor.

"My dear Lady Devonworth," Mrs. Fosberg said, standing to greet her. "I just ordered tea."

Olivia smiled and settled onto the sofa by the woman. "Thank you for seeing me, Mrs. Fosberg."

"You seem quite grave, my dear. Is everything all right?"

Olivia smiled and accepted a cup of tea from the woman. "I'm fine. I hope you're looking forward to the ball as much as I am."

Mrs. Fosberg clasped her hands together. "Oh, I cannot wait! I am coming as Queen Victoria."

Olivia hid her amusement behind her cup. The sweet woman was short and rather dumpy. The fussy clothing Queen Victoria would wear would overpower her.

"The entire town is talking about it. Frederick's partner from San Francisco is coming, and several of his friends. I think you shall raise all the money needed to rebuild the lighthouse."

"I hope so. People have been very generous." She sipped her tea and tried to decide how to broach the subject. "Have you met Mrs. Stewart?" she asked finally.

The woman's smile vanished. "I have."

"How about her husband? He was in town on occasion."

The tea sloshed onto the saucer under Mrs. Fosberg's cup. "Oh dear," she said as it spilled onto her dress. She rang for a servant and asked for a damp cloth.

Olivia bit her lip. Had it been a ploy to avoid the subject? "I heard you and Mr. Stewart were friends," she said.

Mrs. Fosberg's lips trembled. "Where did you hear that? That nosy newspaper reporter, I presume? My son told me he's been asking questions about our family."

"I did not mean to offend you," Olivia said. "I merely wished to ensure you are comfortable meeting Mrs. Stewart at the ball."

Mrs. Fosberg's lips tightened. "I'm perfectly comfortable. Marshall and I were friends. He was a lonely man, and I was lonely as well. Our relationship is hardly your concern, Lady Devonworth, if I may be so bold."

"D-Did he speak of his wife and daughters?"

The older woman put the saucer down with a clatter. "His wife is a cold, heartless woman."

Olivia gasped at the characterization of her mother, then sat back in her chair. Perhaps the truth was not far off. Her mother had always been driven. She knew what she wanted and was determined to have it. "That's what he told you?"

"I heard it from other sources as well. But I'm not at liberty to repeat their names." Her smile came then, but it was strained. "Please, shall we move on to another, more pleasant topic?"

"Of course." Olivia knew when she'd passed the bounds of good manners.

Two days before the ball, Olivia started watching the clock. Harrison was due back. She *had* to tell him the truth when he arrived, even if it meant he broke their engagement. And she very much feared he would. The servants were busy hanging decorations and moving in extra seating and tables. The bedrooms would be ready for the guests to arrive.

When the doorbell rang, she was engrossed in the Kewpie pages of the newest *Woman's Home Companion*. She set the magazine aside and listened for one of the servants to answer the summons. When she heard Harrison's deep voice, she pinched her cheeks and smoothed her hair. Taking care to arrange her skirt becomingly around her, she looked toward the door with an expectant smile.

When he entered the parlor, she took in his attire. Leather jacket and hat, casual clothing. "You're going flying?" She couldn't keep the excitement from her voice. "The plane is ready for testing?"

"Past ready. I've been up in it three times. It performs better than

any other flying machine I've ever seen. Today the comet is supposed
to be as close as it is going to get. Want to come along?"

She sprang to her feet. "May I?"

He nodded. "I have something for you though. I didn't like the
way your skirt was nearly caught in the aeroplane on our last adventure. I bought you an aviator's outfit." He held up a white-bagged
garment. Unzipping it, he revealed a bloomers outfit.

Her mother would be scandalized. Olivia eyed it. The bloomers
ended under the knee and had matching argyle stockings. A leather
aviator's hat dangled from the hanger as well. Oh the freedom of
such an outfit!

She reached for it. "I love it!"

"Get changed and I'll take you up for a lesson. We'll refuel, then
go up again tonight when the comet passes."

She paused in her rush toward the door. "Aren't you afraid at all?"

He shook his head. "Scientists continue to say we're in no danger.
But if they're wrong, being up there or down here won't matter much.
And if we're about to step through eternity's door, I can't think of
anywhere I'd rather be than with you."

She drank in his expression. The quirk in his brow, the daring tilt
to his lips, the tenderness in his eyes. This day held more promise
than she could take in.

"I'll be right back," she said, suddenly breathless.

Carrying the scandalous attire, she rushed to her bedroom. Goldia
turned from putting clothing in the closet. She gasped when she saw
what Olivia held. Shaking her head, she approached her mistress. "Oh
no, Miss Olivia. Your mama would have my hide if I let you wear
them bloomers."

"I'm wearing them." Olivia turned her back to her maid. "Unbutton
me."

Muttering under her breath, Goldia did as she was ordered. "You
go down the back stairs. Don't let your mama see you."

"I'm a grown woman. This outfit is perfectly modest." She pulled on the stockings, then stepped into the bloomers. Turning, she surveyed herself in the full-length mirror and nearly gasped. She was quite the modern woman. No longer a society miss but a daring adventuress. She rather liked the thought.

Twirling, she struck a pose. "What do you think?"

"It's scandalous, miss." Goldia turned away and shuddered. "What if your gentleman sees you like this?"

"He bought it for me."

Goldia put her hand to her mouth and muttered something indecipherable under her breath. Olivia smiled and hurried down to meet Harrison in the entry. When he saw her, his expression warmed. She held out her hand and he took it and raised it to his lips. He lingered overly long in the kiss he placed against the back of her hand.

"Are we ready?" she asked when he continued to stare at her.

He released her hand. "I've got something else for you in the auto."

Jewelry? Shoes? She wondered what might go with this outfit. When they reached his Cadillac, he grabbed a bag from behind his seat and pulled out a pair of coveralls.

She raised a brow. "You expect me to wear these? I hate covering up my new outfit."

"You don't want it to be stained, do you? The engine throws out castor oil."

"Oh, very well. But I'm not putting it on until I have to." She smiled and went around to the other side of the motorcar. She was a free woman. Harrison didn't have expectations of her other than that she be herself. Had that ever happened before? Not in her memory.

THIRTY-FOUR

THE WHITECAPS ROLLED along the blue ribbon of coast below them. The sun had begun its final plunge into the sea, and cliffs threw shadows onto the sand. Harrison steered the plane along the rocky cliffs rising to their right. The engine was performing beautifully, and the new wings handled the winds without a problem.

He glanced behind at Lady Devonworth. Her pink cheeks and wide smile telegraphed her enjoyment. Earlier in the afternoon he'd let her take the controls for a few minutes, and she'd handled them like she was born to fly. He gave her a thumbs-up, and she motioned it back to him with an even wider grin.

The sky began to darken overhead as the sun sank, throwing off pink and orange rays. He wanted to shout, to raise his fists in the air and exult in the experience. Halley's Comet was a bright star overhead. He saw no evidence of the tail. Smelled nothing of poisonous gas. Just the salt-laden breeze.

He was going to tell her how he felt about her tonight over dinner on the beach.

She touched his shoulder and pointed. He looked down at the battered lighthouse she was trying so hard to save. The perfect place. Though she was only pointing out their location, he lowered the flaps and prepared to land. The aeroplane glided on the gentle breeze. Lower and lower. The sunlight gleamed on the water, illuminating the way. He held his breath and set the plane down on the sand. The bumps were gentle. A perfect landing. A good omen for a perfect evening, he hoped.

After leaping from the plane, he secured it with ties, then helped her out. Gulls squawked overhead as they dived for their last attempt at fishing before nightfall. The tide was coming in, bringing flotsam and driftwood.

"Would you get out the basket in the back of the plane?" he asked Lady Davenworth. When she nodded, he rounded up an armful of dried-out driftwood and began to build a fire. He fetched the kerosene lantern and lit it. When he turned around, she had shucked the hated overalls. Her hair had come loose from its pins without the leather cap. He could only stare.

"Hungry?" he asked.

"Not really. It's all too exciting." She raised her arms over her head and lifted her face to the sky. "We're still alive, Harrison."

He grinned. "Are you ever going to tell me your name? I can't call you Lady Devonworth forever."

She paled, then smiled. "I rather like hearing you call me Essie."

It was a grand opening to tell her how he felt, but he didn't have the nerve. Not yet. "I don't smell anything, do you?" he asked. "No poisonous gasses."

She shook her head. "Just the sea."

"Let's take a walk and eat later then." He held out his hand and she took it. The way she wrapped her fingers around his in such a trusting way made him smile.

"Are you laughing at me?" she asked. Her other hand went to her hair.

"No," he said. "I'm just enjoying your company."

She squeezed his fingers. "It's been a lovely day."

They reached the hillside by the remains of the lighthouse. "Shall we sit?" he asked, indicating a flat rock barely visible in the quickly falling darkness. The lump in his pocket seemed bigger, more important.

When should he pull out the box? Before he told her how he felt or after?

She settled on the rock, and he sat down beside her. "I like being with you," he said. He wasn't good with smooth words. He cleared his throat. "I'm not saying this very well." Maybe his gift would say it better than he could. He slipped his hand into his pocket and brought out the ring box. "I have something for you."

Her attention went to the velvet box, and she went very still. She shifted on the rock, and he couldn't tell if she moved a bit closer or farther away. She offered no cues on how to proceed. His fingers were all thumbs as he fumbled to open the box. Now that his proposal was in front of him, he realized daylight might have been a wiser choice. Lamplight wouldn't reveal how lovely the ring was.

He succeeded in prying open the top. The ring sparkled against its black velvet backdrop. Tiny black and white diamonds circled the most magnificent white diamond he'd been able to find. When she gasped, he took heart. "I wanted to give you something no one else would have. Do you like it?"

"I-It's beautiful," she said. She reached for the ring.

"Allow me." He lifted it from the slit in the box and took her left hand. Her fingers were cold. Maybe this had been a mistake. She was likely to laugh in his face.

But she didn't. Her eyes were wide, and her mouth trembled as she stretched out her fingers. He took that as an invitation to slip on the engagement ring. The light from the lantern sparkled on it as she turned it to and fro.

"I'm not good with words, my love, so let me just get this out." He swallowed hard. "I want our engagement to be real. I know I don't deserve you, but no one will cherish you like I will. I'm asking you to trust me. To believe in me. To be by my side as we make a life together."

Her lips parted and he waited to hear the words of rejection he feared were coming.

❧❖❧

The engagement ring took her breath away. So did Harrison's words. Olivia stared at the glittering diamonds, then into his face. His eyes were brighter than the diamonds, more compelling than the comet she'd come out here to see. The pain of knowing that his love would fade when he discovered she was one of the hated Stewarts dimmed her joy. Was it possible his love could withstand the reality of her heritage? When they left this magical place, she had to tell him. It would either all end or he would find it in his heart to look past the Stewart name.

She wetted her lips. "Are you saying you love me?" she whispered. The wind whipped a strand of hair across her face, and she pushed it away so she could study his expression. Surely that was love in his eyes?

He rubbed his forehead. "Didn't I just say that?"

"Not exactly," she said, smiling. "I'd like to hear those words though. I've been waiting days on them."

He lifted a brow and a grin broke the worried set of his mouth. "I love you. I love the way you have to figure everything out. I love your optimism and how smart you are. You make me want to be better than I am."

"I thought you said you didn't have a way with words," she said, her voice husky. She cupped his face in her palms. "I love you, Harrison. I'd be honored to be your wife forever and ever."

A flash of light caught her attention and she looked up, dropping her hands. "Oh look, it's a meteor shower!"

The heavens were a display of fireworks like she'd never seen. Falling stars arced across the sky as they plummeted toward the ground. When she glanced back at Harrison, his face was tilted to the sky. His profile was strong and her soul filled as she looked at him.

He turned toward her, and she knew her whole heart was in her eyes. He palmed her cheek and rubbed his thumb over her lips. Her eyes closed when he leaned forward. His lips pressed against hers, and she exploded with feelings she'd never experienced. Heat swept over her skin, and she pressed closer to him, winding her arms around his neck. She wanted to be closer to him, closer than to anyone.

She couldn't think beyond this moment. Nestled against him with passion arcing between them, she had no concept of time or place. Just the feel of his lips on hers, the taste of his mouth, his arms holding her close. When he broke away, she made a sound of protest and tried to pull him close again.

He sprang to his feet and raked his hand through his hair. "We should be getting back." His voice shook.

As her cheeks cooled, she realized she'd lost her head. She'd totally forgotten propriety. A lesser man would have taken advantage of her innocence. Her trembling legs barely supported her as she slipped off the rock and put her hand in his.

"Can we see the comet?" she asked.

She focused on the heavens and tried to calm her ragged breathing. The sky was filled with stars, some brighter than others. The meteorite shower had ended. She saw the Big Dipper and Orion. The bright northern star was rising. She gulped and dragged in oxygen. What had just happened between them?

He looked up into the sky. "We were supposed to be able to see it, but all I see is Venus."

She'd seen stars when he kissed her. She'd like to experience that again, but the heat in her cheeks still surged when she touched his hand. "We haven't talked about when the marriage will take place."

He tucked her hand into his arm. "I think as soon as possible, don't you?"

Her cheeks flared again once she understood his meaning. What must he think of the way she'd clung to him? Did he think her a wanton woman? Maybe she was. Surely the feelings she'd had weren't normal. Her mother had never warned her of the way her flesh could respond to a man's touch. She'd thought the bedroom side of marriage was something to be endured, something that only delivered the children she wanted, not something to be longed for.

An awkward silence fell between them. She wished she knew whether her behavior had frightened him off.

His fingertip touched the moisture on her cheeks. "Are you crying? I didn't mean to frighten you. I just love you so much. I'm afraid I lost my head a bit."

He was apologizing when it should be her? "Did you think me overly amorous?" she asked. "I shall try to behave better the next time you kiss me."

His choked laugh was cut off as he gripped her shoulders in his hands. "Please don't change a thing."

His mouth came down on hers again and the same passion swept her up in its wake like the tail of the comet they'd heard so much about. Standing on her tiptoes, she pressed against him.

He pulled his mouth away but hugged her close. Her ear was over his heart and she could hear it going crazy. His reaction to her was just as strong as hers was to him. Her hand crept up to touch his face, and his heartbeat marched double time. She nearly laughed. He wanted her too. What a relief to realize she hadn't made him want to run from her.

By the time they flew back, her hair had come loose from its covering. Harrison landed the plane on the field, and Jerry rushed to help her down. She pushed her hair out of her face and steeled herself to tell Harrison the truth on the way back to the manor.

"You need to get home," Jerry said. "Your mother took a spill from her chair."

Harrison stilled. "Is she hurt?"

"A lump on her head, but she's been fretting for you since your father is still away and will be gone at least another week."

He'd be gone for the ball. Olivia managed not to smile.

"I'll go right there if you can take Lady Devonworth home."

"I'm going that way," Jerry said, flashing his grin.

Harrison brushed his lips across Olivia's forehead. "Sorry, honey."

She watched him walk away. She could savor his love for another night.

⌁✺⌁

Harrison found his mother abed when he stopped by her house. He assured himself she was all right, brushed a kiss across her brow, then left her to rest. He paused in the hall and glanced at his father's office.

Since Lady Devonworth had mentioned her doubts about his father's dealings with the Stewart fortune, Harrison had determined to find out the truth.

His mother's butler motioned to him. "Sir, your fiancée called. She was checking on your mother and also asked you to call on her if it's not too late tonight. She said she needed to speak with you."

"Thank you." He waited until the butler went through the door to the kitchen, then Harrison went down the hall to the office and shut the door behind him.

His father's office was sacrosanct. No one came in without an invitation. No one sat in his father's chair, and it was all Harrison could to do to circle the desk and settle onto the leather cushion. No papers marred the surface of the polished desk. He tugged on the lap drawer and it slid open. Nothing there but pens and ink.

He methodically went through every drawer and examined every paper. Nothing was out of place until he picked up a notebook. He flipped through it and saw that the sheets were empty. As he closed it, he noticed impressions on the blank pages. Looking more closely, he realized some pages had been cut out.

He grabbed a pencil and put the notebook under a light. Using a light stroke, he smudged the paper with the impression. A signature began to appear.

Marshall Stewart.

Over and over, all down the page. The signature was the same. It varied in small ways, but the bold handwriting showed up as though someone had practiced writing the name. The only reason for that would be . . . forgery.

He closed his eyes briefly. His fiancée's fears were true. Harrison's father had orchestrated all of this. She had to know about this, but he didn't want to tell her. Not after this evening. Not after the acceptance and love he'd found in her arms. What if she didn't believe he had nothing to do with it?

But if she loved him, wouldn't she believe him? He cut out the incriminating page, folded it, then tucked it into his pocket. He'd put it in his office and tell her about it when he saw her. Honesty was best.

If his father had forged the will, what else had he done? Harrison opened the drawer that held the business books. The men had owned a diamond mine in Africa, and his father had just purchased a second one. Upon his marriage to Eleanor, the Stewarts were to receive half the income from the second mine. He studied the rows of numbers. Both mines appeared to be incredibly profitable, but hadn't Lady Devonworth said Mrs. Stewart's money was gone? With her share from the one mine alone, she should have been extremely well off.

Harrison rubbed his forehead. Could his father have been cheating the Stewarts? Had he misled them as to their financial condition to force them into agreeing to a marriage between him and Eleanor?

He flipped through the remaining pages of the ledger, but they were empty. He lifted the receiver on the telephone and instructed the operator to place a call to Mr. Grayson. When the phone rang and he was connected, he told the attorney what he'd found.

"Are the Stewarts paid anywhere near this amount per month?" he asked, quoting half of the current month's income from the original mine.

"That was the amount transferred last month, Mr. Bennett. Your father oversees what comes in and specifies what goes out to them as well."

"Do you think he's cheating them?"

"The only way to know that is to see how much the mine is actually making, not what he is transferring."

"How can we do that?"

"You'd need to talk to the banker who handles the account."

His father did business with the bank here in town. John North could put him in touch with the right person. "I can do that. I'll let you know what I find out." He hung up and took a deep breath.

If he discovered his father was a swindler, what would he do about it? Lady Devonworth wanted to talk to him, but he was going to put her off until tomorrow. He wanted to get to the truth first.

THIRTY-FIVE

OLIVIA SAT SIPPING lemonade on the terrace with Katie and Addie. This morning she had hustled around the house making sure the bedrooms were readied for overnight guests from San Francisco. Her first load of guests would arrive shortly on the packet, and the real work of hosting the ball would begin.

Bees buzzed a pleasant drone in the background, but she was out of sorts. She'd asked Harrison to come by last night, but he'd made his apologies. Now here it was the day of the ball—their engagement ball!—and she hadn't told him she was Olivia Stewart. How could she tell him today when the tension between them might explode and ruin the festivities?

Hummingbirds flitted from flower to flower in the espaliered planting that shielded the terrace from anyone in the yard. Even the fragrance of hibiscus failed to soothe her.

Katie leaned back in her chair. "I can't thank you enough for all you've done, my dear Olivia. The ballroom should be full tonight."

Olivia rubbed Tiger's ears, and he rewarded her with a loud purr. "And you and Will shall soon be back home. I expect the funds to pour in from the benefit."

"Is your costume ready?" Katie asked.

"Oh yes."

"You shall be the loveliest Juliet of all time," Addie said. She smiled and picked up Olivia's left hand. "You've said nothing about this, though

I've been waiting in agony for you to tell me. When did Harrison give it to you?"

Olivia turned it to catch the light. "Last night, the night the tail of the comet was supposed to show itself, but this was much more brilliant than the comet."

"You've said hardly anything about it to me either, and I've been dying to ask," Katie said. "Why did he give you a ring if you're going to break the engagement after the ball is over?"

Olivia put the cat down. He growled and stalked away with his tail in the air. "We aren't going to break it. I'm going to marry him."

She'd hugged the information close. It was a most delicious secret. Olivia wanted to take out the memories of last night and examine them with no doubts, no familial objections.

Addie leaped to her feet and grabbed Olivia in a hug. "I *knew* you two were meant for one another! I saw the way he looked at you."

"And you at him," Katie added, smiling widely. "I'm so delighted for you both." She sobered. "Have you told him you're Olivia Stewart yet?"

Olivia's elation collapsed. "No. Every time I think I have the courage to do it, something happens and I can't bear to spoil the mood."

Katie put her hand to her head. "But his father knows you! The minute you meet him, the truth is out."

"I know! Thankfully, he's out of town for the ball. Once the craziness of the party is over, I'll pick a quiet moment and tell Harrison."

"He's going to be upset that you waited so long," Addie said.

Olivia bit her lip. "Time just seemed to slip away."

Addie gave her a long look, then shrugged. "When is the wedding?"

Heat scorched Olivia's cheeks. "Soon."

Both of the other women stared at her hot cheeks. Katie glanced down at her plate of cake with a smile. Addie bit her lip but it failed to stop the curve of her mouth.

Olivia stirred sugar into her tea. "I've never been in love before. Is

it—normal—to feel, um, flustered when he kisses me? T-To not want
him to stop?"

Addie choked on the bite of cookie she'd just taken. Katie spilled
tea on her dress. Olivia knew her face must be as red as the straw-
berries on the plate of refreshments. She was totally abnormal. A hussy.
Harrison deserved better than a woman who threw herself at him.

Addie swallowed and the pink in her cheeks intensified. "It's normal when you love someone to, um, want to be with him. Passion
between a man and woman is how it's supposed to be. It's how God
designed it."

"You mean you feel that way too? I'm not a fallen woman?"

The other women laughed. They all looked down at their tea. Olivia's
eyes burned when they didn't answer. Perhaps they would cast her off
now that they knew of her base nature.

Finally Addie glanced up. "I've been married the longest, so I suppose I should answer this. Be thankful you have those feelings, Olivia.
Too many women go into marriage only for convenience or arrangement. They endure the marriage bed with little emotion or feeling.
God designed you to respond to your husband. He looked at the
union of man and woman and said, 'It is good.' And it is."

Katie patted her hand. "And your love for Harrison will only grow
if you let it." She smiled and her dimple flashed. "I'd suggest you plan
that wedding very soon."

"Have you told your mother?" Addie asked.

Olivia shook her head. "She saw the ring, but I think she imagines
it's part of the show. I'll tell her soon."

"He's a wonderful man," Katie said. "There should be no im-
pediment."

"She's uncertain of Mr. Bennett's role in Father's disappearance. As
am I. But Harrison had nothing to do with his father's schemes."

"What of Eleanor's death?" Addie's voice was gentle. "Have you
abandoned any belief that Harrison had something to do with it?"

"Of course. He's saved my life several times." Even as she spoke, she was aware his appearance at the right times proved nothing. He could have hired someone to harm her and then intervened. But she knew him better now. He was not that kind of man.

"Who could be behind these attempts on your life?" Katie asked.

Olivia lifted her cup to her lips. "I suspect Richard Pixton."

"As do I," Katie said. "But I haven't been able to decipher a motive. He gets the money even if you live."

"Not if I'm successfully able to contest the will."

Addie nodded. "And with you and your mother out of the way, he wouldn't have to care for you." She tipped her head in a listening posture. "I think I hear a car arriving. I do believe the ball is about to commence!"

⌁

The bank was nearly empty. It would close for the day in fifteen minutes. Harrison shook hands with John. "Thank you for meeting me here on such short notice."

"My pleasure. I'm on the board of directors—so not an integral part of the day-to-day operations—but I hope to be able to answer any questions you might have."

His father's account included Harrison as a joint signer, but he'd never had the need to do more than arrange deposits and tally outlays. His father managed everything else. He followed John to a back office.

John shut the door behind them and led Harrison to a long table that held a stack of leather-bound books. "I've pulled the account books for you. They are always available for your perusal. I'll leave you to look through them while I tend to another matter. I'll be back to see if you have any questions."

"Thank you." Harrison pulled out a chair and opened the first book.

It didn't take long for his worst fears to be confirmed. The diamond mine was raking in a staggering amount of money, but his father was only transferring a thousand dollars a month to the Stewarts. Not only that, but Harrison saw an even more awful truth: Mr. Stewart had owned 80 percent of that mine. His father had lied to everyone in saying he'd paid for it alone.

So his father had been swindling the Stewarts out of money. The door opened behind him, but he didn't turn until he heard his father's voice.

"Harrison, what are you doing here?" his father demanded.

Harrison stood to face his father. "When did you get back in town?"

"I decided my son's engagement party was more important than business, so I turned around and came back. What are you doing?"

"I wanted to see the books. I have every right."

"I give you a detailed report every month, and you give those a cursory glance. If you wanted more information, all you had to do was ask. Instead you've gone behind my back?" His father closed the door behind them. Perspiration dotted his upper lip. His smile was more of a grimace as he crossed the room to the table where Harrison stood. He glanced at the open book. "What are you looking for?"

"Less than I've actually discovered," Harrison said, suddenly weary. "You've been cheating the Stewarts."

"I've done no such thing," his father sputtered. "Marshall left me in charge."

"Did he really? Or did you forge his name so you could swindle his family?"

His father paled and sank heavily onto a chair. "How do you know that?"

"I found the notebook. There were imprints on the blank pages."

His father's eyes pleaded for understanding. "Marshall's dead. This is my chance to be like the Vanderbilts. I had to take it. It was just going to be temporary until you were married to one of the Stewart girls. The families would be joined and I would give them everything they needed."

"But keep the bulk for yourself." When his father dropped his gaze, Harrison knew he was right. He felt sick. "You cut Mrs. Stewart's money so she would be forced to agree to your demand to marry Eleanor off to me."

His father took a handkerchief from his pocket and mopped his brow. "No one was hurt by this."

"What about Mrs. Stewart and her surviving daughter? You've been raking in the money and forcing them to live on a shoestring."

"Only for a few months," his father protested. "It was to ensure Mrs. Stewart went through with the wedding."

Harrison shut the account book. The thud echoed in the room. "You must make it right, Father."

His father's lips thinned. "I'll not have our name besmirched, Harrison. Keep quiet about this. I'll just start putting more money into their account. I'll tell Mrs. Stewart the mine began producing. Mrs. Stewart will never have to worry about money again. I'll settle a large amount on you and Lady Devonworth as well. You can tinker with your planes the rest of your life in comfort."

Did his father think he could *buy* him? "I don't want your blood money, Father."

"Blood money? I had nothing to do with Marshall's death."

"Rather convenient he died in that mine, wasn't it?"

"Surely you don't think your own father would stoop to murder?"

Harrison tapped a pencil against the financial records. "This much money can corrupt a man."

"His death was an accident, I swear it!"

Harrison studied his father's earnest face. "I hope you're telling me the truth, Father."

His father blotted his forehead again. "What are you going to do?"

"I'm going to tell Mrs. Stewart and her lawyer. They can ask for an audit of the books if they choose."

"If you do, all the money will go to Marshall's illegitimate son."

Harrison stopped on his way to the door. He hadn't thought of that. Perhaps it would be best to keep his mouth shut and ensure Mrs. Stewart and not the shadowy Richard Pixton got the money.

❧

Olivia stood in Stewart Hall's third-floor ballroom and surveyed the decorations. The space oozed glamour with its floor-to-ceiling mirrors festooned with garlands of lilies and orchids. A grand piano was in one corner with a stage for the band, and an enormous vase of roses and orchids sat atop it. The windows sparkled and would let starlight in tonight. The servants had scrubbed the floor, then poured milk onto the wood. The wood now gleamed after the milk had been washed off. There were so many orange trees and evergreen boughs that the space looked like a garden.

"It looks wonderful," Katie whispered. "Olivia, I can't thank you enough for what you've done."

"God brought you when we needed you," Addie said. "Just as he always does."

Olivia turned to smile at them. "I believe we shall raise all the necessary funds tonight. The town has rallied around us. All the ladies are still talking about their tour of the lighthouse grounds and the need for rebuilding. They thought it quite romantic."

"They don't have to stay up all night like Will does," Katie said, smiling. She whirled around the ballroom floor. "I'm going to dance until my feet hurt. I can't remember the last time I went dancing."

"Just don't overdo it, both of you," Olivia scolded. "I shall be watching out to make sure you rest."

Addie smiled. "Our men will be doing the same, I'm certain."

Olivia had never had friends like these two, ones who always pointed to Jesus in all circumstances. Her faith had been strengthened so much since coming here. She was beginning to believe she could be who she was inside.

She left her friends arranging flowers and went down to greet her guests. Mr. and Mrs. Broderick, a prominent family from San Francisco, arrived first. Mr. Broderick pressed a check for a thousand dollars into her hand, and she was nearly overcome with his generosity. She escorted them to the parlor to take refreshments. The Fremonts arrived next. Olivia admired Mrs. Fremont's elaborate Marie Antoinette gown and hairstyle and took them to join the other guests.

Her smile faded as she went back to the foyer. A familiar set of shoulders was getting out of a car. Mr. Bennett. What was she going to do? She had to avoid him until she could talk to Harrison. She hiked her skirts and raced for the ballroom.

THIRTY-SIX

CHAMPAGNE FLOWED WITH the conversation. Harrison stood still in a swirling kaleidoscope of brightly colored costumes and masks. The participants in the polka swept by him, and he stood out of the way, laughing as he saw the townspeople dressed in costumes ranging from peasant dress to Queen Victoria. The ballroom was packed, and heat shimmered in the air from all the bodies. The party spilled from the ballroom to the first floor and out to the lawn. He couldn't guess how many were in attendance. Hundreds? The whole town and the neighboring towns of Ferndale and Eureka, as well as the nobs from San Francisco.

He still hadn't seen Lady Devonworth and wasn't sure he would recognize her in her costume. Then he heard her laugh. He turned to see a beautiful woman with dark hair cascading to her waist. She wore an elaborate gown. Her dance card, a vellum paper with a tiny gold pencil, was attached to her wrist by a pale green ribbon. It looked empty, and he hoped she'd saved all her dances for him. She wore a white mask, but he recognized her pointed chin and full lips.

He bowed in front of her. "Romeo at your disposal, miss. Can I talk you into dallying in the moonlight with me?"

She fluttered her fan at him, and a smile curved her lips. "You're most outrageous, Romeo." She put her gloved hand on his arm. "I need to talk to you anyway. You've been avoiding me."

He led her to the center of the ballroom. "Ladies and gentlemen, can I have your attention?"

"What are you doing?" she whispered, glancing around. "Is your father here?"

"He's outside, I believe." He realized he hadn't introduced her to his father, but he'd gone too far to stop now when hundreds of eyes were fixed on them. "Folks, I'm the luckiest man alive. You all know the beautiful Lady Devonworth has consented to be my bride. As a token of my love, I have something special for her, and I want you all to share our joy."

He lifted the lid of the box that he had been carrying under his arm. The necklace she'd tried on at the jeweler's her first day in Mercy Falls glowed in the shimmer of candlelight. The ladies around him gasped, but he was waiting to see his Essie's reaction.

She put her hand to her mouth. "You remembered! It's exquisite!" Her fingers touched it, then she pulled her hand away.

"Let me." He took the intricate platinum chains from their resting place and stepped close enough to lay the piece onto her skin. The necklace was heavier than it appeared.

"I hope I don't break it," she said.

"It's not as fragile as it appears." He fiddled with the clasp on the back of her neck and inhaled the aroma of her perfume, something sweet like honeysuckle. He stepped back. "There. Take a look."

She went to stand before one of the ornate mirrors. "It's beautiful," she said, touching the lacy filigree.

"You look quite lovely," he said, his voice husky. He'd never seen her look more beautiful.

"I want one," a woman dressed as Cleopatra said to her right.

Other women agreed, and Harrison grinned as he realized he'd just likely sold more diamonds for his father. Where was the man anyway? Last time he'd seen him, his father had been talking to some nobs outside. He watched Lady Devonworth in the mirror.

She glanced at his face in the mirror and their gazes locked.

"I shall wear it with pride," she said, her fingers touching it.

He saw doubt and love in her eyes. "Is something wrong? You said you needed to speak with me."

She bit her lip. "There are several things I need to speak with you about. But in private."

He gestured at the smiling guests promenading around the floor. "The ball is a success. Let's pass the plate for the Jespersons while they are all in a spending mood."

He motioned to the footmen and instructed them to pass around silver platters. Lady Devonworth's smile grew as a mound of checks and cash grew on the plates being handed around. After the servants carried off the booty, he swept his fiancée into a dance. Holding her in his arms was the one thing he'd longed to do all evening. Her head barely came to his chin as he whirled her around the floor. Others joined them after the first pass around the floor.

He paused when a familiar form came to the doorway to the ball-room. "My father is here. I need to introduce you."

"Later, in private," she said, her smile fading. "I need to tend to a few things. I'll be back." She squeezed his forearm, then disappeared into the flutter of color and movement around him.

After half an hour, he went in pursuit but couldn't find her, so he wandered back downstairs where men were in the smoking parlor. They were discussing the disappointing appearance of Halley's Comet. He leaned against the wall by the fireplace and listened to their conversation.

A footman offered him a glass of champagne but he refused. Another footman announced a buffet supper was ready in the dining hall. He peeked inside to see if his fiancée was there. She stood talking to Mrs. Stewart at the damask-covered table. Even the heady aromas of creamed oysters, turkey, lobster salad, and salmon mousse failed to tempt his appetite when he was so concerned about what she needed to discuss.

A smatter of laughter echoed in the night, and he saw Jerry and his vaudeville friends performing their play on the wide porch. Harrison took his drink with him and went to watch. It was a comedy about four men from different walks of life. Jerry played a coal miner's son, and his passionate speeches about social equality made Harrison stop and think about how his father treated his employees. Maybe he'd been too hasty to disengage himself from the businesses. He could make changes that could bring a better life to their workers.

When the play ended, he went out to the lawn, where he found Eugene talking with a young maid, Brigitte, under a small alcove. Harrison plopped onto a chair beside them, glad to be out of the crush of people. Before he could say anything to Eugene, he saw Lady Devonworth making her way through the crowd to him.

She stopped when she saw him. Her attention went from him to Eugene. Her eyes widened. "Do you know this man, Harrison?"

He glanced at Eugene and saw his valet lift a brow. Harrison shrugged. "He's my valet, Eugene."

She rubbed her forehead. "I'd hoped you didn't know him." Her voice was a stricken whisper.

"Essie, what is this all about?" he asked. He rose and took her hand, but she pulled back. "What's wrong?"

She glanced from Eugene to Harrison. "Which of you is going to explain this to me?"

Harrison spread out his hands. "I don't know what you are talking about, darling." He pitched his voice low and gentle, aware people were glancing their way.

"Why were you hiding him without telling me?" She broke off on a sob and took a step nearer. "Please tell me there was a good reason for this. I didn't believe you would hide this from me."

"I don't understand what you're saying." He put his hands on her shoulders, but she shook them off.

"Do you think I'm blind, Harrison? That I couldn't see the resemblance to my father?"

Her father? He was totally confused.

"What's going on here?" Mr. Bennett's voice boomed from behind him. "Your voices are carrying." He glanced at Lady Devonworth and his eyes widened. "Miss Olivia?"

Olivia? "Father, this is my fiancée, Lady Devonworth."

"I suggest you have a talk with your fiancée, son." He reached over and ripped the mask from Olivia's face. "This is Olivia Stewart."

Harrison rocked back on his heels, and his gaze went to her as she stood with her head up and her eyes blazing. "Olivia? You're a *Stewart?* Is that why you refused to tell me your first name?"

A crowd had gathered around them, and he heard the name Olivia Stewart whispered from mouth to mouth. Her mother was white and motionless at the table, speechless for once.

"I tried several times to tell you," Olivia said. "That hardly matters now. What about Eugene?"

"Eugene?" He turned to his valet. "Do you have any idea what she's talking about? Who is it you resemble?"

His valet was grave. "I'm afraid I know exactly what she is saying, sir. She is speaking of my resemblance to my father. And her father."

The words fell like boulders, hitting him hard, stealing his thoughts. "Y-Your father?" He stared at Eugene, then to Olivia. "Wait, are you saying . . ."

"I'm saying I'm Richard Pixton." His steady gaze bored into Harrison. He turned and plunged off into the dark.

❧

"Come back!" Olivia sprang after the man, as much to avoid Harrison's stricken expression as to catch Richard. She raced through the crowd, but he disappeared in the throng and she lost sight of him.

Harrison reached her. She stared into his face, desperately wishing he would be able to explain away his part in this. "He's gone," she said.

"He won't have gone far. I'll find him." Pain contorted his features. "Let's go to the library."

Every eye watched them exit. Olivia held her head high but nearly lost her composure when her gaze met Addie's. Her friend's eyes were brimming with sympathy. Olivia stepped into the library, and Harrison shut the door behind them.

He swept the mask from his face and stared at it in his hands. "I didn't know he was Pixton."

"I believe you," she said. She steeled herself for his questions and accusations. "I wanted to tell you who I was, but you'd made it perfectly clear you could never love Olivia Stewart. I couldn't find the words to tell you."

He opened his mouth, then closed it again. "It appears my distrust of the Stewart family was well-founded. You're as deceitful as your sister. I hate lies."

Olivia clasped her hands together. "It wasn't exactly a lie. I do possess the title of Lady Devonworth."

He turned the mask over in his fingers. "Why did you hide your identity?"

"I wanted to find out what happened to Eleanor and thought I might accomplish that better if no one knew I was Olivia Stewart." The explanation felt weak, even to her. "After someone tried to throw me off the boat, I also feared to reveal my identity, in case the murderer made another attempt."

"I would have protected you," he said.

Olivia shriveled under the contempt in Harrison's eyes. They'd had a measure of trust between them, and it was gone now. Scattered and destroyed like his plane. She'd gotten used to seeing admiration in those brown orbs. Now they were cold, so cold.

"I *had* to find out what happened to her," she said. "My mother wanted me to marry you in Eleanor's place, but I told her I wanted to see if we would suit first. Once the masquerade was in place, I felt trapped. I planned to tell you, then you informed me that you wouldn't marry Olivia Stewart if she were the last woman on Earth. I wasn't sure what to say after that."

"You thought I killed her."

She hung her head at his accusation, unable to deny it. "I didn't know you then."

"So you went into this deception to try to prove I murdered her." His voice was shaky. "I honestly thought you loved me."

The pain in his voice stopped her heart. "I-I'm sorry, Harrison. I didn't think you killed her once I got to know you better."

"Yet when you saw Eugene, you assumed I knew he was your brother."

She bit her lip. "I was overwhelmed. I'm sorry. I should have trusted you more."

"Yes, you should have." He tossed his mask onto a chair. "Our entire relationship has been a masquerade. How appropriate." He turned and exited the library, leaving the door gaping behind him.

"Harrison!" she called after him. When he didn't turn, she slumped onto the desk chair and struggled not to give in to tears. This was her fault.

After a few moments, she rose on stiff legs and went to the parlor with a smile pasted onto her face. Her guests turned curious faces her way, but she moved through the crowd reassuring them that all problems had been smoothed over. If only it were true. By the time the grandfather clock chimed four in the morning, she was limp with the effort of keeping the smile in place.

"We want to tally the donations," Addie said. "Are you okay?"

Olivia managed a smile. "We'll talk about it later. Let's find out if the ball was a success, at least as a benefit."

"Want to do the honors?" Katie asked.

"Go ahead." Olivia didn't have the brain for figures tonight. She watched as the other women counted.

Katie glanced up, her eyes shining. "It's nearly twenty thousand dollars, Olivia!" She choked up and tears filled her blue eyes. "I can't believe it."

"Believe it," Addie said. "God always sees our needs."

"I was beginning to believe that until tonight," Olivia said. Her vision blurred and she grabbed her hanky to mop her eyes.

Addie embraced her. "What did Harrison say? Was he terribly angry and hurt?"

Olivia clung to her, inhaling her friend's comforting perfume. "He was. I feel terrible. But there's more. His valet is Richard Pixton."

Addie stiffened. "Pixton? The man we've been looking for?"

Olivia nodded against Addie's shoulder. "So all this time that we've been looking for the man, he was right under our noses." Fresh tears poured down her face. "Richard is the one who has been terrorizing me. Calling on the speaking tube. He's the one behind Eleanor's murder. He tried to kill me too."

Addie hugged her. "Oh my dear, I'm so sorry. But this isn't Harrison's fault. I can't believe he would have known this."

"He said he didn't. I believe him." She mopped her eyes again. "But he's hurt and angry I didn't tell him I'm Olivia Stewart, and he has every right to be."

Addie bit her lip. "I was afraid of that."

Olivia sniffled. "I know I should have told him."

"Have you gone to the constable yet?" Katie asked, putting her hand on Olivia's back.

Olivia pulled away from Addie. "Not yet."

Addie squeezed Olivia's fingers. "Olivia, trust God with this. He is there for you."

"Thank you, Addie. Pray for me." Olivia swallowed hard and pulled away. "I'm going to go see Harrison."

"Ask God to open your heart and eyes," Addie called after her.

Olivia rushed from the room. She grabbed a shawl from the foyer and stepped out into the night air. She could call for a car but she'd rather walk. Stars glittered in the black bowl of sky. Cicadas sang around her as she walked up the driveway. Walking through the silent town, she felt a presence. Were her friends praying for her? She was sure they were.

"Where is the truth in all this?" she asked God. "What is my purpose? Surely you have more plans for me than to live a vain existence of spending money and trying to impress people."

God could see into her heart. Better than she could see herself. If he had stirred some kind of desire for more in her soul, shouldn't she listen? Shouldn't she explore the parts of herself that God brought to light? She'd been doing that, but now she wasn't sure. Maybe it was selfish to want more than she had. To want a noble purpose.

"I'm going to do better, God," she said. "I'm going to listen more. Be thankful for everything you give me and hold it with an open hand. Even if you want me to be poor. Even if I have to give everything to this unknown brother of mine. I want to become the person you see. Even if it means letting go of Harrison too."

There was no lightning overhead, no dove flying up from the shrubs. But she could have sworn she felt God smile. Smiling herself, she quickened her step. Harrison's house loomed in front of her. There was a light on. She'd thought she would have to rouse him and Richard from bed.

Please, God, let him listen. Let him still love me. Squaring her shoulders, she stepped onto the porch and pressed her finger on the buzzer.

THIRTY-SEVEN

HARRISON PACED THE floor of his billiards room. Nealy followed him. He hadn't wanted to notify the constable, but it had to be done. If someone had asked who his best friend was, he would have named Eugene. To discover he'd been lying all this time—and was almost certainly the man who murdered Eleanor—made Harrison doubt everything in his life. His eyes burned and he rubbed them.

Olivia hadn't cared enough to trust him with her identity. That could only mean she had never trusted him at all. And she was a Stewart. Now he marveled that he hadn't seen it for himself. No wonder she knew all their business.

When the doorbell sounded, he stopped and glanced at the mantel clock. Nearly five in the morning. Only the constable would come at this hour. He strode down the hall and threw open the door.

Olivia stood on the porch. She still wore her Juliet costume and the necklace he'd given her. "May I come in?" she asked.

He stepped aside and turned his back on her as he retreated to his office, the closest room. The sooner she stated her purpose and left, the better. He heard her shut the door and greet Nealy, who had stayed behind. Traitor dog.

He flicked on the light in the office and went to stand by his desk as she appeared in the doorway. "What are you doing here at this hour?"

"I needed to talk to you."

He narrowed his eyes at her. He saw she still wore the ring as well. Why hadn't she taken it off?

She didn't look away from his glare. She glanced around. "Is Richard here?"

"I have no idea where he is. I haven't seen him since he ran off."

She twisted a long lock of hair around her finger. "He left town?"

"I'm not privy to his secrets. Nor yours."

A breeze fluttered through the window behind him and ruffled the papers on the desk. A storm was blowing in, but it was nothing compared to the storm in his soul.

Her attention never left him. "You totally trusted him?"

"I didn't suspect *you* weren't Lady Devonworth," he pointed out.

She had the grace to flush. "How long has he worked for you?"

"Four years. I counted him as a friend. My *best* friend. I hate to see him behind bars."

"Don't you even care that he killed my sister—that he tried to kill me?" Her voice broke.

He nearly moved to comfort her but stopped himself. "Of course I care. I told the constable to arrest him."

"Has he?"

He shrugged. "I haven't heard. When you rang the doorbell, I thought it was Brown."

The wariness in her eyes faded, and she gave a tentative smile. "I believe you, Harrison. I was just shocked at first when I realized he was your valet. I'm sorry."

"Why were you so quick to jump to the wrong conclusion?"

Her eyes pleaded for understanding. "I've been dressed up and posed just like the Kewpie dolls. Perfect hostess, obedient daughter, scion of society. It's hard to believe anyone would love me for myself and not for what I can do for them. I allowed my doubts about myself to carry over to you. I was wrong."

His anger began to ebb. "I only wanted you, Olivia. Not your name or your status."

Tears filled her eyes. She took a step toward him. The wind picked up again. The gentle breeze changed to a sudden gust that caught the papers on the desk and blew them across the room. She stooped and began to pick them up.

"I'll get them," he said.

She reached for a paper and froze. She snatched it up and stared at it, then up at him. His gut clenched when he remembered one of the papers on the desk. The forged signatures.

"Would you care to explain this?" she asked, holding out a paper. Her voice sounded thick.

He knew what it was without looking. "I was going to tell you about it."

"You forged my father's handwriting. You let me hope he was alive." Her voice was disbelieving.

He shook his head and took a step toward her.

She backed up, tears spilling down her cheeks. "I wanted to give you the benefit of the doubt. I wanted to believe that there was a good reason for Richard Pixton to be under your roof. You had me convinced I was wrong."

He reached a hand toward her, then dropped it when she flinched. "No, Olivia. It's not what you think. I found that at my father's house. See the pencil rubbing? I did that trying to figure it out. When I saw what he'd done, I confronted him about it. There's more I need to tell you about all of this, but not until you calm down."

"I'm perfectly calm, thank you." Her gaze searched his. "I want to believe you, Harrison." Her voice broke off in a sob.

"I had nothing to do with any of this, Olivia."

She passed her hand over her forehead. "I'm so tired I can't even think. I'm going home now. We'll talk about it later." She lifted her gaze and studied his face. "Can we get past this, Harrison? I want to. If you could understand how devastated I was by Eleanor's death, perhaps you could understand my determination to know the truth."

He thought about telling her he loved her, but he still couldn't wrap his mind around the fact that she was a Stewart. He let her turn and rush from the room. Moments later the door slammed.

❧

Tears poured down Olivia's cheeks as she rushed back to the manor. Harrison had shown no willingness to forgive her for hiding her identity. And heaven help her, she still loved him. What a pathetic fool she was.

The manor was dark as she made her way to her room. She closed the door behind her and fell onto her bed before she let out the sobs crowding her throat. Her life was in ruins.

She lay on her back and watched the stars through the window. Her fingers crept to her lips and she remembered the night he'd kissed her for the first time while stars fell from the sky. Burying her face in her pillow, she wished that day back again.

"Olivia." The words echoed from the speaking tube. "I need to talk to you."

She bolted upright. Her father's voice. She grabbed the speaking tube. "I'm on to you, Richard. I won't be taken in again."

Ghostly laughter floated up the tube, then the voice faded away. How dare he come here and taunt her? He knew she wouldn't fall for his ruse now. He'd done it to torment her. How had Harrison let such a viper into his household?

Tiger curled up against her and she caressed his soft fur. He was a comfort tonight. His ears flickered and he looked toward the door. Her skin prickled when he tensed. Was someone listening outside her door? She bolted upright.

A board creaked and she struggled to see her door in the moonlight. Was the knob turning, or was it a trick of the light? Before she could decide, the door eased open and a figure stepped inside. A woman's figure.

Olivia relaxed. "Goldia, what are you doing up at this hour?"

The light came on, half blinding her. She put up her hand to shield her eyes and realized it was her housekeeper. The door shut behind Mrs. Bagley. Swiping at the moisture on her cheeks, Olivia sat up.

"Is something wrong?"

"Yes, miss, we have a crisis. Could you come with me?"

Olivia swung her legs to the floor. "Of course. What's wrong?"

The housekeeper put her fingers to her lips. "It's your mother. Quietly, Miss Olivia. Your mother was most adamant that I didn't rouse the Jespersons."

Just like her mother to want to smother any gossip. "Is she ill?" Olivia rushed toward the door and followed the housekeeper into the hall. Instead of turning toward her mother's room, Mrs. Bagley turned left toward the stairs. Olivia followed Mrs. Bagley down the staircase to the first floor. She started past her to the parlor, but the older woman grabbed her arm.

"She's not there, Miss Olivia. This way." She beckoned for Olivia to come with her to the back of the house toward the kitchen.

What was her mother doing in the kitchen? But when they reached it, the woman continued out the back door toward the carriage house. Were they leaving the premises?

"Mrs. Bagley, where are we going?"

"She's in the carriage house, miss. She's had an accident."

An accident? What would her mother be doing wandering around the carriage house? Olivia darted past Mrs. Bagley and ran across the backyard. The carriage house was across the driveway and at the back of the property. What could her mother have been doing all the way out here where only servants went?

She reached the structure and stepped into the dusty space smelling of gasoline and oil. "Mother?" Straining to see in the dark, she could only make out the shrouded shapes of the automobiles.

The door slammed behind her, and a man's hard hands grabbed her. A rag was thrust into her mouth, then he wrenched her arms behind her back. The man propelled her toward the smaller automobile.

She worked her tongue around the rag. It wasn't stuck in very far and she managed to get it out of her mouth. It fell to the ground in the dark as he shoved her forward.

A scream tore out of her throat, and he clapped his hand over her mouth. "If you make another sound, your mother is dead. Understand?"

She nodded, and he took his hand away. "Richard?" she gasped. "What do you want? Where is my mother?"

"Get that rag back in her mouth, Jerry."

Jerry? Olivia strained to see the man's face. The sliver of moonlight through the window showed a slimmer, shorter man than Harrison's valet. Jerry and Mrs. Bagley were in on this too?

"I can't find the rag," he muttered. "You have a hanky?"

"No," Mrs. Bagley growled.

Olivia heard a woman moan. The sound came from behind her. "Mother?"

"She's here and if you scream, I'll kill her first," Jerry said.

"Whatever Richard is paying you to help him, I'll pay you more if you let us go," Olivia said. "I promise you won't go to jail."

"Richard?" Mrs. Bagley laughed and shoved Olivia. "That milquetoast nephew of mine has nothing to do with this. He's much too *forgiving* to mete out justice where it's due."

"Nephew? You're Lulu's sister? The one she went to live with after leaving our house?" Olivia struggled to see the woman's face in the dark. "What do you stand to gain if I'm dead?"

"If you're all dead, Richard will get everything. He'll share it with the aunt who raised him. But it's not about the money. It was never about the money."

"It's just revenge then?" Jerry's grip on her arms never slackened. The only way she would be free of him would be if he let go.

"Your father gave everything to you and your sister. He let his wife toss Lulu to the dirt. She went quite mad, you know." Mrs. Bagley's voice rose.

"Mother, don't," Jerry said. "Stay calm."

"Calm?" Mrs. Bagley's voice rose to a near shriek. "The Stewarts are to blame for everything. For the way we lived hand to mouth. For Lulu's death by her own hand. They have to pay for their sins. I've waited and waited for God to do it, but he has let them prosper. So I have to do it."

"But you'll go to jail. No one will believe this was an accident. You'll be found out."

The woman's smile was chilling. "Jerry will testify he saw Frederick Fosberg sabotage the plane. And we also have his gun in our possession. He'll take the fall, not us."

"Fosberg tried to kill us?"

"He tried to kill Harrison. He was convinced Eleanor killed herself because she was afraid of having her reputation besmirched. Of course, Harrison had nothing to do with it—Jerry threw her over the cliff—but Fosberg's rage suited our purposes."

"It was Jerry on the boat," Olivia said. "He tried to kill me."

Mrs. Bagley shoved her. "Enough talk. Let's end it, Jerry."

Jerry shoved Olivia toward the roadster. He wrapped a rope around her arms, then lifted her into the seat and tied the rope to something on the floor that she couldn't see. She opened her mouth to scream, and he stuffed a vile-tasting rag into her throat. From the oily texture it must have been used to wipe grease off the cars.

She began to work the rope but it refused to loosen. Straining to see in the dark, she realized her mother was slumped unconscious against the other door. Olivia's scream tried to work its way past the rag, but all that emerged was a choked gasp.

The next moment she heard something splash. The stench of gasoline choked her. They were going to set the carriage house on fire!

THIRTY-EIGHT

HARRISON SAT FOR a long time just staring into the flickering fire. All his bright hopes for the future were gone. His father was a swindler, maybe worse. He still wasn't convinced his father hadn't orchestrated Mr. Stewart's death. The man he would have trusted with his life had betrayed him. Worst of all, the woman he'd meant to spend the rest of his life with believed him capable of killing her sister and plotting her own death. And she'd deceived him.

"Sir."

He looked up to see Eugene—Richard—in the doorway. The proper response would be to leap to his feet and restrain him until the constable could be summoned, but Harrison couldn't dredge up the will to do it.

"Why, Eugene?" he asked simply. His valet would always be Eugene to him, not this Richard fellow.

Eugene stepped into the office. "I'm not behind Eleanor's murder. I know that's what Miss Stewart thinks. You believed her too. I saw it in your face. That's why I ran."

"The constable is looking for you. Why have you come back?"

"To make sure you know the truth. I had nothing to do with any of this."

"Then who has?" Harrison asked.

Eugene hung his head. He went still, then picked up the forged signatures on Harrison's desk. "What is this?"

"My father forged the paper giving him control of the mine." Harrison rubbed his throbbing head. "If you didn't kill Eleanor, then maybe he did."

Eugene shook his head. "My cousin did this, not your father."

"What? How do you know?"

"It's known in town that if you want a well-done forgery, you go to Jerry."

"Jerry? He's your cousin?"

Eugene nodded. "Your father wouldn't sully his hands by doing this himself."

"And the one from Mr. Stewart to Eleanor? He would have done that one as well?"

"It would make sense."

Harrison frowned. "What would be Jerry's connection to this? Was he simply hired to do the forgery? Why would my father want Eleanor dead? Or Olivia? He forced Eleanor out here to marry me. He had much to lose by their deaths. But you didn't."

Eugene held his stare. "I would not take their money or their lives, sir."

"Then who is behind this? Who else stands to gain from eliminating the Stewarts?" He saw Eugene pale and glance away. "Who, Eugene?"

Eugene put his hands in his pockets. "Jerry himself. When Mr. Fosberg told Eleanor about the new will, Jerry came to me chortling about how life would be different when I possessed all the Stewart money. That we could take over the estate and be as good as anyone else in town."

"That's not proof," Harrison said.

"There's more, sir. A few minutes ago I overheard Jerry in the Stewarts' garden. He was talking in another voice."

"Probably practicing for the vaudeville play he'll be in. The same one he performed tonight at the ball."

Eugene shook his head. "He sounded like my father. I heard him say, 'Olivia, come down here.'"

"Why would he say that? You mean he was practicing to coax her from her room again?" The pencil in Harrison's fingers snapped. "He was the one who lured her outside, then tried to kill her?"

"That's what I suspect," Eugene said. "I came straight here."

Harrison leaped to his feet. "He's in the house with Olivia! I must get to her immediately."

"I'm sure he would do nothing with a houseful of guests." But Eugene followed him to the hall.

Harrison called Nealy, then went directly to his car. He slid behind the wheel of the car that was parked along the street. The engine didn't turn over. "Come on, come on," he said.

"We'd better walk," Eugene said.

Harrison got out and followed his valet as they ran toward the Stewarts'. Nealy raced after them. As they rounded the corner, a red glow lit the predawn sky.

"Fire!" Harrison seemed to be moving in slow motion though his legs pumped beneath him and his chest burned with exertion. "The carriage house!"

The property seemed impossibly far away. As he raced up the driveway, he detected no shouts of alarm. All the guests were probably sleeping off their exhaustion from being up all night. "Fire!" he screamed again at the top of his lungs. He prayed the servants would hear him.

What if Olivia was in that building? Considering the danger she faced, an unrelated fire would be an unlikely coincidence. Horror seemed to encase his legs in ice. Was he never going to arrive? Panting, he reached the end of the house and ran for the backyard, shouting for the servants as he ran. He rounded the back corner.

The carriage house roof was in engulfed in flames. Embers shot into the air and fell like the falling stars they'd seen that night he first kissed her. He ran for the door and tried to open it, but the doorknob was scorching hot. He took off his shirt, wrapped it around his hand and tried again, but it was locked. With his hand still encased in his shirt, he punched his fist through the glass, reached inside and unlocked the latch, then managed to get the door open.

Smoke and heat poured out of the doorway. He screamed her name above the roar of the flames. Stepping into the inferno, he choked on the smoke and peered through the hideous scene straight from a nightmare. "Olivia!"

Someone touched his shoulder and he looked back to see Eugene in the blazing building with him. "She has to be in here!" Harrison yelled. Holding his arm across his nose and mouth, he began to kick at the flames.

He wouldn't find her alive. The inner conviction nearly made his knees buckle, but he refused to give in to despair. Nealy began to bark. The dog grabbed Harrison's pants and tugged. He let the dog drag him forward. "Olivia!" he called again.

A movement caught his eye in the seat of the roadster. He leaped to the automobile and found Olivia, her eyes half closed and her head lolling against the seat. Her mother was beside her.

"Eugene, here!" He tried to pick her up, but she was tied. It took precious moments to loosen the rope, then he raised Olivia in his arms and ran with her toward the exit. "Get Mrs. Stewart!"

Fire crackled overhead. Burning timbers began to rain down on their heads, and the doorway seemed too far away. He leaped over a blazing rafter and felt the heat of it on his legs as he reached the other side. Looking down, he realized his trousers were on fire, but he felt no pain. He didn't stop to beat out the fire but rushed for the clear air he could now see outside. He burst through the space into the yard where a group of guests were huddled together watching the blaze.

Laying Olivia on the grass, he made sure her clothing wasn't on fire. It was only then that one of the guests took off his jacket and smothered the flames on Harrison's trousers. Harrison caught a glimpse of burned flesh and wondered when the pain would start.

He spotted Mrs. Bagley and Jerry watching the blaze from the porch. Her face fell when she saw Olivia on the grass. She grabbed Jerry's arm, and they disappeared inside.

Eugene exited the carriage house with Mrs. Stewart in his arms. The hem of her nightdress was smoldering, and Harrison tossed the jacket to Eugene, who beat at it until the fire was out.

Olivia seemed unhurt. He cradled her in his arms and took the gag from her mouth. Her eyelids fluttered and she swallowed.

"Water!" he called to the shocked crowd. "Shh, don't talk," he told Olivia. "I've got you." He held her close. "I can't lose you, Olivia." He rocked her back and forth.

"I prayed you'd come," she said, her voice hoarse.

He pressed his lips to her forehead and thanked God they'd been in time.

Her lungs burned with every breath she drew. Olivia opened her eyes and coughed. She tried to sit up, but gentle hands pushed her back. She realized she was in her bed. The scent of smoke still clung to her even though someone had removed her smoky clothing and replaced it with a clean nightdress.

"Lie still, darling." Harrison's face shimmered in her vision.

She blinked and his face came into focus. "Mother!" She tried to rise again, but his hands on her shoulders held her down.

"She's fine. Eugene got her out." Time enough later to tell her about her mother's burns. They weren't life threatening and would heal without disfigurement.

"Richard didn't try to hurt me," she said past the pain in her throat. "It was his aunt and cousin."

"Eugene told me."

"Where are they?"

"In custody. Brown caught them fleeing town. Jerry is telling the constable everything."

She clutched his forearm and drew it away so she could take his hand. "Harrison, I'm so sorry. Can you forgive me?"

"I already did, the second I realized I might lose you." He raised her hand to his lips.

"There was no excuse for how I acted."

"I'm not without blame. I was too proud to make you listen to me. I believed the worst about Eugene too, and I was wrong." He slid his hand under her back. "I'm going to raise you up. Ready?"

She nodded, and he lifted her to a seated position. Her vision swam again, then cleared. "I need to see my mother."

"She's resting. I spoke with her. The doctor is with her now."

"Did she have many burns?"

He shook his head. "Mostly on her ankles, but they will heal. He was concerned because of her age. He wanted to check out her heart and lungs, but he said he thought she'd be fine. He treated your burns and the one on my leg."

She coughed, her lungs still hurting. "You were burned?"

"Just my leg. I'll be fine."

"What's going to happen to them—the Bagleys?" she asked.

His lips flattened and his eyes narrowed. "They'll be tried for your sister's murder. And for trying to kill you and your mother."

There was a tap on the door, and he turned. "Come in."

His valet poked his head into the room. "I wondered if I might speak to Miss Olivia?"

Richard stepped into the bedroom when Harrison nodded. Olivia stared at him. In the daylight he looked even more like her father. And he was her brother. She struggled to wrap her mind around that fact.

"I wanted to personally apologize," Richard said. "And to assure you that I had no idea what was happening until this morning when I heard about the forgeries. I really thought Eleanor killed herself."

"I don't understand," she said.

Harrison smoothed her hair. "Eugene says Jerry is the person to go to when someone needs a forgery."

"So he forged my father's signature onto the agreement with Bennett?"

Harrison nodded. "And he wrote the letter we thought was from your father."

"Why would he tell Eleanor to cut off all ties with the Bennetts?"

"The constable said Jerry was trying to cozy up to Eleanor. He had hopes he could win her. He didn't know of her relationship with Fosberg," Harrison said. "When he found out, she had to die to prevent the attorney from laying any claim to her money."

"What of hearing my father's voice? Was that you, Richard?"

He shook his head. "I went to talk to my cousin Jerry early this morning as the guests went off to bed. I found him in the garden practicing speaking in your father's voice."

"I don't understand," Olivia said. "Jerry was the person I heard?"

Richard nodded. "He's always been good at mimicking voices."

"He did an excellent job in the play," she said. "All this for money." She would have given the Bagleys all the money they wanted if they'd only spared her sister's life. Olivia rubbed her head. There were sore spots. Burns most likely.

"They wanted revenge more than money," Harrison added.

"She hated our family so much," Olivia marveled. "It seems extreme."

Richard nodded. "My aunt had a hard life that was made even harder after my mother died. When your father built the grand house here, the only job she could get at the time was as his housekeeper. The more she saw the differences between his life and the life we lived, the more deranged she became. I often heard her say she could do a better job running the estate than the Stewarts did."

"Did they have anything to do with my father's death?" She had to know.

Harrison shook his head. "If anyone did something wrong there, it was my father. He maintains your father's death was an accident and I tend to believe him. But even if that's true, he took the opportunity to swindle your mother. I found evidence in the books that the diamond mines are producing millions of dollars, and my father is paying only a fraction of that into your accounts."

It was all so overwhelming. "Now what?" she asked.

"I told Father he has to fix it. All of it. And turn himself in."

"Will he?" Richard asked.

Harrison's jaw hardened. "If he doesn't, I will."

Olivia stared at her new brother. "Now what, Richard? We need to get to the bottom of the will."

He shook his head. "The document makes no difference to me. I'm not going to take your money. It's not right."

"I think Father wanted to right a wrong," Olivia said softly. "It's clear that you will never let my mother want for anything. You're a good man. I believe we can trust you."

He swallowed hard and looked down. "I can't take your money."

"I'm going to talk to our attorney. Will you accept whatever just settlement he suggests?"

He raised his eyes and stared at her. "If you insist, Miss Olivia."

"Just Olivia," she said. "You're my brother, and you saved my life tonight." She tightened her grip on Harrison's hand. "You and Harrison."

A sheen of moisture gleamed in Richard's eyes. He bowed. "I'll take my leave now, Olivia, and let you rest."

"Wait!" She held out her hand. "I want to know why you don't hate us like the rest of your family."

"I used to," he admitted. "After my mother hung herself."

Olivia squeezed his hand. "I'm so sorry."

His Adam's apple bobbed and he blinked rapidly. "Thank you. I got into trouble as a teenager. Petty theft, breaking windows. A cop in the San Francisco suburbs caught me, but instead of arresting me, he made me go to church with him."

"And you came to know Jesus," Harrison said.

Richard nodded. "That changed everything. I couldn't harbor bitterness like that. So I just . . . let it go. I was free. Bitterness binds you. Look at my aunt and cousin."

She shuddered and released his hand. "Don't go too far. I want to get to know my brother better."

A ghost of a smile flitted across his face. He nodded and closed the door behind him.

"I did the same thing to him that you did to me," Harrison said. "Even though I'd known and trusted him for years, I believed he had duped me."

She tugged on his hand until he sat on the edge of the bed. "So are you still going to marry me even if I'm poor? *And* a Stewart?"

He grinned. "I thought you *were* poor until I saw the accounting books. I'd rather support my wife myself. Are you sure you still want to marry me knowing we are going to have to work hard to make a go of the business?"

"Trying to talk your way out of it?" she teased.

He leaned down until his face was just inches from hers. "Not a chance, darling. I'm not letting you get away. When will you marry me?"

"Today?" she suggested.

"I'll get the preacher." His eyes were serious.

Heat settled in her cheeks. "We could make it soon," she whispered. "But just a small wedding after everyone is gone. I'm done trying to impress people."

"We'll have it on the beach at night. Right where I kissed you under the falling stars. If we're lucky, it will happen again."

"There are enough fireworks when you touch me that we don't need falling stars," she said, pulling him down to kiss her.

A Letter from the Author

Dear Reader,

I hope you've enjoyed this third excursion to Mercy Falls as much as I have. I've learned about Halley's Comet, the first cars and airplanes, and what people at the turn of the last century ate right along with you. Such fun!

I'm so thankful you were all willing to take this little sidestep with me to historical romantic mysteries. I hope it delivered my usual blend of mystery and romance while giving you a glimpse of an earlier time.

I love and appreciate every one of you and the way you spread the word about my books. I love hearing from you, so e-mail me anytime at colleen@colleencoble.com. And if you are a Facebook or Twitter fan, you can find me there as well. I love to interact with my reader friends!

Much love,
Colleen

ACKNOWLEDGMENTS

IS IT POSSIBLE that *The Lightkeeper's Ball* is my eighteenth book with my Thomas Nelson family? They are truly my dream team! Publisher Allen Arnold (I call him Superman) is so passionate about fiction, and he lights up a room when he enters it. Senior Acquisitions Editor Ami McConnell (my friend and cheerleader) has an eye for character and theme like no one I know. I crave her analytical eye! It was her influence that encouraged me to write a historical romantic mystery, and I'm glad she pushed me a bit! Marketing Manager Eric Mullett brings fabulous ideas to the table. Publicist Katie Bond is always willing to listen to my harebrained ideas. Fabulous cover guru Kristen Vasgaard (you *so* rock!) works hard to create the perfect cover—and does it. And of course I can't forget my other friends who are all part of my amazing fiction family: Natalie Hanemann, Amanda Bostic, Becky Monds, Ashley Schneider, Andrea Lucado, Heather McCoullough, Chris Long, and Kathy Carabajal. I wish I could name all the great folks who work on selling my books through different venues at Thomas Nelson. Hearing "well done" from you all is my motivation every day.

Erin Healy has edited all of my Thomas Nelson books except one, and she is such an integral part of the team. Her ideas always make the book better, and she's a fabulous writer in her own right. If you haven't read her yet, be sure to pick up *Never Let You Go* and *The Promises She Keeps.*

My agent, Karen Solem, has helped shape my career in many ways, and that includes kicking an idea to the curb when necessary. Thanks, Karen—you're the best!

Writing can be a lonely business, but God has blessed me with great writing friends and critique partners. Hannah Alexander (Cheryl Hodde), Kristin Billerbeck, Diann Hunt, and Denise Hunter make up the Girls Write Out squad (www.GirlsWriteOut.blogspot.com). I couldn't make it through a day without my peeps! Thanks to all of you for the work you do on my behalf, and for your friendship. I had great brainstorming help for this book in Robin Caroll, Cara Putman, and Rick Acker as well. Thank you, friends!

I'm so grateful for my husband, Dave, who carts me around from city to city, washes towels, and chases down dinner without complaint. Thanks, honey! I couldn't do anything without you. My kids—Dave, Kara (and now Donna and Mark)—and my grandsons, James and Jorden Packer, love and support me in every way possible. Love you guys! Donna and Dave brought me the delight of my life—our little granddaughter, Alexa! Though I tried my best to emulate her cuteness in the scenes with Jennie, I'm sure I failed!

Most importantly, I give my thanks to God, who has opened such amazing doors for me and makes the journey a golden one.

Reading Guide Questions

1. Do you ever feel you are insignificant and nothing you do matters? Why or why not?

2. Do you have a dream you have been too intimidated to pursue? Maybe even too afraid to name it? What is it?

3. Name characteristics of some of the true friends you have had. How important is it that they point you back to God?

4. Have you ever altered your behavior because of others' expectations the way Olivia did? What allows you to be yourself?

5. Do you know anyone who has allowed bitterness to fester? How can you help that person forgive and let go?

6. Family expectations were very different for children a hundred years ago. What would you have found the most difficult about growing up in that era?

7. Society at the turn of the last century was also preoccupied with appearances and impressing other people, much as we see today. What can you do to keep from falling in the hole of materialism?

8. What do you want badly enough that might tempt you into compromising your integrity?

9. Olivia was wrong for keeping her secrets from Harrison. At what point should she have admitted her identity?

10. God sees us as we are inside. Does this comfort you or intimidate you?

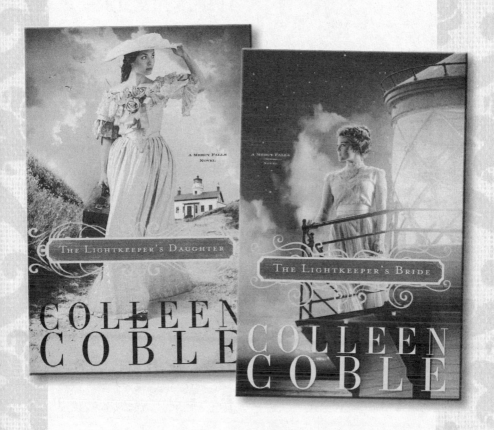

THE ROCK HARBOR MYSTERY SERIES

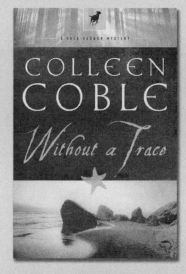

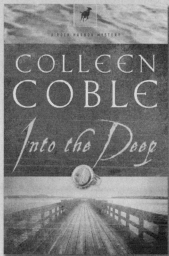

ALSO AVAILABLE FOR YOUR eREADER

ABOUT THE AUTHOR

RITA-FINALIST COLLEEN COBLE is the author of several best-selling romantic suspense series, including the Lonestar series and the Rock Harbor series. She lives with her husband, Dave, in Indiana.